Forty On 70

A Journey of Faith and Healing

By Philip D Bliss

Book 1 in the series: The Pop-Up Pastor

2nd Edition

Published By Fulcrum Publishing

A division of The Fulcrum Center

Forty On 70

Fulcrum Publishing
www.thefulcrumcenter.org
www.thepopuppastor.com

ISBN Paperback: 979-8-9851038-3-0

ISBN Hardback: 979-8-9851038-4-7

ISBN e-Book: 979-8-9851038-1-6

Dedication

This book is dedicated to Christians everywhere who
continually rely on God but still have struggles
in their daily lives. Our God loves us more than
we know, and if we persevere, He will see us through.

Author's Note

This book was written in obedience to God. When you are sitting on the couch, and God says, "Write a book about a guy that travels along Interstate 70," you are left with a choice. You either find out where Interstate 70 begins and ends, or you go about your day and ignore God. I was obedient.

My intention is to entertain and teach. It is not intended to say, "Hey, this is the way it is so deal with it." As a pastor, author, and fellow human being, I realize we will not always agree on everything, especially when religion is involved. I hope you approach this book the way it is intended—as entertainment first, and if you are interested, as teaching. But if you disregard the learning, I sincerely hope you are entertained.

Get ready to embark on a journey. I purposely wrote it as if someone jotted down their ideas and put them into a book. You will see his struggles; you will feel his pain. Let's get the message out that a relationship with God is the greatest thing you can ever do for yourself.

Reason for 2nd Edition
When I first published this book, I found a big mistake at a pivotal point in the book. Two paragraphs were intertwined and even the best readers would have said "What?" So, I fixed it. But the printing company had already pre-printed several books so I had to unpublish and re-publish as a second edition. With only 28 copies in print (all paperback), they are somewhat of a collector's item now.

God bless you, and thank you for reading Forty on 70.

Chapter

1

A bag of roasted peanuts changed my life forever.

The day started like any other day in early summer. The sun burned warm and bright. I left my wife, Jane, and my son, Timmy, at our home in Albeth Heights, Maryland, right outside of Baltimore, to travel to a local grocery store.

My trek focused on picking up supplies for a trip that would begin as soon as I arrived back home. We planned to drive straight through to Yellowstone National Park. Our trip would include three days of driving time, five days of sightseeing, and travel back through Chicago on Interstate 80. Jane had always wanted to see Chicago, and tall buildings fascinated Timmy. We had planned this trip for months. With the day upon us, excitement and anticipation waited in the wings.

While standing in the checkout line about to place my items on the belt, I had a sudden realization—I had left my wallet sitting on the kitchen counter, and I had no cash on me. I did what most husbands would do in this situation. I grabbed my cell phone, called Jane, and begged for forgiveness for disrupting her packing and preparation so she could bring my wallet to me.

Although the local Harris Teeter grocery is two miles from our home, I had worked my way into a sticky situation this time. Instead of staying local, I went to a store I frequently visited on my way home from the office each day. The H Mart in nearby Ellicott City had a variety of foods usually not available in other retail stores. With a long trip in front of me, I desperately sought a particular brand of roasted peanuts. The day was fresh, and I knew I would have time for the more extended voyage.

I called Jane, and she was unhappy I did not stay local but said she would be right there with my wallet. She jokingly said it would cost me longer driving hours so she could sleep later in the evening. After our call, I explained my situation to the store manager and pulled my cart to the side to avoid disrupting other customers. He agreed, and we even laughed at how this happens more than anyone realizes.

Knowing it would take her a few minutes to load Timmy into the car and another ten minutes to drive to the store, I became only slightly concerned when twenty-five minutes had passed. At the forty-five-minute mark and four unanswered phone calls later, I became more nervous. Fifty-five minutes had passed since I first called her when my phone rang, and it was Jane, according to the caller ID.

Noise on the other end of the line indicated the caller stood in traffic. My heart sank as I heard a male voice introduce himself as a trooper with the Maryland State Police. A tragic automobile accident on Interstate 70 involved my wife and son. He informed me I should immediately go to the hospital.

Tears welled in my eyes as I listened, but did not respond. The trooper asked if I was okay and if I understood. I finally answered and told him I would go to the hospital. I left the cart full of items, including five bags of my favorite roasted peanuts and the bouquet I had purchased for Jane, and rushed to the hospital.

Spotting a doctor at the Emergency Room (ER) registration desk, I announced my name. He took me aside and informed me Jane was in surgery and her condition was critical. Timmy did not survive the accident. I fell to the floor, screaming in anguish. How could this have happened? I immediately blamed myself, allowing condemnation to flood my spirit.

I can't imagine anything more painful in this world than hearing the words "He's gone" when someone is speaking of your eight-year-old son. Those words turned my life upside down and inside out that day, now more than a year ago. When in similar situations, I've known people to lose their faith. Thankfully, God kept me going and continues to do so day by day.

After I had calmed down, the trooper from the scene found me and explained what had happened. The police chased a car theft suspect who twisted down an exit ramp, going the wrong way. He didn't even try to avoid anyone and drove into oncoming traffic. Unfortunately, he crashed head-on into Jane and Timmy. The force caused the car to slide to the left, and an oncoming semi-truck hit the right side of Jane's minivan. The impact killed Timmy instantly. He didn't suffer. Jane received severe head injuries, two broken legs, and a fractured collarbone besides multiple scratches from the shattered glass.

The twenty-year-old driver had stolen the car as a prank. Being the son of an influential businessman in Baltimore, anxiety over his dad's anger caused him to evade the police. He reported he did not realize he had gone the wrong way down an exit ramp and thought it was an on-ramp. A broken arm, a bruised jaw, and the painful lifetime memory of what he had done became the young man's only injuries, along with his tarnished police record. But he survived; my family didn't. Forgiveness did not come easy for me, but God helped me make it a reality.

Forty days later, I signed the papers to give the hospital staff permission to shut down the machine keeping Jane alive. She had no brain activity, and her extensive injuries showed she had no hope for survival. I was heartbroken and distraught, as my hand shook so much I could hardly sign the form. But I also knew I would see her and Timmy again someday in heaven. Dealing with her angry parents, who both said I should have waited longer, became a grueling task God also had to help me navigate. I knew in my heart God had spoken to let her go. So, I did.

The remainder of the summer blurred by filled with family and friends offering condolences and sympathy. Through the hurt and pain, I never lost my faith in God to restore all I lost. I didn't know how he would do it, but I trusted he would get me through my agony.

I sold the house in Albeth Heights and moved into a downtown apartment closer to my office. After seven months, anger with God consumed me. I could hardly think of God without balling my fist. Somehow I could still hear Him though, and He told me to resign my role as a part-time pastor, which I held for twelve years. So, I gave a four-month notice and walked away from my passion for serving others, at least in that capacity.

In early May, I awoke from a strange dream, confident it came from The LORD. I dreamed I saw a sign indicating I was on I-70 EAST, but it had the familiar jargon I saw every day I drove home from my office in Baltimore. Columbus 420, St. Louis 845, Denver 1700, Cove Fort 2200. As I read the sign, I saw a red square around Cove Fort. I became confused because I knew I would travel westbound to see this sign, but the sign showed eastbound.

The next night, I dreamed I stepped into a red car, drove, and saw the familiar I-70 EAST sign. But the sign indicated: Cove Fort 1, Denver 10, St. Louis 20, Columbus 30, Baltimore 40. The dreams perplexed me so I asked God what they meant, but I did not receive the answers I desired.

In the eleven months since the accident, I refused to travel on

Interstate 70 eastbound at all. I drove to various places westbound but would find a new way home every time. This area of Maryland is big enough that it is possible to arrive at a destination without a great deal of deviation or extra time.

A few days after my dreams, The LORD responded to my question, His answer shook me to my core

I prayed about what to do for a few more days before I became convinced The LORD wanted me to make a trip across the country from Cove Fort to Baltimore. To put the plan into action, I purchased a car, requested delivery to Beaver, Utah, booked a flight, and researched various stops along my way. When May gave way to June, the time to make the trip honoring my wife and son and to finally travel on Interstate 70 eastbound for the first time in a year had come. I did not know what I would discover, but I knew God was with me and would guide me. My role in the journey became clear; to stay close to Him in prayer.

For many, this may seem like an unusual method of recovering from tragedy. For others, it may sound like complete nonsense. As I reflect on it now, I see the wisdom of God in what I did—helping people to know God better, explaining in a
short time what I had tried to explain in twelve years as a pastor. Establishing and strengthening a relationship with God through His son is the greatest thing we can do for ourselves in this life.

Chapter

2

Relaxation evaded me as the Great Salt Lake came into full view. It was vast, significant, and amazing to behold. My ears popped as they acclimated to the change in atmospheric pressure during our descent to the airport. Four hours had passed since I left Baltimore's Washington International Airport at noon. My watch had auto-adjusted to reflect the two o'clock local mountain time zone.

It was my first flight ever into Salt Lake City, and I took in the scenery. From the sky, the homes looked neatly spaced and resembled teeth in a zipper. The skyline was much bigger than my hometown view of Columbus, Ohio, but smaller than Baltimore. A building caught my attention. It resembled a castle, I believed it to be a church. Snow-capped Rocky Mountains extended as far as I could see, which reminded me I was no longer close to home. I tried looking out the window across the aisle, hoping to get one last view of the Great Salt Lake, but it faded into the distance. We leveled off as we approached the ground.

"You're not an LDS, are you?"

I glanced in the direction of the voice which addressed me. "I am not sure what you mean," but after the words came out, I put it all together.

He confirmed it for me. "LDS, Latter-day Saints. You're not from around here, are you? You're not from Salt Lake City."

Curiosity piqued within me as I wondered what I had done to give away my "tourist look."

"How could you tell?"

He pointed out the window. "Lake Stink. Locals have seen it enough and don't glimpse it out the window when we approach." He held out his hand, gesturing a handshake to which I obliged him. His grip was firm and dry. "I am Joe Smith."

Without thinking about it, I raised my right eyebrow, which he must have interpreted as a question. He quickly added, "No, not Joseph Smith, founder of the Mormon church."

I laughed, "It's nice to meet you, Joe. I am Jake Anderson."

Joe pointed again out the window and continued his educational rant about the water basin entirely behind us. "The locals call it Lake Stink because there are shallow areas, and I guess gasses leak out, and it causes a stench twice a year. "

"Oh!" I nodded with a look of intrigue. I am an information guru, so hearing any bit of new knowledge was something I enjoyed.

"My wife grew up a mile from the lake. It's how I know so much. I moved here in 1999 with her because she wanted to return to her hometown. We used to live in Boulder, where I was a successful lawyer. But now," he paused slightly and looked down, "I am a mailman."

I could already sense Joe's disappointment. I do not believe it stemmed from his working for the United States Government as a postal carrier. No, I believed he gave up a lot for his wife, and I sensed resentment in his voice.

"She said I would be happy here. I mean, I guess I am. I am healthy, and our son is healthy. The weather is nice." He paused, and with a big smile, continued, "I have a grandchild coming next month."

"Congratulations."

The excitement once on his face became gloomy. He turned his head to the left so I could no longer see his eyes. I watched as he raised a hand to wipe a tear from his left eye. A small moment of awkward silence occurred, and I gazed out the window again to notice the ground hundreds of feet below. The seat belt sign, though it had been on for the last twenty minutes, flashed with a ding, reminding us it would not be a suitable time to stand up. A roar filled the cabin as the flaps on the wings extended to increase drag and slow us as part of the plane's thrust reversal system. A loud screech sounded as the plane's wheels touched the runway. The noise became louder, and as quickly as it began, subsided seconds later. Another smooth landing.

"I don't want my grandchild not to choose for himself, that's all." Joe glanced back at me. The redness in his eyes confirmed my suspicions. He had become teary-eyed.

"A choice?" I asked as we taxied toward the terminal.

A man in front of us stood and reached for his luggage in the overhead compartment. I had to chuckle as he lost his balance and fell quickly back into his seat as the plane made a sharp right turn. *Amateur,* I thought to myself.

Joe smirked a little at the impatient man. He thought for a moment as he made eye contact with me again. "I want him to choose his own life and not be forced into the LDS church like his mother forced his dad, my son."

I nodded my head to show my understanding. "So, you are not a Mormon, but I take it your wife is?"

"Correct."

"And you don't want your grandchild to be one?" I paused, reflecting on the information previously provided. "Is it a boy?"

"Yes, Rankin David Smith. My middle name is Rankin, and my son's name is David." He chuckled, and I could tell his mood returned to a joyful state. "We are not original in this family. We keep re-using names. My dad was Joseph Rankin Smith, too, but again, not the one who started the LDS church."

I laughed at the thought. I knew the Joseph Smith he referred to died 175 years earlier. I also knew this man's pain. During my ministry, I had counseled many individuals struggling with the expectation of carrying on the family's faith traditions. The generational ideology plagued families across denominations. One needed little evidence to know the Joe Smith before me was not a fan of the LDS movement, nor of the fact, his wife must have convinced his son to remain in this tradition.

The eager man in front of us stood up again and retrieved his bag. He continued standing as the plane pulled into the terminal bay. The seat belt light went off, and almost at once, the cabin filled with the sounds of metal clanging as passengers unbuckled their seatbelts. I always waited for the hustle and bustle to end before I even tried to leave.

Joe continued, "I was raised Catholic. Every Sunday and the occasional Saturday, we would be in church. Up and down, up and down." He shot a convincing look my way. "St. Joseph's church was the name, ironically. I felt like it was not my choice, but it was my parent's choice for me, and when I was eighteen, I went off to college and never went to church again. Well, until I met Cheryl."

He paused and looked down. I knew he relived a painful memory. I thought to ask if I could pray for him, but I heard The LORD speak, *listen, Jake.* So, I sat and listened to the remainder of his story.

"We were both freshmen at Colorado Mesa University in Grand Junction, where I grew up, and in the political science track, so we had a lot of classes together. We hit it off, and four years later, after graduation, we were married. I went on to law school, and she stayed home to raise our son." He paused, and with a critical look, he raised his hand and said, "It's not what you think. David was born ten months and one week after our wedding. It's all good."

I laughed at his apparent need to remain pious.

"So anyway, the entire time at Mesa, neither of us attended a church service. We attended a lot of parties together, but never once went to a religious gathering. I assumed she was not religious, and I wanted to get out of the religious monotony."

Passengers continued to file out of the plane, and I wondered how long the conversation would last. Would the flight attendants need to ask us to leave? I glanced back and forth but also tried to remain focused on Joe's story. I was not in a hurry, but it seemed Joe was not either, and I didn't know if he planned to deplane or not.

"So, to make a long story short, Cheryl told me about a year into our marriage that she wanted to move back to Salt Lake City and join the Mormon Tabernacle Choir. She wanted to attend the SLC castle. You probably saw it from the sky as we approached."

It took me a minute to understand what he meant, but I pieced it together. Salt Lake City Castle, or as I thought silently to myself, *the Latter-day Saints temple*, Joe had confirmed it for me. He waited for a response from me. I simply nodded.

Joe and I noticed a single file line had formed in front of us. His voice became louder and faster as he tried to finish quickly. "Anyway, I don't want my grandchild or son to be a Mormon, but I won't bore you with the details. Can you pray for me?"

"Right now?"

"No, we have to get off this bird. I mean, I can tell you are a praying man."

I was curious how he knew me to be a man of prayer. No one had ever said that to me before when I was on a plane, but it was true. I pray daily. I decided not to stress over this apparent God-given knowledge and responded I would pray for him.

He stood first and walked toward the now smaller queue before us. I grabbed the only thing I had boarded the plane with, my Bible. Joe turned around and raised his hand to wave goodbye.

I stood behind Joe, and I was the last passenger to leave the plane. The pilot stood by the cockpit, thanked us for flying, and told us to enjoy our time in Salt Lake City. We walked through the tunnel. I grabbed Joe's arm and said, "Joe, can I give you a scripture verse for your wife?"

"Yes, that would be fantastic. I was going to ask you to do so. Man, you are close to God, aren't you?"

I smiled. "Well, I try to be." We continued to walk, and as we entered the terminal, Joe rushed to a set of empty seats. He turned back and looked at me with eagerness.

Why did I say I try to be? I never liked when someone said those words because when we try to be, we will fail. When we surrender to God and submit our lives to His will, there is no try. We simply do and be.

"Do you have about five minutes?" Joe asked with excitement in his voice.

I glanced at my watch. It was two twenty-eight. According to my schedule, the rental car pickup was not until three-thirty. I decided I could spend a few minutes with him, so I approached and took a seat in the boarding area.

"My wife thinks she is becoming like God. Well, it's almost like she thinks she is going to be a god, I guess. I don't know the full belief. We don't talk about it much. But she believes she will someday have a planet of her own, and others will worship her like God in heaven." I was about to speak, offering advice, but he cut me off before I began. "She drank the Kool-Aid, obviously." As the anxiousness rose in him, he spoke louder. "She believes since eternity is an exceptionally long time, after this life, she will be transformed to a god and yeah, rule a planet or something. I mean, have you ever heard of such a thing?"

"Actually, I have Joe. It's no longer a fundamental belief in the church of Latter-day Saints, but early church scholars proposed this doctrine, or speculation, as they often call it. I have never actually met anyone who genuinely believed it until…"

"Oh! I don't believe it!"

11

"No, Joe, I didn't mean to imply you did. I was saying I have…"

"That you never met a crazy person like my wife. She is crazy. Certified. The certificate is hanging on my wall in my house."

I laughed. "About the verse, Isaiah 43:10 comes to mind."

"I am not sure I know what it means or says. Is it the one about the eagle's wings?"

"No, you are thinking of Isaiah 40:31, but the numbers are all the same. 43:10 says before me, there was no god, and none will come after me. So, this may be something you can share with her to see how their doctrine manages it."

Joe stood up, put his hand on his chin, and walked in a circle while I observed. He repeated it as he walked. "Isaiah 43:10, no other gods after me." He continued to pace back and forth while reasoning in his mind, "So that means she can't become a god. I mean, they know the Bible; they trust the Bible. They believe they are the only ones who understand the Bible, so surely, she will understand this. There are no other gods that come after the one true God." He circled back, stopped before me, and smiled. "Thank you, umm. What was your name again?"

"Jake. Jake Anderson,"

"That's right," he said as he snapped his fingers. "And why are you here in Salt Lake City?"

I stood, eager to tell someone my story. "Well, I am from Maryland, and I came here because I am traveling to Beaver, where I will pick up a new car. I plan to drive to Baltimore along I-70, but I am taking forty days to do it."

His eyes expanded, and his jaw dropped a little. "Okay, good luck with that."

It was not the response I had predicted, but how often do you meet someone who says they are traveling along Interstate 70 for the joy of doing it. I was not sure if he wanted to wait around for the details of what I had planned. I assumed not.

"But why not start in Fillmore?"

"Excuse me?"

"Fillmore is closer to the start of I-70. If you drive to Beaver, you will go past 70 and could get on there. Why go to Beaver?"

"I don't know." My head turned, and my eyes shifted. "I just 'know' I am supposed to start in Beaver and did not consider any other starting locations."

We both remained silent for a moment until I realized something Joe had mentioned on the plane. I wondered if, but I quickly dismissed it as not likely. I continued to stare at the ground for a few seconds and asked, "Joe, if I may change the subject for a moment. You said…"

"Sure, change it. I am finished talking about my family issues. I am sure you are done hearing about them, too."

I offered a nervous laugh before continuing. "You said you were from Grand Junction." Joe nodded. "I knew a girl from Grand Junction, too. Any chance you ever heard of Gina Taylor?"

"Tall, red hair, pretty?"

The description fit her well, and as I tried to figure out Joe's age earlier, his baldness, large girth, and gray goatee had me believe he was much older than me, but what he said next surprised me.

"I went to school with Gina Taylor. Graduated a year ahead of her. Nice girl, very intelligent, if I remember correctly."

"Yes!" I blurted enthusiastically. "I believe she was class valedictorian, but I lost track of her about nineteen years ago."

"I believe she went to Ohio State for a time and finished at…"

"UC Denver." I could not believe he had graduated with my sophomore year college girlfriend. I knew Grand Junction was not vast. I planned to visit the city, but this was too much for the "It's a small world' cliché." It didn't seem possible. A girl with whom I spent most of my days walking on High Street between my Lane Avenue apartment and classes near the Union went to the same high school as a stranger I spent four hours with on a plane. This encounter could not be by chance. I wondered if the rest of my journey would cause this much excitement.

"Yes, that's right. Hmm, small world."

"Yes, it is Joe. Yes, it is."

Feeling bad I had changed the subject on him, I asked Joe if I could pray for him, and he agreed. When we finished, I asked Joe if he understood what it meant to be a Christian. He assured me he did. He said he had learned all of it in the catechism classes in his youth. I explained to him if he would focus on his relationship with God and not treat it as an obligation, his wife may never leave the Mormon church, but it would make his life with her more enjoyable. Encouraging him to live a life worthy of the gospel, quoting Philippians 1:27, he said he understood and would. In my heart, I knew his concern for his grandchild was more significant than his desire to strengthen a relationship with God. It saddened me, but I knew convincing him would not be easy. I glanced at my watch again and noticed several minutes had passed.

"I need to get going, sir. But I will continue to pray for you and your wife. Try to remember what I said about your relationship with God, too."

Joe winked and walked away. As I turned to see where he had gone, I could hear him say once again in a faint voice, "Isaiah 43:10." He weaved his way into the crowd of people, and seconds later, I could not distinguish him from anyone else in the airport.

I proceeded to the baggage claim to retrieve my luggage and walked to the concierge desk for my rental car. After signing some papers, saying a prayer, and grabbing something to eat at a Chick-Fil-A, I drove away. I knew Interstate 70 was my ultimate destination, but Beaver was in my sights first. I passed through Fillmore and glimpsed briefly at Interstate 70 as I continued toward my goal.

Chapter

3

The rental car slowed as I lifted my foot from the accelerator. I signaled my intention to exit as the GPS voice echoed through the cabin. The sound, though I had grown used to it, suddenly startled me this time. I passed it off as adrenaline and anxiety mixed.

"Take exit 112 State Route, Beaver, and then turn right."

I coasted to the stop sign at the end of the off-ramp. I made the obligatory three-second pause and did as commanded; I turned right. Along the two-lane road, I saw no grass. Seeing red dirt and sand everywhere, I wondered if the locals even owned lawnmowers. I didn't imagine many homeowners paid for someone to grow grass in their yards, so many accepted the sand and rock as standard. I passed a sign showing Butch Cassidy had been born in Beaver. What caught my attention most was the charging station. It looked like a park and ride area with gas pumps. But these gas pumps did not pump refined petroleum. Instead, they plugged into electric cars and charged them with electricity. It was the first time I had seen such a thing. I nearly drove the rental car off the road as I gawked at it, trying to take in every detail.

As I continued, the female voice from the GPS informed me my destination was on the right. I was glad she told me because I would have driven past the car dealership had she not. I noticed a sign showing my destination, Davidson Ford.

I turned into the dealership and saw a quaint little building sitting in the middle of a vast parking lot. Behind the building, I glimpsed several garage doors, and I assumed it was the shop. Before me, several rocking chairs sat in front of the white, glass-covered storefront. I noticed a pattern as well, blue, white, purple. They repeated to make a line of six chairs to the left of the single glass door. To the right of the door was the same setup, but this time in reverse. I did not see any handicap markings, however, I did not want to choose the spot near the door. Instead, I took the location in front of the second blue chair from the left.

It is always nice to get a new car. But more than the excitement of getting a new car, I felt the excitement of being able to stretch my legs for the first time since I had left the airport. I looked at my watch as I moved the gear shift to park—5:58 p.m. I had a half-hour before they closed. I exited the car, took a deep breath of fresh air, stretched my weary legs, and walked toward the door. An older gentleman sat in the white rocker and continued to look ahead as if I didn't exist.

"Evening, Mr. Anderson. I am glad you made it."

I stopped, startled and puzzled. I was over 2,000 miles from my home, and this man addressed me by my last name. I glanced behind me, but I found no one. When I turned back to face him, he looked at me and smiled.

"What? Scare you, son? Didn't expect to be called by your name here in the small town of Beaver, Utah?"

"Well," I paused as I thought about what to say, "I guess I am a little surprised, yes."

"The name's Solomon. Solomon Davidson. I am the proprietor and founder of this here establishment, and I know who you are because, well, son, let's face it." He pointed toward the rental, "You pull in at six o'clock driving a car with a Texas plate. It has a sticker on the windshield which tells me it is a rental. You got out of the car stretching your legs, and since I don't think you drove here from Texas, I guessed you to be Jake Anderson from Baltimore, here to pick up the car you purchased. If I may add, you probably grabbed that vehicle in Salt Lake City and drove here."

I laughed slightly at his reasoning. He was good. It all made sense now.

"Son, you don't have to be a prophet to figure that one out. You stick out like a toe you broke on a bedpost."

Interesting choice of words. I walked up and stuck out my hand to shake his. "Jake Anderson, but you already know."

"Son, I know a lot more. But let's get those keys for you so you can begin your journey."

His handshake was firm and confident. But how did he know about my journey? I reasoned with myself this time. I had flown to Utah to pick up a car. Of course, I started on a trip. *Oh, he is good. He is really good.*

Solomon opened the door for me, and I walked in. I turned to speak with him but could see the door shutting behind me, and he sat again. To the left, I could see a young couple with a small child talking to a salesperson about an SUV parked in the showroom. Straight ahead, I saw a long counter, and printed beneath it was: Welcome to Davidson Ford. I surmised I would probably find someone to help there, so I walked the twenty feet to the four-foot-high creation. Walking toward me at the same time was a young man who looked familiar to me. The older man outside resembled this man. The name tag read Ray Davidson.

We met at the counter simultaneously, and he greeted me with a standard "Can I help you, sir?"

"I am Jake Anderson, and I am here to pick up my new Ford Fiesta."

"Yes, sir. Right over there." answered Ray, as he directed my attention toward the right side of the showroom. Beyond the glass, I could see the front of a shiny, new, red car. I took a few steps to the right and stood in amazement as I saw my new car for the first time. Ray had stepped around and behind the counter, presumably to grab paperwork, and I walked closer to the window to view the car.

I approached the window and took in the various aspects of the vehicle. I glimpsed a shadow flying over before a bird dropped some guano on the hood of my new car. For a moment, I didn't know whether to laugh or be angry. My mouth dropped in astonishment.

"I will make sure we get it cleaned up for you, Mr. Anderson," Ray said as he stepped behind me.

"It's not necessary."

"Well, sir, unless you are in a hurry, it is no problem, and if you are not, I believe my father sitting outside would like a moment to speak to you. Would that be okay?"

I glanced at my wrist again. My jet-lagged body told me it neared eight o'clock, but my watch showed it was two hours earlier. I didn't have to check-in at the hotel at a specific time, and it was a mile away, so I decided I could spend a few minutes with Solomon. "Sure, I would love to talk to your dad."

"Great, we will get her all washed up for you, sir." He showed a face of excitement. "Oh, can you sign here, sir? It says you are taking delivery of a new Ford Fiesta, red. Here is the odometer reading, three miles. Here is the price you paid and the amount you financed. Oh wait, I see." He looked me in the eyes, "You paid cash for it." He looked back at the paper and said, "This is the date of the sale. Information about the warranty is here, and this shows you have a ninety-day temporary tag. Finally, please sign there." Ray handed me a pen, and I scribbled my signature.

"Can I ask you something, Mr. Anderson?"

"Please, call me Jake, and yes, sure."

"Well, it is really none of my business, but the guys who work

18

here, we, um, well, we have never sold a car to someone outside of the Utah, Nevada, New Mexico, or even Colorado area. Once a man from Idaho bought a truck. Anyway, we are wondering, you know…"

"Wondering why someone travels across the country to pick up a car he paid for in Maryland?"

With this, Ray seemed timid and did not want to continue with the question. He looked to his right, and I saw another curious mind looking our way. I tapped the pen on the counter a few times as I thought about what to say next. Ray fumbled with other papers on the counter. "It's okay, guys." I waved for the other man to join us.

He pointed to himself and mouthed, "Me?"

I nodded and waved again. "Come on over and hear the story." The door closed behind me, and as I turned, I saw the young couple with the child walking out. The sales associate who had been with them made his way to where we three gathered.

"Well, it may seem unusual to many but to those who know and trust God as much as I do, it is…"

"I trust God!" the man who had joined us last spoke up.

I nodded at him, "Good, you will understand this. I have wanted for a long time to get to know God more. I gave my life to Christ at age eleven. I spent the last twelve years as a part-time pastor in a mainline denomination, and I, well, I…" I didn't want to talk about the accident at the moment. "Let's say I had a tough year. So, I prayed one night God would tell me what I should do. I laid it all out. I said I would do anything." I saw if anyone had questions. All eyes and attention focused on me. "The next day, a thought formed in my mind. I live near the eastern end of Interstate 70, near Baltimore. I asked myself, 'Where is the beginning of Interstate 70?' I thought for sure it was somewhere in California.

Jim, the salesman, nodded in agreement. "I wondered where it ended. So, it's Baltimore?"

I continued, "Yes, at a Park and Ride. It's a pretty neat place. So, that night I had a dream. I dreamed I drove east on 70, but I knew I had gone west because I saw a sign that can only be seen westbound."

"Whoa, was it God?" asked Frank, the man I had waved over to join us from the office.

"Well, Frank, I believe it was," I commented as I read his nametag.

"God doesn't talk to me, and I don't dream."

"Yes, He does, Frank. He does talk to you. You need to learn how to listen and to look for His ways of communicating," added Ray.

I agreed.

I looked at Frank, "He loves you, Frank. He wants you to know Him better, and He said to me just now, 'Tell Frank, I hear all he has asked for, and when I reply, he has already moved on.' Does that mean anything to you?"

Frank took a step back. His eyes widened, and he looked at Ray, Jim, and back at me. "Yes. It does. I know exactly what you mean. Wow!"

I spoke again, "So I knew God spoke. I said, 'Okay, God, I don't think this is a coincidence.' Remember, I said I had a rough year, and I asked God how I could recover. I thought about the start of the interstate and the dream. But I had another dream, too." I paused once again for any feedback but heard none. "The next dream was like the first, but I specifically saw myself in a red car this time. I also saw another sign which said Interstate 70 East and another listed cities with numbers."

"Numbers like miles to the city?"

"No, Jim. It was more like the days, I think. The Cove Fort line had one, Denver had ten, each city had a small number, and finally, Baltimore had forty."

"So, what do you think it meant" asked Frank.

"I didn't know, but when I woke up, I heard God say forty

days. Feeling confused, I kept praying. Finally, after a few days of back and forth, I approached my boss, who also is my best friend and business partner. I call him my boss, but we are genuinely 50/50 partners in our company. I told him I wanted to take forty-five days (about one and a half months) off work. At first, he scoffed and asked if I quit. I told him no. I wanted to take a day to fly to Utah, the next day drive from Cove Fort, Utah, to..."

"That's where I-70 begins," Jim interjected.

"Yes, it is. I told Sean I was going to drive from Cove Fort, Utah to the Park and Ride, and I would take forty days to do it."

Excitement in his voice, Ray exclaimed, "Wow, what a story."

I reflected on the moment with Sean a little over a month ago and ten months after the accident. If I went into more detail, I knew I would become teary-eyed, so I told them, "He accepted it and said, 'Have fun. Be safe. You deserve a break, and, come back when you finish.'"

"Wow, without question, he let you do it?" asked Jim.

"Well, he couldn't say no. He had once taken a four-week vacation to Europe for his honeymoon, so it was a no-brainer."

"God said that to me?" inquired Frank.

I could tell what I had said bothered him, so I tried to encourage him. "Yes, Frank. And stop listening to garbage music. It pushes you away from God."

Laughter broke out as Jim and Ray knew what I referred to, as did Frank, but I did not know what it meant. I would often speak what came to mind, knowing it came from God, but I did not always understand why.

"That's quite the story, Jake," Ray said, as the laughter calmed down. "Hey, if you don't mind and if you have a little time, can you tell my dad the story? I am not sure what you believe about prophets and apostles. Many Christians don't believe they exist anymore, but my dad is a prophet to all who know him. I don't mean a fortune-teller; I mean a prophet. Now, I don't mean like an Old Testament prophet. He doesn't tell people about judgment. I mean, like the prophets of Ephesians 4. Do you know what I mean? He is an encourager and teaches people about what God is saying to them."

I nodded in agreement as Ray spoke, "I know what you mean, Ray, and I believe. I would be glad to talk to him. Are we finished here?"

"Oh, yes! I will get your car cleaned up again and have it ready for you in a few minutes." Ray shook my hand and thanked me for my business. Frank walked away with his head down, and Jim followed me to the door. He opened it for me and said it was nice to meet me before turning around and going back inside.

The young couple still sat in their car. She made funny faces at the child, and he laughed. Seeing this brought back a fond memory of my wife and son. For a moment, I tried to relive the day that never happened. *What if this could have been us at Yellowstone.* I reflected on it more when Solomon spoke up.

"Can you sit for a spell, young man?" Solomon now sat in the purple rocker but still on the left side of the door. I walked around him and took a seat in the white rocker. The sun hung high above the tree line, suggesting the daylight hours would soon diminish. I imagined what it might look like in Baltimore.

I did not expect a wooden rocker to feel so accommodating. I almost wanted to stand back up as I remembered I had been sitting for several hours. *How am I going to drive all that way?*

"Asking yourself how you are going to make this journey, are you, son?"

I froze. It was surreal. It was almost as if Solomon knew me or read my mind or both. However, in that brief awkward moment of silence, I remembered how I would do this to my mom and dad. I would tell them things I knew before they ever told me. I knew what he had done, but it was still surreal to experience it for myself.

"Sorry, son, I didn't mean to startle you. And please know if you think I am a mind reader or psychic, put that notion right out of your head. There is no way at all I can read your mind. Anyone who says they can is full of hogwash. There is no ESP or any other thing. Everything I say to you, I hear God speak to me through His Holy Spirit. That's the only way. It's a gift given to me by The Almighty. Oh, some people believe they can read minds, and some can predict your thoughts, but son, I am here to tell you they are not hearing from God. They hear from the enemy." Solomon stopped rocking and looked at me. "I am a bit of an unusual person, some would say. But I believe, son, you know what I mean. Am I right?"

"I am not sure what you are saying, sir."

"First, there is no need to call me sir. I realize I am your elder, and I am sure your family raised you properly and with manners, but please, call me Solomon. Or if you wish, you can call me Saul."

"Which do you prefer?"

"You know what happened to the two Sauls in the Bible, right?" Without giving me a chance to answer, he continued, "So, let's say I prefer Solomon. My wife likes to call me Saul, though."

"Okay, Solomon. I need to ask. You seem to know a lot about me, and it doesn't seem all of it is from observation only. Can I ask how? Is it Google?"

"Google?" he looked at me. "What's a Google? Oh, it's that iPhone thing."

"Well, yeah, something like that." I could not help but laugh.

"Son, I think you know how I know."

I still did not understand what Solomon tried to say to me. I did not want to be rude, but I wanted to tell him his logic made no sense. I looked at the sun and back at Solomon, who looked at me the whole time.

"Son, you have a strong prophetic anointing." He waited for my response. When I did not give one right away, he added, "I think you know this, too, but you have never understood how to use it. Am I right?"

I was shocked and did not know how to respond, so I humbly nodded.

"Now, please tell me if I am wrong. I am human, and I can make mistakes. The LORD knows there are many demons in this here town. But I am sure I am not listening to them. I hear from God. It's a gift and a craft He taught me. Tell me if I am wrong." Once again, he waited for a response. "Are you okay with me doing this, Jake?"

I nodded.

"Okay, you have known since you were a child you were different. You probably made predictions at first. As time went on, you may have known people were going to visit or call. You knew when someone would get sick, or you knew the teacher would call on you, am I right?

"Umm, yeah. All those things. Especially the teacher thing. I used to hate school because of it."

"And you were never sure what to do with it. You didn't know how you knew. You probably were taught psychics were bad, and they are. That's occult stuff. That's demonic through and through. Oh, they hear well, but not from God. They hear demons speak to them. About you, now, I didn't know this until you got out of that there car." He pointed at the rental. "But when you did, your spirit connected with my spirit directly and through the Holy Spirit of God, I heard, 'This man has a strong prophetic anointing. He will save people from the very gates of hell.' Do you believe me? Do you understand what I am saying?"

"Yes, I do, Mr. Davidson. I believe you. I thank you, too, because yes, you are right. I thought there was something wrong with me, and I tried to suppress it for many years."

"Okay, there is one more thing, son. The enemy has a hand over your mouth. When someone said you were wrong, it made you afraid to speak what God spoke to you. So today, God said the enemy's hand is released." Without asking, he grabbed my jaw softly, but I still winced a little. "He is releasing you to speak, for God has ordained you to help many on this journey."

I sat in amazement, but I knew it was all true.

Solomon closed his eyes. He turned to me and laid his hand on my shoulder. He opened his left eye, and asked, "Is it okay if I lay hands on you and pray for you?"

I agreed.

He closed his eyes and prayed, "Father, bless and anoint this man to be your servant as you have so ordained. Teach him and lead him in the ways of your calling on his life. At the right time, in your time, let him know and understand the meaning of what you have for him. In Jesus' mighty name, Amen."

"Amen. So, you are referring to Ephesians chapter 4 and not 1 Corinthians chapter 12?" I asked Solomon.

"Exactly, son, Paul tells us the Holy Spirit has called some to be apostles, some prophets, some evangelists, some pastors, and some teachers. You, by the way, are a teacher, too."

Many aptitude tests I had taken to become a pastor showed I had a knack for teaching. Everything he said resonated in my spirit. I praised God under my breath.

Solomon stood up, walked out into the parking lot, threw his arms up in worship to God, and prayed. I could not hear what he spoke, so I stayed back and waited. When finished, he returned to his seat next to me. He stared ahead for a few brief seconds before speaking. "So, Jake, I still don't know the whole story, and if you don't mind telling me, I would like to know why you came to the great state of Utah to buy a car when you could have purchased one in Maryland?

I did not mind telling him the story again, and I explained how I talked to Sean, moved into my plane ride, and how I spoke to Joe Smith in Salt Lake City. I explained how I heard God speaking to me, the dreams, and how I knew I was supposed to make this trip."

"Religion!"

I was not sure, once again, what he tried to say to me. I wished he would speak in more words. "Religion?"

"Religion is man's attempt to reach God. Religion teaches you find God in a church. I believe God doesn't want you to be involved with the spirit of religion. He wants you to infuse His Spirit into the minds of people stuck in religion so they can find freedom in Christ." He stood, shook his head side to side and searched for words to say. "Jake, Hebrews 10:25 says do not forsake the gathering together as many have."

I nodded. I was familiar with the verse.

Solomon continued, "It's one of the most insanely misused verses in the entire Bible. When the author of Hebrews wrote those words, there were no four-wall churches. He said, 'Don't forsake the gathering in The LORD's name.' In other words, prayer. I could go on and on, but The LORD says to me right now you will understand this as you travel." Solomon sat back down next to me.

I sat there waiting for more. I thought I understood. I know a church is a building and God doesn't dwell in a church, but I also knew He would be present in churches with the gathering of two or more. "God doesn't like religion, does He?"

"No!" I could hear the anger in his voice. "He despises it! He wants us to have a relationship with Him, and if we have a relationship, He will allow the buildings and the stained-glass windows and the people with smiling faces and their hands in the air. He allows it because He knows the church is His people, and where they meet or what they do when they meet does not matter as much if they know Him personally. That's where growth occurs, where a person is changed. The church is a facilitator, but the church is not the relationship."

God had connected me to Solomon uniquely. I repeated the phrase, which stuck with me the most. *If they know Him personally, that's where growth occurs.*

"He wants us to be in a relationship with Him first, seeing Him as a friend, a loving father, and as a righteous judge. But one full of grace and mercy. On one side, we have people who want all of God's love and the power of His spirit, but on the other side, we have people who want to remind us how awful and how sinful we are. There is little middle ground, Jake. Why do you think the Romans crucified Jesus in the middle? God wants us to come back to the middle and meet Him. It's the easiest and freest place to be, it is a place where His protection over us is the greatest. It is a place where we can confess our sins and find His grace and mercy. It is a place free from the religious rules and rituals and abhorrent teachings and sayings of the…," now Solomon raised his hands and made air quotes "of the 'church leaders.' Jesus paid a hefty price on the cross, and God only wants us to understand it and not add to it all the nonsense we have added. God loves us. He wants us to know Him. But He also knows our being and how we operate.

"He knows we created churches to reach Him, and He allows it, but He wants us to know Him through our hearts and not through a beautiful building. A church building should be a place we can worship without getting wet. It should never be the thing we worship."

I could see tears rolling down Solomon's face as he finished speaking. I agreed with him. As a pastor, I saw too much religion, and it bothered me. I also concluded, like Solomon, that a relationship was more important. I heard God's voice whisper to me. *I will explain more.* Great joy came upon me.

We had been talking for fifteen minutes. I knew I would have to wrap up this conversation soon. It had been fabulous to spend time with him, but I needed to rest for the next day, my first day on the road.

I saw Ray drive my car around to the front parking lot. It gave me joy to see it clean and ready for me, but it also comforted me to know the rental company would come to the dealership later to

27

pick up my rental. I stood up and walked to the leased car to grab my suitcase and belongings from the trunk.

Ray handed me the keys, and I pushed a button to pop the hatch. It looked spacious, and I could smell the new car smell. *This is going to be fun.* I set my luggage in the space behind the back seat. I closed my eyes and silently thanked God for all of His provisions. After closing the hatch, I walked back to the front of the store, where Solomon still sat. Ray had walked into the store and turned the deadbolt on the door. I extended my hand to the man who had prayed over me and given me a lot to consider.

Solomon stood and shook my hand. "Young man," he said, "it's not about how many people you will reach. It's not about how many people will know your name. It's about how many people you will allow God to impact through your actions as you speak the name of Jesus, our Lord."

"I need to write that one down, sir."

"Yes, son, you should. Reflect on it often because of this journey you are taking. God, indeed, ordained it. He called you, and you were obedient to listen. Son, you will see and discern what others cannot. There will be many joys along the way, but there will be a trial of enormous proportions you will face. Forgive her; she is a lost soul. She needs your help."

"Who?" I asked.

"The LORD will provide in His time. Be blessed." He turned, fumbled for a key in his pocket, unlocked the door, and went inside.

I walked back to my new car, sat down, and took a deep breath of that fresh car smell.

Within minutes I pulled into the Days Inn. I set my alarm for seven o'clock in the morning, turned on the television, and set the sleep timer to shut off the device in one hour. As I lay in bed, I prayed aloud, "Lord, I am not so sure about this prophetic anointing thing. I mean, that's controversial. I know what the Bible says, but why don't churches teach on it? What do I do with it? Should I tell people I am?" I decided a lion doesn't have to roar for someone to know it is a lion. I relied on God's leading.

After rolling over to my side, I continued my prayer, "You sure have made this past year easier to handle. I know I will always miss Jane and Timmy, and I know the pain will get easier, but God, if you can use my situation to help others, please do it." I slept well and rested my weary body.

Chapter

4

I am not a fast runner. My dad used to tell me I was flat-footed and I ran like a truck. I have a fear of dogs after being attacked by a Great Dane when I was seven. So, I did not take time to find the size of the canine barking out horrific sounds upon my arrival. I was over 2,000 miles from home, in an unfamiliar place. I was already both nervous and eager to explore, but now I was terrified. This was my first stop, and it did not start out well for me.

I had walked up to the old stone fort, admiring the trees growing within its 100-foot-long walls, when I noticed a sign showing it would be closed from May 27 – June 5. I didn't have time to be disappointed by the news because I heard the dog, and I ran at once.

There I was, probably 400 yards away from the stone fort and at least 385 yards from my car. I bent over and dug my fingernails into my thighs as I tried to catch my breath. The pain in my skin, for a moment, took away the attention of the burning pain in my lungs. I was out of shape, and I proved it by gasping for air, trying to catch my breath, and the entire time listening for the beast to approach. I heard nothing and prayed he gave up and went back to protect his domain. I could not help but wonder, *Is this dog some sort of security for the site while they are closed?* I stood up and looked around. There were no homes, at least not in which people lived. I recognized the cabin and blacksmith shop from the pictures I had seen of the historic site.

Why is there a dog here?

Confident the danger had subsided, I walked slowly and cautiously to my car. At that moment, it was my protection, but it was still a great distance from me. I realized how far I had run. If the car did not have only thirty-five miles on the odometer, I would have considered the thought of abandoning it to avoid having to face one of my greatest fears. Thankfully, my mind rationalized again, it was my only means of returning home. But if the beast had its way, I would not live past the next few minutes. I looked in all directions, not sure what I was looking for, hoping beyond hope perhaps someone would be there to rescue me. I found no one. I only saw rocks, red dirt, and the dog.

Halfway between me and the car, he sat on the side of the road. I stopped and began a stare-down with him. I started breathing normally, but my legs still burned. As if an angel had turned up, I saw a car approaching us both from the northwest— my redeemer. But no, it was not a car. It was a mirage. I winked and rubbed my eyes. The vehicle was gone; well, it was never there.

Processing thoughts quickly and still hoping for a car to approach, I watched as the dog stood up and walked away. I left, too. When he stopped to look back at me, I stopped, too. I made sure he knew I had no intention of getting closer to him. In the distance, I heard a rustling. A hawk flew from the tree in the courtyard of Cove Fort. The dog sprinted toward the building and continued around the north side and out of my sight.

Lactic acid had built up in my legs, and I had slowed to a casual walk. I took into consideration the red dirt surrounding the building. It was dull, yet screamed of heat, and I imagined it was as hot as it looked. But I realized the warmth I felt emanated from the steamy pavement burning into the souls of my New Balance size thirteen sneakers. The dog was now out of sight and the hawk flew away. *Would the dog return for me?*

Across the flat desert landscape, beyond the fort, I saw a tiny figure walking toward where I assumed the dog must be. I wanted to scream at the rodent to run the other way, but I studied the object to see if it was a groundhog. It was too big for a squirrel. As the brown, large object moved closer, I could identify it as a beaver. Considering the dog would be distracted by the large-toothed mammal, I tried to move more quickly toward the car.

The piercing sound which had sent me running sounded again, like an alarm blaring from a security system. It was the dog barking. My body seized with fear, but this time I knew the dog was not coming for me. The beaver, hearing the sound as well, stood on its hind legs and sniffed twice, batting its left paw in the air. Recognizing the danger, it turned and ran in the direction from which it came.

I seized the opportunity and sprinted toward my car. My vision darkened from a lack of oxygen in my bloodstream, but I decided I could make it to the car and could pass out there. In my mind, I believed the state patrol or a backpacker would find me and get me the help I needed.

I reached my destination, and the dog was not in sight. I fumbled in my pocket for my fob, and instead of unlocking the door, I pushed the panic button; The horn honked. Having given up on the beaver and wanting to figure out what caused the ruckus, the dog investigated and quickly rounded the corner of the 150-year-old fort.

I heard the bark and didn't consider shutting off the panic button but grabbed my door handle, threw it open, and sat down. I watched as I slammed the door shut with a bang. The dog ran within three feet of my car, tried to halt, and kicked up a cloud of dust in front of him. Feeling safe now that I was in the vehicle, I watched as the beagle wagged its white and brown tail and panted.

I took in the canine's features—primarily brown and white with black blended in on his back in spots. His head was all brown except for a golf ball-sized black spot between his eyes. This caught my attention as it seemed to be a perfect circle, and if I had a golf ball, I probably could have filled the spot with it. His snout was white as were the tips of all four legs and paws. He was a pretty dog, but he had scared me into next week.

A beagle? It was a beagle. The way the dog sounded while it chased me had me believing for sure I would face an English Mastiff or worse. But it was much smaller and even looked like it may be a puppy. My mind drifted back to my neighbor's dog, back in Columbus, the one that attacked me while I grew up. It was not a beagle, but this beagle barked like it was a Great Dane. The hound breed is known for its deep howls, and this little animal sure had a loud bark. My thoughts returned to *why?* Why was there a dog near the old Cove Fort when the place had been shut down for days already and would be three days more before it opened again?

The entrapped humidity in the car caused me to sweat even more than I had been from my jog, and I turned the car on and rolled down the window. "Hey boy," I said as the dog wagged its tail even faster. "Are you lost, boy?"

I noticed he did not wear a collar. He seemed lost, but, he seemed like he planned to protect the fort. The conversation between us ended abruptly as the beaver had made its trek again. The beagle pursued his prey, and I took this opportunity to put the car in drive and return to the interstate.

My visit to Cove Fort proved not to be what I had hoped. The adrenaline rushed through my veins as a witness to the fact. My heart had stopped beating so rapidly, and I pushed back in my seat, rolled my window back up, and took in the new car smell. As the fort and the dog both faded into the distance of my side mirror, I made a mental note not to journal the encounter out of embarrassment. A beagle. Who gets chased by a beagle?

Chapter

5

I could have visited many small towns, but I wanted to see Elsinore, Utah. It started during my trip planning. I looked for towns along Interstate 70, and Elsinore jumped out at me. They built a water tower and featured pictures of its progress on their town's Facebook page. This intrigued me, so I stopped and visited.

Luscious green grass caught my eye as I approached the town hall building in Elsinore. It was a welcome change, having seen nothing but tumbleweeds, lava rocks, red dirt, and a vicious small dog for the last twenty-five miles. In front of the building, in the carefully manicured lawn, stood a pergola with a picnic table underneath it. Two people sat at the table.

I parked at the first available spot near a curved cement sidewalk separating the beautiful grass landscape and leading to the town hall entrance. I saw another vehicle in the next zone and assumed it belonged to the couple sitting at the table. Part of me said I should not bother them, but *it's all about the relationships*.

I slipped the car into park and looked around at my surroundings. Across the street, I saw a post office, and above the building, on the horizon, was unmistakably a water tower. I recognized it from the pictures I had seen on Facebook and smiled. I knew I was in the right place. I pushed the button on my dashboard, and the car engine shut down. I glanced to the left and saw the man and woman at the picnic table watching me. The woman had her back to me but occasionally turned her neck to look at me.

As I exited the car, the heat of the day reminded me how nice Utah was during the summer. It was hot but not at all humid, and it was still early. I even thought for a moment I could get used to living in a place like Elsinore. A climate without humidity was a nice thought. I raised my arms to the sky and stretched with a hearty motion upward, and moved toward the curved sidewalk. The woman turned to look at me. The man's reaction told a thousand tales. His gray eyebrows turned in, and wrinkles on the side of his eyes became more defined as he spoke softly to the woman in front of him. His face returned to normal, and I could tell he observed me peripherally, although he made it obvious.

I approached the pergola, raised my left hand, and greeted them. "Howdy!" and as soon as I said it, I wished I had not. *Howdy? Really Jake?* I wished I had given the standard *Hi.*

"Howdy yourself, young man," said the older gentleman. "Something I can help you with, sir?"

I gradually made my way to the edge of the picnic table so I could see them, and they could see me without squinting or turning their heads. "My name is Jake Anderson, and I am from Maryland and am here to…"

"Maryland?" the woman interrupted with an excited look on her face. "I have friends in Maryland. What part?"

The man looked at her with stern disdain, suggesting it was rude to ask, or maybe he thought it to be disrespectful to interrupt. Either way, it was easy to see how unhappy he was with her. I discerned at that moment they knew each other well.

"I am from Baltimore, ma'am."

"Well, it is nice to meet you, Jake. My name is Ralph Adams, and this here is my secretary, Marian." Ralph extended his hand to shake mine. He had a firm grip and rough skin. "I am the mayor of Elsinore."

"It's very nice to meet…"

"My friends are in Cumberland," interrupted Marian. "What brings you to Elsinore, Mr. Baltimore?" Marian's voice was deep but feminine. She had the rough sound of a woman who had smoked most of her life. It was a trait I recognized from many older women in my family. I guessed her age to be in the late fifties or early sixties as her hair was dark but spotted with gray, and the wrinkles around her eyes and mouth also indicated her age and likely smoking history. But it was her comment that caught me off guard. *Mr. Baltimore?* I guess they don't get a lot of tourists from Baltimore in Elsinore.

Without thinking, I answered her question. "I am passing through on my way along Interstate 70. It is rather complicated, but I can explain."

Marian continued, "Well, we have about thirty minutes left before we head to church if you want to sit a spell.

I had nowhere else to be. "I would love to. And if it is okay with you, I would like to join you for your service today."

"That would be fabulous. We don't get many visitors in this small town, so we would welcome the change," said Ralph.

For the next twenty-five minutes, we discussed my trip. They were amazed a sign existed in Baltimore mentioning Cove Fort. Of course, they preferred it would have indicated Elsinore. Being ten minutes from the beginning of Interstate 70 prevented them from this honor.

When Marian asked why I made the trip, I didn't mention my family, but I told them it was all because of a bag of roasted peanuts and a desire to serve God. I don't know if they grasped the entire reason I made the trip, but I tried to explain my obedience to God. They were not alone in their lack of understanding. It was day one, and I had not fully grasped the concept yet either.

When the time came to leave, Marian spoke up first. "It's time to go, my love."

Ralph most certainly recognized the expression on my face. "Oh, she's not just my secretary. She is also my wife."

I nodded my head several times. "Thank you for explaining."

We all laughed as we stood, stretched, and walked to our cars.

Reaching the parking lot, Marian walked to the passenger side of an older model Dodge Caravan. "Tell him about our church, Ralph." She opened the door and disappeared into the vehicle.

"We are a very spirit-filled non-denominational church, son, but I have to be honest. Some people think we are fake. You seem to be a man of great discernment and wisdom, so I will allow you to decide for yourself." He opened the door of the minivan and was about to sit. He looked back at me. "Follow me, we are minutes from our church, son." Ralph turned and sat down backward before groaning as he pulled his legs inside.

I remained standing at the edge of the sidewalk. I could feel the heat emanating from the blacktop as my toes hung slightly over the concrete walkway. I looked toward my car. *Should I follow? Or should I go on? Find another town.* I decided I would visit their church. I couldn't abandon the trip already, and as I reminded myself, I had nowhere else to be.

As I drove behind Ralph's van, I processed what had happened and followed blindly behind. I did not realize the traffic light had changed from yellow to red, and I did not stop. Moments later, I saw a police officer behind me with his lights flashing. Thankfully, I traveled with the mayor of this small town, and he had turned right into a parking lot of what was undoubtedly a church. I parked behind him, and the police officer pulled in behind me.

The building was small. A white steeple sat atop the roof and extended twenty feet above the peak. In it was a bell, and a cross sat on top of it. The church was white and had two stained glass windows on the side. Visible in front of me was a red double door with a small but unreadable sign. It reminded me of a small Methodist church I had visited in Adena, Ohio, many years ago.

The police officer pulled up behind me. Ralph exited the van and gingerly made his way to the side of the police car. Since the officer pulled me over, I remained in my vehicle with my hands on the wheel. I watched in my side mirror as Ralph laughed, and I could see the officer pointing at my car before he turned his lights off, backed up, and pulled away. I exited the vehicle.

Ralph walked over to me with a smile on his face. "If you are going to run the only red light in town, make sure the only cop in town is not sitting at the only gas station in town when you do so."

I looked back at our route. I could see a gas station sign, and I could also see a traffic light. "Ooops."

"It also helps if you are going to run the red light to be following the mayor of the town. But so you know, I will have to have Marian make him a pumpkin pie now."

Marian had come to the front of my car as Ralph talked, and we all three laughed. We walked toward the door, and I could make out what the small sign indicated on the center of the left door. "Elsinore Christian Church - Pastor Ralph Adams."

"You're the mayor of this town and the pastor, too?"

Marian laughed. "I knew you would get a kick out of it when you found out."

"Yes, son, I've been pastor here for thirty-five years. Only been mayor of this wonderful town for three years." Marian opened the right door, Ralph opened the left door, and they both motioned me inside. "Welcome, young man."

I stepped inside, and I smelled what I could only describe as a sweet smell. It had a lemon scent. Cleaning solution filled the air. Ralph must have recognized me sniffing because he said, "Yes, our janitor does go heavy on the pine cleaner, but he does one heck of a job for us."

As we walked in, many people addressed Ralph as Pastor Adams, and a few called him mayor. A young girl ran up to him, grabbed his leg, and said, "Pastor Mayor, I am so glad to see you." "I'm glad to see you too, Becky. Are you ready to love on Jesus today?"

"I am, Pastor Mayor." She turned and ran back to the pew with her mom.

I saw ten pews on each side of the church. The first five on each side, from the front, were empty, but the remaining five on each side were nearly full. *It looks like I will be in the first pew today.* As the thought passed through my mind, Marian grabbed my arm and led me to the right.

"This is our guest seat," she said and pointed to a leather arm chair with beaded arms. "That is, if you want to sit here. Otherwise, you will have to sit in the front on this side." She pointed to the right set of pews before us.

"This will do," I said, and I took a seat. I watched as Ralph walked toward the front, greeting everyone as he walked up. Marian took a seat on the left side in the fourth pew back. Ralph continued up the two small steps leading to a small chair behind the pulpit. An organ played loud music as he sat down, and everyone raised their hands including Ralph and Marian. *Should I put my hands up?* I continued to observe. The organist finished playing after what seemed like five minutes, and Ralph stood up.

"He's alive!"

"He's alive indeed," came the sound of all voices in the church in unison. I guessed there were about eighty men, women, and children in the small white church.

Ralph continued, "Our God has forgiven our sins."

"Jesus is our Savior," came the reply in unison.

"He sent us the great counselor."

"Spirit fall! Spirit fall! Spirit fall!"

I even said *Spirit fall* with the last iteration.

"My friends," Ralph spoke, "today, we have in our midst a special guest."

"Thank you, Jesus," shouted Marian.

"Today, in our guest seat is Jake Anderson, from Baltimore, Maryland."

"Welcome, Jake!" Again the voices were in unison, but no one looked back. They continued to look straight ahead.

"Last year, after the tower was completed..."

"Thank you for the living water!" someone on my side of the church yelled out.

"The LORD gave me a dream, and He said a gifted young man would visit our church. I believe that man is here today in our midst."

Several jumped to their feet, dancing and throwing their arms in the air. "Praise Jesus! Spirit fall! Our God lives!" Moments later, the organ played again. Marian danced, too. Ralph looked around until his eyes met mine. He did not dance but occasionally threw his arms in the air.

The excitement continued for about six minutes until Ralph finally motioned both arms up and down, and everyone sat. Ralph opened his Bible and read.

"The Spirit of the LORD is on me because he has anointed me to proclaim good news to the poor. He has sent me to proclaim freedom for the prisoners and recovery of sight for the blind, to set the oppressed free, to proclaim the year of the Lord's favor."

"My friends, freedom for Sara is coming." Ralph threw his arms in the air with palms lifted to heaven. He tilted his head back, and for a moment, I thought I heard him speaking in tongues. But it was once again interrupted with loud praises, dancing, and the organ playing loudly.

As I walked out with Marian and Ralph an hour later, I approached my car and considered my next move. I wanted to visit a few small towns on my way to the Triangle Mountain campground, but I also felt some hunger pains. Ralph's message was good, but he talked about freedom for Sara, although he never mentioned who Sara was. His daughter, I presumed.

I wanted to journal my experience and wondered if I might find a McDonald's nearby where I could sit in solitude for an hour. But Marian had other plans, and it became apparent she would not take no for an answer. She had invited me to their home for lunch. With intrigue about Sara, I agreed I would visit. She said she had made lasagna, a Sunday tradition for the last six months. I approached my car when Ralph reminded me. "Oh, and Jake, make sure you don't run the red light this time."

We both laughed. While in the car and driving away, I prayed out loud, "God, thank you for this experience. Thank you for Ralph and Marian, but Lord, who is Sara? I pray for her freedom wherever she is, and I pray she receives the freedom she deserves."

Chapter

6

Ralph navigated his minivan into a gravel driveway. At least I
thought it was a driveway since there was an opening in a tree line
big enough for a car to fit in. However, the gravel we drove on
was as red as the gravel and dirt mix in the yard. The trees were
tall, and most were pine. I could feel my car's tires crunching a
few pinecones as I passed between the small trees lining the
driveway. All other trees in the distance were near the same
height. I estimated them to be forty feet tall.

The house was a white rectangle shape with a red metal hip
roof. A white fence adorned the front of the home, and pleasantly
planted in front of the structure were manicured shrubs. As I
approached from the right side, I could see the house was square,
and the porch continued to wrap around to the back.

Ralph continued toward the back of the home, and I was
unsure if I should follow or stop where I was. I stopped, leaving a
thirty-foot gap between us. I put the car into park as I saw Ralph
exit, grab his hip, wince in pain, and motion me to join him. We
went in through the back door. When I was younger, my dad
always said back door friends were the best type of friends to

have. But I always thought it was because my mom never wanted us to use the front door since it was only a short distance to the highway.

I stepped out and could feel the day's heat hit me, but, again, it was a dry heat, and no humidity existed. I walked along the fenced-in porch toward the back of the house. I followed Ralph into the back door as Marian had gone in first. The home was beautiful. For as far as I could see, hardwood floors adorned the home. I noticed a distinct cream color tint to the walls, and halfway up each division was a chair rail with a wallpaper design I immediately recognized as a Navajo theme. We walked into the kitchen, and I could see a long line of white cabinets along the wall in front of me. To the right, I saw a small dining area. One would have to pass through what looked like a half-hexagon archway to get to it. To the left, past the cabinets, was a similar archway entry to what I assumed was the living room. In the corner of the front of the house stood a wood-burning stove. I could see the hardwood and Navajo chair rail wallpaper in the room as well.

"Your home is beautiful," I said as I continued to take in the new surroundings.

"Thank you," replied Marian as she tended to the oven.

A sweet smell of Italian food filled the air as she opened the oven door, and my mouth watered. Ralph had disappeared to the right side of the kitchen to a room I could not see well. I stood waiting for instructions while taking in the tantalizing smell of Marian's lasagna.

I felt something brush against me. "Meow," said the orange cat, weaving in and out of my legs as it purred. "Meow." I was about to bend down to pet him when Ralph returned. The cat darted to the left toward the room with the fireplace.

"I see you met Malachi," greeted Ralph as he raised his left hand, motioning for me to walk to the dining area to my right.

"Love that name."

43

"Sara named him," Ralph said, pointing at Malachi, who had returned to the kitchen. "She loved him."

I was at a loss for words. I wondered if Sara was Sara Adams, the daughter of Ralph and Marian. I was about to speak but remained silent. Malachi decided I was not a threat and slowly walked back to the living room. He turned his head around one last time, almost to double-check the stranger in his home before he continued out of sight.

As Marian scooped piping hot lasagna to plates, I broke the silence. "You've mentioned Sara twice." I turned to Ralph to study his reactions. "Is she your daughter?"

"Yes."

I immediately discerned the thought of her had brought some potent emotions to the forefront of his mind. Marian interrupted us as she walked in and set a plate in front of me. It looked as delicious as it smelled. She left again and returned with two more dishes. One she placed in front of Ralph and the other on the table across from me. She left one more time and returned with three glasses in one hand and a pitcher of water in the other.

I looked at Ralph and saw a tear rolling down the side of his face. He closed his eyes and folded his hands.

"Let's say a blessing for the food." Marian sat down, and I closed my eyes. "Father, thank you for the food we are about to eat. Thank you for the dream and confirm for us, please, if this fulfills it. Bless our food and our souls. Amen"

He mentioned the dream again, as he had done in church. Did he think I was the one to fulfill the dream? I didn't know how I could be of any help.

Our lunch was silent and delicious. None of us spoke a single word while we ate. I scraped my plate with my fork and took one last bite. I glanced at Ralph, who now stared at his empty plate. My eyes met Marian's, and we both looked at Ralph again. "Ralph?" I asked. He looked up from his catatonic gaze and met my eyes. "Can I pray for your daughter? Sara, is it?"

Ralph pushed his plate away from him. Marian stood up and grabbed it. She motioned for me to provide her with mine as well. Ralph took a drink of his water and finally broke his silence. "Do you like Muslims, Jake?"

"Sir?"

"Muslims, Jake. Do you like Muslims?"

I processed this question quickly before stating my opinion. "I don't judge people based on their choice of religion nor their ethnicity nor gender."

"Yes, of course. Mark 12:31 and Matthew 22:39. Love your neighbor as yourself. I believe it, and I lived that life until about four years ago. When Sara met Sadiq, I welcomed him into my home and treated him like a son. But he will never receive my forgiveness for this."

I am big on offering forgiveness. I preached on this probably more than anything at all. I get irritated when I hear someone say they refuse to forgive someone for various reasons. I also felt Ralph's pain. I knew there was more to this story, and he wanted to tell it. "I'm listening" was all I could say, while silently hoping he would continue. I also prayed for him from my heart.

"Christmas, two years ago. Sara left the house the next day, the day after Christmas, and that is the last time we saw her."

Marian had returned to the dining room and gathered more plates, napkins, and anything on the table by this time. The look on her face was one of disgust, anger, and hurtfulness. She did not like this story.

"Let me back up, but I will be brief. Sara met Sadiq at UCLA. She brought him here to meet us, and he was polite, kind, and courteous. He spoke incredible English, and he wore jeans with holes in them, so he seemed to be Americanized if you know what I mean."

I nodded.

"But on Thanksgiving, she told us after New Year, Sadiq was going to Egypt to visit his parents. He lived in the United States with his uncle for ten years, and he wanted to see his parents. He wanted Sara to go with him. At first, her mother and I were concerned. Mainly because she didn't have a passport and only partially because the whole Middle East was volatile, but he lived in Egypt and not someplace like Iran or Iraq, so we helped her pay for her ticket. We expected a phone call a week later, once she was settled and had time." Ralph looked at me and quivered. Marian had returned, and she, too, had tears in her eyes. She walked up to him and put her arm around him.

Marian looked at me and spoke for her husband. "The phone call did not happen until after New Year's day, last year. It had been over a year since we heard from her."

I was shocked. My jaw dropped, and I leaned back in my chair.

Ralph wiped his tears. Marian walked back to the kitchen. "She also dropped a bomb on us." He shook his head. "She wasn't in Egypt. Sadiq had lied. He was Iranian, and she was living in Tehran. But it gets better. She told us we had a two-week-old grandson named Atash. That means fire. I have a grandson I will likely never see, and his name means fire. So not only have I lost my daughter, I lost my grandson, too."

Marian walked back in once again, wiping her hands on a dishtowel. "We knew she was in trouble. I could hear it in her voice, but she could not say much." She sat down. "When she was young, we used to have a code word for danger. If she ever called us and said, 'Today is a great day for a bike ride,' we would know she was in trouble."

Ralph jumped in. "I answered the phone, and I said hello, and I heard my daughter say 'Hi Daddy...'" He choked back more tears before continuing. "'Hi Daddy, isn't today a great day for a bike ride?' Now, praise God, I kept my composure, and I replied with yes, dear. It is a great day for a ride. I think your mom and I will do it today."

"I grabbed the other phone and jumped on the call," Marian

said, pointing to a phone hanging on the wall to the right of where I sat. "She said she would not be home for a while but was looking forward to the bike ride. She said she was well, and she apologized for not calling sooner."

"Did she tell you she was living in Iran?"

"No," said Ralph, now perfectly composed. "She said Cairo was so incredible, and she loved it there. She said she was not sorry for letting us know all was fine, but she was so involved in day-to-day life with Sadiq, and she was working with her father-in-law in his chemistry business."

"Wait, she said she was married?" I asked.

"Yes," continued Ralph. "We didn't know she was married, but she gave us clues. She had gone to school for chemical engineering, and she made a point of telling us Sadiq's father owned a chemistry business. Still, she knew he did not tell the truth because she couldn't answer any questions about it. But now, she told us she worked for this business."

"It was then she told us about Atash," Marian added. "But we still don't know if this was some sort of signal, too. The agent we spoke to seems to think it was some sort of code, too."

"Agent?"

"Yes," added Ralph. We contacted the police, who in turn contacted the state department. They traced the phone number we caught on our caller ID, and that is how we knew she was in Iran. But the government is not doing much to get her back for us."

"Ralph, we don't know for sure."

"It's been over a year since I last heard from my daughter. I have not seen her for two and a half years. I would say they are not doing much."

In the ensuing minute of silence, as we all searched our thoughts, The LORD spoke to me in his unique way and told me, "Tell them Boston." I questioned The LORD. It didn't seem right. I heard it again. So, I mustered up the courage to speak and said, "God says I should ask you about Boston."

Ralph stood up, as did Marian. They looked at each other. "Praise God!" they both said in unison.

"At Sadiq's uncle's home?" asked Ralph.

"Pardon me?"

"Sadiq's uncle lives in Boston, and it is where Sadiq lived before traveling to UCLA for school. That's where they supposedly were before leaving for Egypt. This makes sense. Yes, they must be back in town. Or did they even go? Has this all been a big lie? But we tracked the phone number."

"Yeah, when are we supposed to go?" asked Marian.

Supposed to go? Her answer perplexed me. "I am not sure you are supposed to go anywhere, Marian. God said ask them about Boston. He didn't say you should go there."

We sat together and prayed God would give them wisdom and understanding and direct them about Boston. Sara had written down Sadiq's uncle's address, and Marian had found it while looking through her room for any clues for the agents. We prayed, and we talked. As the hours continued to pass by, I realized my plans to stop in Aurora and Salina were not likely to happen. But I knew I was where I needed to be. These people had pain, and they needed and wanted to talk.

Four hours after our lunch, Marian talked to her sister about getting plane tickets to Boston, while Ralph and I discussed the book of Acts. We were both interested in how the church grew and established itself in the ancient world. We both agreed what we do as today's church was not at all what God had initially intended. Still, we also decided God uses imperfect people in all of His grace and mercy, whether they are in a four-wall church or roaming the streets, as long as their heart is in the right place.

The fourth hour became the sixth hour. Marian kept insisting they fly to Boston and started looking for tickets. Ralph told her he preferred to alert the agent in charge of the case. He was sure they had scoured Boston looking for her.

I gave the couple my cell phone number and accepted their offer to stay with them for the evening. Triangle Mountain would have to wait. Before bed, I sat alone with Ralph. We had finished our conversation about the book of Acts, and I felt a strong desire to pray for Sara. I walked to Ralph's chair, and I placed my right hand on his left shoulder. "Ralph, I want to pray for you."

"Sure, Jake. Go ahead. I will take all the prayers I can get."

"Lord, God of heaven, Maker of all things. Giver and Sustainer of life. I pray for my friends Ralph and Marian. I pray they find their daughter. I pray they forgive Sadiq. I pray you will pour your spirit upon Ralph and Marian and use this experience in their lives to help them grow in a relationship with you. Help them, Father, to trust you. Help them overcome obstacles and help them both see you as the wonderful Father you are. Please help them to clear their minds and seek your face. I ask you to do this, Father, in the name of your Son, our Savior, Jesus Christ. Amen."

As I opened my eyes, Ralph was crying. He reached over and turned off the lamp sitting on an end table by his chair. I walked back and sat on the couch. We looked at each other before he spoke.

"Jake, what did you do?

"Excuse me, sir?"

"Jake, no one has ever prayed for me like that and had such an immediate impact. I cannot explain it. As you prayed, I felt warmth in your hands, and I suddenly felt like I could forgive Sadiq. I always said I would not forgive that man unless my daughter was returned unharmed."

"God is good, Ralph. God is good."

"Yes, all the time, but what did you do?"

"I prayed. God did the rest."

"Well, He has blessed you with great power. I feel so incredibly new and alive now. You know what? I feel confident I am going to see my daughter again. For the last year, I wanted to have a funeral for her. I wanted to try to forget her. I felt she was lost and probably dead. But you have inspired me not to give up."

"Well, sir, I did not do it. I am a vessel. God has inspired you through the Holy Spirit."

"Yes, I know."

But did he know? I had run into so many people afraid to tell me they did not understand what I meant. Our Christian society sometimes fosters pride. Many will ask for more details or a better understanding, but we often don't ask and act as we know. Ralph was a prime example. He had been a pastor for a long time, so he was "expected" to not only have a strong relationship with God, but to know all of the answers. I knew this was not the case.

I never expected him to know, but I sensed he knew the inspiration came from the Holy Spirit. I knew he believed it, but I didn't trust he truly understood what it meant. I had done nothing but pray. In some regard, perhaps God had worked through the Holy Spirit to bring spiritual healing to Ralph. I was not sure.

When Ralph had said earlier he would not forgive, I knew he was in bondage. Unforgiveness is a bitter root which entangles a person's soul. When we harbor unforgiveness, we often believe we are in some way paying someone back for the harm they may have caused us. But I knew the damage only came to the person who would not forgive. It was a powerful tactic of the enemy. I wanted to carry on the conversation with Ralph, but I witnessed his head droop. If I had not spoken up and said I would like to go to bed, he would have likely fallen asleep in the chair.

Chapter

7

The tent was up, and the air mattress was full. I was lucky to be given the last camping location with electricity. It was a two-outlet socket, but I only needed one to blow up the air mattress. Yes, it was June, but I knew I would not need a fan nor a portable AC unit. My plan all along was to sleep in my larger six-person tent or with someone who offered to let me stay as Ralph and Marian had. I had the money for hotel rooms, but I wanted to take time to be close to God in the creation He made. When I arrived at Triangle Mountain, they were full, so I had to continue until I came to a place called Masons Draw, near Moab.

The location reminded me of the story of Ruth and Boaz since Ruth was a Moabitess woman. But I also chose this campground because it is rare to have wooded areas in Utah; however, they do exist, and this campground had trails through trees. I spent Monday, Tuesday, Wednesday, and Thursday nights at the campground in Utah. Friday morning, I packed up, with Colorado in my sights.

While at the campground, I kept to myself for the most part. During the day, I would take long hikes on trails at the various parks near Moab, and sometimes I would sit on a log or a manufactured bench and pray. I prayed for myself. I prayed for Ralph and Marian and their daughter, Sara. I prayed for Joe Smith and his family. I prayed for the Davidson family.

I also prayed for my deceased wife's parents. They still took the tragedy hard. July 12 was a little over a month away, and it would be the first anniversary of Jane's death. I had long forgiven the inexperienced driver for smashing into them, but I know my father-in-law, for one, had not yet.

I spent most of the day Monday relaxing and praying. I would walk a few hundred yards and stop and pray. Around five o'clock, I went back to my tent, made dinner for myself over the fire, and fell asleep in my chair. I awoke an hour later as the sun stopped its scorching heat for the day. It was still two hours from setting for the evening, but the heat had significantly diminished.

The following two days were much the same. I would walk, I would pray, I would pray while walking. I felt like I became closer to God, and I pieced together many events. Thursday, I took a new trail, one I had not traveled before. I had to walk a mile to get to it. Once I arrived at the head of this new path, signs indicated a two-mile loop. About halfway through the walk, while sitting on a log drinking some water, I heard a voice call out to me.

"Hey friend, got room on that log for me?"

He looked older. I guessed him to be close to seventy. He walked with a stick in one hand, and I could see his other hand behind his back. He had white hair that peeked out on the sides of his ball cap. I recognized the logo; it was an Angel's baseball cap. He wore an orange-padded vest and a long-sleeve white shirt. Blue jeans adorned his legs, and a pair of hiking boots protected his feet. As he approached, I could tell it was a leash he carried with his left hand, and a dog in tow sniffed the sides of the trail. As the man walked, the dog would sniff until the leash became tight. He would trot a few steps and start the process all over again.

"Sure, there is plenty of room, have a seat. Take a load off and catch your breath."

"Oh, I haven't lost any breath I need to catch. I may be old, but my God has blessed me more than you know." He stopped walking, sat down on the downed tree approximately three feet in diameter; it made for the perfect bench height.

The dog with him continued to sniff out his new territory. The man set his walking stick between us and offered his hand in a welcoming fashion.

"Jake Anderson. Nice to meet you. And yes, I agree, Our God is mighty gracious to us." He didn't offer his name in return, but I didn't feel the need to ask it.

"He is indeed, young man." He looked to the left and whistled before saying, "Come on, boy. Come see our new friend."

I finally caught a better glimpse of the man's companion. It was a young brown beagle pup with a dark spot the size of a golf ball between its eyes. His snout and the bottoms of all four feet were the whitest of whites. I wanted to jump and run, but I fought back the fear that gripped me, and I said to the man, "I think the dog and I have met before." As the dog drew nearer, he let out a loud howl which quickly confirmed it for me. I stood, but my mind told my legs to stay, so I don't think I looked as if I was ready to run. But I was. "This is your dog?"

"Yes, yes. Do you say you met him before? What makes you say such a thing?"

"Well, let's put it this way. If you found this dog at the old Cove Fort site, I definitely met him before."

"You don't say!" The older man looked at the dog, looked at me, and back at the dog. "Well, what do you know, Zion? He saw you at Cove Fort, too." He looked back at me. "He's not yours, is he? I mean, you didn't mean to leave him there, did you?"

"Me?" I pointed at my chest with my right index finger. "Leave him?" I laughed. "No, but he did give me quite a scare the other day when I saw him there."

"And what day did you visit?"

I had to think for a moment. *I was there Sunday.* "Well, I guess it was Sunday morning."

"No kidding." He looked at his watch and mouthed something to himself. "That was several days ago." He looked back down at the dog. "And how did he look when you saw him? Was he in good shape?"

"Well, he chased me and scared me to pieces, that's for sure."

"Little Zion scared you? I can't imagine." Zion sat at the man's feet, waiting for his owner's hand to caress his body. "This little guy was almost dead when I found him last night. But I gave him some water, and we got some food for him, and he perked right up. No tags on him, so I am not sure who he belongs to."

"Yeah, I noticed when I saw him. I couldn't take him with me, and I figured someone would come to get him, so I left him alone."

"Oh, you must not be from these parts?"

"No, sir. I am from Maryland."

"Oh, I see. Yeah, people around here are constantly taking dogs and cats to Cove Fort, and well, I heard someone say they found a sheep there one time, too. It seems to be a tradition, though I find it to be a pretty lousy one. If you want to get rid of a pet, drop it off at the fort. If you want a pet, go pick one up."

I was shocked by what I heard. But it also explained why I ran into this dog at the fort. I was thankful the man with no name had stopped and picked up Zion. *Interesting name.* "Did you say his name is Zion?"

"Yes, that is the name The LORD gave me when I asked him what I should call the fellow." He reached down and rubbed

Zion's ears. "You know what Zion is, young fellow?"

"Sure, it's Jerusalem and also a mountain."

"Yes, indeed. Zion is the place our Savior will return to, but there is an old Jewish tradition that the word Zion was the term they used to graft in a foreign grape to the natural vine. The process of the grafting was called Zion."

I learned something new. But if it was true, it made sense because Jesus told us that He is the vine, and we are the branches, and He has grafted us into this vine. "I have never heard that."

"No, I guess you would not have. I mean, if you look in the dictionary for Zion, it will say what you said. It may even call it a Christian term, but Zion is as Hebrew as it gets."

"Interesting that you said Hebrew and not Jewish."

"Oh yes, I get that a lot. But I already know that you know why I said it that way."

"You do?"

"Yes, I knew as soon as I walked up that you were a powerful man of God, with great understanding and knowledge. You know all Jews are Hebrews, but not all Hebrews are Jews. Am I right?"

I smiled as I recalled my first lesson on this teaching. "Yes, I know that. Jews are from JEW- DUH and Hebrews are all descendants of Abraham, Isaac, and Jacob."

"Indeed. The LORD favors you highly, sir. Best of luck with your journey." He stood up and walked away. I was unsure if this was the end of our conversation, and I was about to speak when he turned to me and said, "It's okay when you spend a few days in Denver. You'll need it, and there will still be plenty of time left for the other states." He turned and walked again, with Zion now traveling in front of him.

"But...," I stammered. "I..." I was at a complete loss for words. So, I watched him walk up the trail. I looked down, closed my eyes, and thanked The LORD for the encounter. I prayed for about one minute straight. As I opened my eyes, I saw a twinkling of light on the ground by my foot. I reached down to grab a golden coin I knew had not been there earlier. I picked it up and walked at a brisk pace, trying to catch the man and Zion. But as I reached the top of the small hill before me, where the path leveled off for a mile, I saw no one.

I stopped, looked around, and this time jogged up the trail. In the distance, I could see a young couple coming toward me. I stopped, and as they approached, I raised my hand to motion for them to stop. They slowed and continued jogging in place as I asked, "Did you see a man and a dog walking this way?"

The man said, "We've been on this path since the parking lot, and you are the first person we've seen all day."

"And how far is the parking lot?"

The man looked at his watch. "We've been jogging for eleven minutes now. So, if you will excuse us." They both ran past me and started down the hill toward the downed tree.

"Come on, God!" I shouted out loud. But I spoke silently to myself. *What was that? Who was that guy, and where did he and Zion go?* I looked through the trees, hoping to glimpse someone not on the path. Signs everywhere along the trail warned hikers to stay on the course to avoid rattlesnakes and other dangerous wildlife. I am sure the joggers didn't see him. I mean, I could have been visited by an angel, but Zion? That was the dog I saw at Cove Fort. I reasoned that the joggers didn't see anyone, and I probably sat there longer than I realized.

Shortly after this encounter, I arrived back at my tent, packed everything up, and left for Colorado. I had seen enough of Utah, and it was glorious, but I was ready to get back on the road and see where The LORD would lead me next.

Chapter

8

Grand Junction, Colorado, has some sentimental value to me. My girlfriend from my sophomore year in college grew up here, and of course, Joe Smith from the plane did, too. I didn't plan to spend more than a day here while traveling on my way to Denver, but when I arrived late, I found my way to a Motel 6 near the airport and slept in a bed instead of on an air mattress.

When I visited the Grand Junction visitor center and discovered all Grand Junction had to offer, I stayed a few extra days and left it up to God which church I visited, if any. I had many choices, including a Christian Church, at least two Latter-day Saints' churches, and a handful of non-denominational churches. I prayed and let God lead me to The Cradle of Christ Church on Orchard Avenue.

Friday morning I visited the church, and it was open. I had a wonderful conversation with the pastor, Tom. My first question was how the name came about. He explained when he and his wife started the church, they had come to this decision on a Christmas Eve, and they felt the name embodied what they wanted to share…that God's love came on Christmas and came to stay. It was the most interesting name for a church I had ever heard.

With a cup of hot coffee in hand and sitting in his study, I explained I planned to travel along Interstate 70 and take forty days to do so. He was fascinated and asked if I would stay until Sunday and if I wanted to speak. I hesitated at first, but I decided I would do it. I had not spoken from a pulpit in several months, but I was comfortable with doing so, and decided I would use one of my favorite sermons, The Felix Syndrome. As I explained the sermon, Pastor Tom was thrilled and thought it would go over well.

When we ended our conversation, Pastor Tom joined me for lunch at a local restaurant called Taco John's, and we continued our discussion about Grand Junction, the love of God, and Ralph and Marian. Pastor Tom said someone like Sadiq would never be welcome at his church. I questioned why.

"Because they cause problems. We are a conservative establishment, and we can't have disruptions like that. Besides, these days, public opinion is important, and we want to share God's love, and sometimes people like Sadiq bring out the worst in people."

"Pastor Tom, let me make sure you understand what I mean by the Felix Syndrome. In Acts 24, Felix used to like to listen to Paul speak. But when Paul spoke about striving to be righteous as Jesus is righteous, Felix would throw him out. Now Felix was anti-Semitic, though he was a freed slave, so listening to Paul at all was interesting. What's more, I will speak about loving all kinds of people and how Paul encouraged this, too."

"Yeah, Yeah, I get it. Felix was progressive, and Paul was conservative. I think it fits well with my church. We are conservative. So, what do you think of those tacos? Pretty good, huh?"

I could not believe what I heard. I tried to reason that perhaps I didn't understand what Tom said instead of him not understanding me. I decided I would continue to pray to see if God wanted me to be there and found a few other churches I could have attended. Pastor Tom picked up the check, and I left a twenty-dollar bill for the tip. Jane had been a waitress in college and always told me how she loved to tip heavily.

We shook hands before parting ways. Tom drove to the east, while I went west, until I came to a park known as Long Family Memorial Park. I parked near an open field and watched a mom teaching her son how to kick a soccer ball correctly. It brought back memories of Jane and Timmy playing in our backyard in Albeth Heights. I closed my eyes and prayed, asking God if I was still doing the right thing. He calmly assured me with His still small voice that I was faithful to His will.

While driving back to my hotel, I passed underneath Interstate 70 and by a coffee shop called Octopus Coffee. I wondered if their coffee was eight times stronger than national chains. I made a mental note to check it out in the morning. I pulled into Motel 6 and considered going for a swim because the pool was still and empty, but the grumbling in my stomach suggested I should not. I am not sure if it was the tacos or something else, but I was not well.

I watched the local news channel in the evening and learned there had been a gang-related shooting in Denver. Two young men were dead, and authorities searched for another man in connection with the murders. A picture of a heavily tattooed Caucasian man with multiple piercings on his face appeared on the screen. While I am sure many were already passing judgment on this young man, I reminded myself that God loved him, too, and for all I knew, that young man could be a pastor someday. I became honest with God. I told Him I would probably not want to listen to a man with a skull on his cheek. "Could he be a pastor, God?"

Beyond doubt, I heard in my mind, "I spoke through a donkey, didn't I?"

Yes, God, you certainly did. That was the last thing I remember before I fell asleep. The sleep timer shut the television off an hour later.

Larger, more modern, expensive, and way too much were the words I used to describe the Cradle of Christ Church. I arrived an hour before the eleven o'clock service, and this time I went in through the main entrance. I followed the office signs during my visit a few days earlier, and the church seemed smaller then. As I walked through the main doors, into what I later learned was "the intake area," two women stood behind a solid oak desk, waist-high and in a semi-circle shape. They welcomed me, and the lady on the right offered me a coffee mug. On it was a picture of Pastor Tom, another turn-off for me. Had it been a picture of a cross or even the traditional Catholic rendition of Jesus, I would not have been as offended. The lady on the left must have noticed my facial expression because she said, "We want people to become comfortable with our wonderful pastor. He doesn't like his face on the mug, but we have found it helps break the ice for newcomers.

I smiled approvingly, but in my mind thought *you caused more ice for me, ma'am.* I looked around, hoping to see Pastor Tom, but I noticed small gatherings of four or five people in small groups. Some stood, drinking from their pastor image mugs, while a few groups sat in various sitting areas. Beyond the crowd, I saw four sets of double doors leading to the sanctuary. I walked to the center of the worship area when I heard a familiar voice from the side.

"Pastor Jake, what a pleasure to have you with us."

I turned in time to see Pastor Tom adorned in a black full-length robe with a green stole that had a white chalice on one end and a brown loaf of bread on the other end. I remember thinking it looked cartoony. I smiled and offered a warm greeting. "Good Morning, Tom."

The lady on the right, the one who handed me the mug, gasped loudly.

I turned to see what had caused this when Pastor Tom shook his head and said, "Jake and I are on a first-name basis. It's alright, Janine." He watched my eyes as he spoke, and I turned my head but in a split second turned back to look at him again. He gave Janine a stern look. When he glimpsed me looking at him again, he immediately turned it into a smile. "Bless you, young lady, for your service in our intake area."

Interesting. This guy demands to be called Pastor Tom. I didn't know, but now I did. *Can I leave now, God?*

"Pastor Jake, please let me show you around The Cradle of Christ."

Okay, that sounded weird. I was mad at myself for thinking of leaving. I still wanted to explore as I believed it was an interesting name for a church. I wondered if the story had more details. I followed Tom (and from the moment I witnessed his overbearing approach and knew of his desire to be called by his title, I called him Tom) to the sanctuary.

"I want to show you what makes this church so special. I held back from telling you Friday because I wanted you to see it firsthand."

We continued walking down the long auditorium-style

sanctuary. I looked around at the plush stadium seating. I estimated it held at least a thousand. I looked to the ceiling to see lights and catwalks, and I looked to the sides and saw enormous speakers and televisions. *This place looks more like a television studio than a church.* When we finally reached the confluence, I counted eight rows of seating. I redid the math in my mind. *At least 1,500, maybe more.*

In the shape of a half octagon, the stage had three steps on all sides. The blue Berber style carpeting was crisp under my feet as I stepped up to the platform. The pulpit was three feet wide and made of five-inch-thick hand-carved glass. Atop the glass structure, another glass platform laid perpendicular to the glass post holding it. I decided if I saw Tom's image in the pulpit, I would leave immediately. As we reached the top of the forum, I turned left to see the pulpit's surface. I did not see it.

"This way, Jake. I want to show you why we built this church."

I turned back, and Tom motioned me to follow him. I could see a white octagon on the floor beyond where he stood. It was eight feet in diameter on all sides. *They should have called it the church of the immaculate shape.* I immediately felt a check in my spirit as I had that thought. I grieved the Holy Spirit with my thoughts. But I still found it funny.

"Right here." Tom walked to the center of the octagon and stomped his right foot down. His robe kicked up slightly, revealing his black wing-tipped shoes and white slacks before it fell back in place, covering both. "Right here," he said again.

I walked closer and looked down at the white carpeted stop sign resemblance. I almost expected it to say STOP, but instead, it had in faint gray letters the word heal.

"Heal?"

"Yes! You can see it. That means you are anointed."

I looked at him. "I mean, it is faint, but it says heal. It's right there." I pointed at the floor.

"Yes, Jake. I see it, too. But not everyone can see it." Tom looked around the auditorium. The loudness picked up as people entered. "Beth, Beth, please come here."

I turned to see a young girl, probably ten or eleven, walk up to the stage and up beside me.

"Beth, what do you see?"

Beth looked up at me and back at the floor. Her face was as straight as the blond hair that stopped at her shoulders. She put her hands at her side, grabbed the sides of her knee-length dress, and bent over slightly. "I still don't see it, Pastor Tom. I only see the white carpet."

"Thank you, go back now."

Beth turned around and walked back to her parents. I watched her mom speak as her daughter approached the edge of the third row of the second column of seating. I am not a lip reader, so I was unsure what she asked the young girl, but I guessed it was "Did you tell him no?" I squinted, hoping to discern more, but Tom grabbed my attention again, but not before I saw the young girl nodding in agreement.

"It was at this spot right here, twenty years ago, I had a gun in my mouth. This building sat on a field owned by my dad. He wanted to make it a park. I came here at this very spot, and it was here I wanted to take my life. But God showed me a hexagon around me, like a stop sign and I…"

"An octagon?"

"Huh?" Tom leaned down as if he had not heard me.

"Octagon, Tom. You are standing on an octagon."

Tom looked at me. "Yeah, Yeah, sure. I stood here, and God showed me this octagon and said, "I have healed you in this place."

"Interesting."

"So, I threw the gun on the ground, fell on my knees, and prayed. I said God make me a pastor, and I will build a church here for others to find healing as you have given me. I did. My father passed later in the year, and I inherited a lot of money. I started planning to build this church. We have been here for seventeen years now, and only a handful of people can see the gray letters that say heal. Only anointed people."

"So, do people get healed if they stand here?"

"Oh yes!" he threw his hands in the air and spun around, dancing, and speaking in tongues. The act continued for three spins. He stopped and repeated it. "Oh yes! People come to visit us from all around to find healing here. We are well known in this region."

I didn't tell him, but after listening to his story and the story behind how he almost took his life, I felt it didn't add up. I wondered if a demonic presence spoke to him that night, one which led him to build this church with the octagon healing spot on the side of the stage. My discernment kicked in, and my mind went back to the words of Solomon Davidson, *Son, you will see and discern what others cannot.* I prayed silently as Tom continued to recount the church's building, how he secured a contractor, and that many cannot see the word heal. I only caught bits and pieces of what Tom said to me.

My mind was all over the place, and I asked God if I should leave. Without warning, I heard a loud commotion coming from the back of the church. A man yelled, and Tom and I both looked to see what happened. My thoughts filled with the voice of Solomon and The LORD at the same time. *Give her grace. She needs your help.*

Tom moved toward the source of the argument. I could see an older, nicely groomed gentleman wearing a black suit with white pinstripes, and I estimated he was six foot three because he seemed to be taller than me. He yelled at a young girl. This girl stared at him with intent and occasionally would throw back a few words at him. He pointed at us as we walked up the aisle. Her eyes never left his.

Clashing significantly with her hair, she wore a long yellow dress that touched her knees. I could see as I approached, purple coloring on the ends of her long, otherwise brown hair. She had a tattoo on her left arm, in the shape of a heart. Coming off the heart on four sides were zig zag lines that led to smaller hearts. Each heart was red with a shadowy black outline. I surmised she was probably five foot five, but she was a little taller with the heels she wore. I could see the man yelling at her looked at her hair and tattoo. I observed Tom walk toward the back of the church. I followed but stopped briefly to talk to Beth and her parents.

"Beth, did you see the word heal, but tell Pastor Tom you did not see it?"

She looked at her mom, expecting she would be her voice. Her mom did answer for her. "I am sorry, who are you?"

"Sorry, ma'am, my name is Jake Anderson, and I am visiting from Baltimore. I know others can see the word heal printed on the carpet. I was curious if your daughter saw it, too."

The woman looked at her daughter first and turned behind her to see how far Tom was from us. He had stopped to speak to someone several rows back. "Yes, we all see it. It's a big joke. We call it the pastor's new circle." She and I both laughed at the reference.

I was about to continue the conversation when I heard the man yell from the back of the church. I moved toward the commotion. I didn't hear all of the conversation, but I had listened to what I needed to hear.

"See, now you will understand. The pastor is coming. He will tell you." The man looked at Tom and lowered his voice. He pointed at the young girl. "She says she wants healing for her mom, and I tried to tell her that first, we don't do proxy healings, and second, that we cannot let her stay here today with the demons that are obviously all around her and maybe even in her." He motioned his hands up and down as he spoke.

"Okay James. I will handle this. Would you mind helping Randy with the sound system up front? We have a guest speaker today." Tom looked at me and pointed to the front. "Pastor Jake, if you want to go with James, he will adjust your microphone."

I had to decide. I wanted to be obedient to The LORD. I asked again, "*Lord, what do I do?*" I heard nothing this time, but I knew in my heart I needed to stay and observe how Pastor Tom handled the conversation. "If it is, all the same, I would like to listen to what this young girl has to say. God has a powerful love for her."

The young girl looked at me with a straight face. I could see the anger ease up in her when I said this, but her voice did not show the same as she spoke. "I came from Denver. I left at four o'clock this morning, and all I want is to have you touch this cloth so she can be healed. I know the Bible says this is possible. Someone told me a guy named Paul did this, and I want to help my mom heal." Her voice changed from anger to sorrow as she uttered those last words, and I could see tears run down her face.

Tom glanced at me disapprovingly. I could tell he wanted me to leave. I wonder if his actions and words would have been different if I had, but I knew I was supposed to stay. I knew God had a great love for this young, confused, and scared purple-haired girl. He looked back at her and tried to place his hand on her shoulder, and said, "Let's go out in the foyer and talk."

The girl shrugged his hand away and took a step back. "No!" she screamed. Many heads turned to see who had said it. "If you will not heal my mom, fine, let her die, and you may as well bury me too." She cried harder, and her face turned red.

Tom must have taken the gesture from her as a sign of disrespect. "Young lady, don't raise your voice with me and don't push me away like that. Do you not know who I am? Have you not heard what the Bible says? 'Psalm 105:15. Do not touch my anointed ones.'"

I rolled my eyes; thankfully, no one saw it. I had dealt with this type of pastor in the past—
anointed and untouchable.

"I am the anointed pastor of this church, and God has raised me for a time such as this. Someone like you will not disrespect me."

I couldn't contain myself. I had seen and heard enough. "Someone like her?" I stepped in between them as it almost seemed as though he was about to strike her. I may have even saved him from an assault charge, though I doubt anyone in the church would have corroborated the matter.

"Tom, this has gone far enough. I am going to take this young lady, and we are both leaving now. Maybe you should go with James and do your sound check because you, sir, are speaking today, not me." My voice was stern but respectful.

"Jake, Jake, Jake. Come, let us reason together." He turned and tried to put his arm around me, guiding me toward the stage. I held firm, so he stopped and turned to me again. "This young girl is clearly a child of the devil. Look at her hair, and what on Earth is that ungodly tattoo on her arm?"

"Why don't you ask me what it is?" The girl said through labored breathing as she wiped the tears from her eyes.

"Yeah, why don't you ask her instead of being so judgmental?" I paused slightly, but Tom did not reply. "1 Samuel 16:7. Are you familiar, Tom?"

"It's Pastor Tom!"

"Oh! My fault. I guess we are not on a..." I held up my hands and made air quotes as I said, "first-name basis anymore." With that, I turned and addressed the young lady. "Hi, my name is Jake Anderson. I am not from this church. I have no part in this church, and what happened to you is very sad. I am leaving, and if you want to leave, too, I will gladly talk to you about your mom, and we can pray for her."

"I am leaving, but alone!" She stomped her foot, stumbled a little as she lost her balance, and reached down and pulled off her shoes before storming out of the sanctuary.

Tom and I watched her walk out. I turned to him, awaiting a reply. He said nothing. I looked around and saw many people who filled the sanctuary look at us. "Pastor Tom, The LORD loves you and all the people here. But he is not pleased with your pride and self-righteousness. He is not pleased with how you handled this situation nor with how you manage this congregation and building. Hear now what The Most High God of all creation says today: 'I am loving and forgiving and patient, but I will not subject my people to such leadership. Change needs to happen, and if leaders do not return to me, I will cause weeds and pestilence to overrun this building. Mildew will adorn the walls, and gophers will make dens beneath its foundation.' Now you can believe it or ignore it, but this is what God is saying to you today."

Out of the corner of my eye, I could see Tom clench his fists. The muscles in his neck flexed, and I prepared myself for what came next.

"Are you now a prophet? Do you think you are better than me? Do you not know what I have done here?" He loosened his fists and raised his hands, and waved his outstretched arms left to right to show me the congregation he had built.

"Yes, I know what you have done." I turned and walked out.

"The LORD rebuke you, Satan!"

I did not respond. Instead, I watched as a sea of people parted before me, allowing me to walk through the same door I had walked in earlier. I wanted to reach down and act as if I was dusting off my shoes, but God spoke and said, "*No.*" As I walked by the intake desk, I set the mug on the edge. The lady on the left turned and gave a shocked look.

"I have plenty of mugs. Someone else needs this more than me."

I continued to the door and walked out. I scanned the parking lot hoping to find the purple-haired girl and didn't see her, so I continued toward my car. As I approached, I heard weeping. I walked past my car, and in the next row of vehicles and two cars over, I saw her, sitting on the ground, sobbing.

"What's your name?" I asked.

She jumped and looked at me before turning her head. "Leave me alone, please."

I walked closer and squatted beside her. "What happened in there disgusted me. There is no reason to treat anyone that way. God loves you, and He wants you to know Him."

"He gave up on me several years ago." She stopped crying, but she partially hyperventilated. "And trust me, I deserve to be given up on."

My knees ached from the squatting, so I sat on the ground. I left some space so as not to be too intrusive. "God doesn't give up on anyone. He is not like you and me. We can give up on people pretty easily, but He never gives up on anyone. Not for any sin you may commit. Not for any reason at all."

She didn't respond, but she started breathing normally. She looked around, almost expecting someone to break up this conversation we had. She looked down at the ground and watched her feet as she wiggled her toes. I watched, too, begging God for the right words to say.

"What's your name?

She didn't reply.

"Did I hear you say you came here from Denver? I am not from around here, but I bet it is still a few hours away."

"Charlotte," she finally spoke.

"You're from Charlotte? North Carolina?" I asked quizzically.

Her head turned toward me. Her eyebrows turned in toward her nose. I sat and waited as she shook her head and looked at her toes again.

"Charlotte is my name. I have lived in many places, including Denver, which is about 245 miles from here. "

I was impressed she knew exactly how many miles Denver was to the east. I took her word for it but knew I would find out as Denver's Brown Palace was on my itinerary as a place to visit. It also made me think her journey from Denver was likely a long one. If she had brought a car, she would be sitting in it crying, yet she sat by a car, and I guessed it was not hers.

"Hi, Charlotte. My name is Jake, and it is nice to meet you. As I said, I am not from around here. I am from Maryland, and if you need a ride to Denver or anywhere, I am heading that way." With this, I stood up. The asphalt burned into my slacks, and I wondered how she could still sit on the ground. I reached out my hand and offered to help her stand as I stood up. She ignored it, pushed against the car with her left hand, and rose to her feet.

"I can hitchhike. That's how I got here, and is how I will get home."

My heart ached for this girl. I could sense she had been through a great deal in her young life. I wanted to help her, but I would not force her to take my offer. I decided I would pray for her and be on my way. I glanced at my watch. 10:24 a.m. I was unsure when other churches in the area started their services, but I was confident I might find an eleven o'clock service somewhere if I tried.

"Charlotte, it was nice to meet you. I am sorry for what happened in there." I paused and pointed back at the church, "And I want you to know it proves not all churches are the best for all people. I hope you find the help you seek, and I hope you consider God is not done with you. He has told me in the last few moments you will see He has grand plans for you." I tried once again to shake her hand, but she looked at it and swiftly turned her head away. "Well, best of luck to you." Within seconds I was back in my car.

I closed my eyes and prayed silently for Pastor Tom, the church, and Charlotte. I also prayed God would direct me to the next church. I opened my eyes moments later, and from the corner of my eye, I saw Charlotte standing at the passenger side of my car.

"My feet are burning up. Will you please unlock the door?"

I smiled and pushed the unlock button on my fob. She opened the door and sat down before I could even reach the handle of my door. I prayed again, asking for direction and protection. I didn't know how old this girl was, but I guessed she might be in her early twenties. Her background was unknown, and I wondered for a moment if I was being set up.

Chapter

10

Charlotte sat silent next to me as I contemplated what I would do next. God spoke to me and told me to drive and He was with me. It comforted me knowing He would protect both of us. The drive was quiet, and I did most of the talking, except for the occasional yes or no from Charlotte. I was not sure if she was nervous or not at all interested in my story. I told her about my decision to travel from Utah to Maryland. "That's nice" was all she had to say about it. I told her about the crazy dog named Zion. She found humor in the fact I had to run.

I brought up the incident again and asked why she traveled from Denver to that church. She spoke and told me she had lied about hitchhiking from Denver. She had been in Grand Junction for the past two weeks and stayed with her uncle. He had told her about the church. The cloth, she told me, was not for her mom. But her mom was sick, she said. The fabric was an excuse to get into the church. She thought they would let her in if she said she needed healing for someone. Her uncle had told her they would chase her out because of her hair and tattoo. She would not tell me, but I wondered if she needed healing for herself. I was confident she did.

"How old are you?"

"How old are you?" she quickly replied with a voice of disgust.

"I am thirty-eight."

"Well, I am much younger than that."

"Twenty?" I glanced at her. Her toes wiggled, and her shoes sat in her lap with both hands, holding them in place. She now seemed nervous.

"I am over eighteen if that is what you are worried about." She continued looking down while she spoke. I didn't reply again and focused on driving. "You can drop me off in Rifle."

"Rifle?"

"Yes, it's a small town close to here. I have friends there, and I will walk to their house."

I looked at my gas gauge. It neared empty, and I decided Rifle would be a great place to fuel up. My stomach grumbled as well, and I remembered I had skipped breakfast.

"Hey Siri."

The familiar beep came with the comfortable female voice. "I'm listening."

"Charlotte and I are hungry. Where is the nearest place to eat?"

"Did you want directions to Charlotte, or are you looking for places to eat?"

Finally, Charlotte laughed, and I did, too. I told Siri I was looking for places to eat, and several options popped up on the console screen between the two of us. Charlotte let go of the death grip on her shoes and pointed at the screen. "Mean Jean's is a great place for Sunday brunch."

"Ok, Mean Jean's it is." I caught a glimpse of Charlotte smiling before she looked at her wiggling toes once again.

The rest of the drive to Rifle comprised of talking about my business, Sean Morris, and life in Baltimore. I never mentioned

Jane and Timmy. I asked questions about her life, but she would not answer. I was not sure if her mom was in Denver or Rifle or if she even had a good relationship with Charlotte. As we approached the exit, I saw a sign for a local fueling station. I told Charlotte I planned to get gas first, and she could direct me to Mean Jean's for some food. She agreed. As I pulled into the gas station, I checked my text messages before I set my phone in the center console, exited the car, and started pumping gas. I went to the back of the car and popped the hatch. I had been keeping track of how many miles I had traveled with each refueling. I had planned to crunch the numbers when I returned home and analyze my driving. It was part of who I was.

I am a data nerd, and I always looked for ways to make data work for me. I fumbled around in the trunk, looking for my journal when the pump clicked. I remembered my journal was in the glove box inside the car. I closed the hatch, and before moving back to pull the pump handle out, I noticed Charlotte had turned and watched me.

I remember feeling sorry for her again, wondering what her story was, and if she would ever tell me. My eyes met hers. Her eyes widened considerably, and she gasped. She raised her hand, pointed, and shouted something when I felt an incredible pain in the back of my head. I remember falling to the ground and grabbing my head. I lay there, stunned. I felt like I had blacked out, but I also was aware. The pain was incredible. I wondered what had happened. What had hit me? How did this happen? Only seconds passed, but it seemed like minutes. Before I blacked out, I watched as my brand-new Ford Fiesta pulled away from me, leaving me lying on the ground beside a gas pump handle.

Chapter

11

I heard the faint beeping of machines around me. Oxygen pumped into my nostrils, making a hissing sound. The room was dark except for the sunlight piercing through gaps in the drawn blinds. My head ached, and my mind was groggy. I tried to turn to the left and to the right, but it seemed to take more strength than I could muster. With chapped lips, I opened my dry mouth. It felt like sandpaper. I tried to raise my right hand, but it would not move. Someone had tied my arms down with restraints. My eyes blinked several times, trying to focus and adjust to my surroundings. *Where am I? A hospital?*

I could not understand why—trying to recount what had happened as my mind awoke. I remembered talking to Sean about an extended vacation. I remembered talking to Joe Smith on the plane. *Isaiah 43. Sara Adams. Pastor Tom.* The memories returned to me. *Charlotte, Rifle, Mean Jean's. Charlotte. Where is Charlotte?* I tried once again to lift my arms. I could feel my strength returning as I gained more awareness of who I was and where I was. "Charlotte," I yelled as loud as I could. *My car! Charlotte!*

I could see the outline of a person walking in the room. A thin young man with dark hair and dressed in blue from head to toe came near. He put his hand on mine and spoke, "Your niece is fine, Mr. Anderson. She is getting something to eat, and she will be back soon. How are you feeling?"

He knows my name. My head shook from side to side as I continued to struggle with what had happened. Why was I in the hospital? "I am fine. Where's Jane? Is Timmy okay?" As soon as I asked the questions, my memory returned.

"I am not sure who Jane and Timmy are, Jake. Is there someone we can call?"

"No, no, never mind. Where is Charlotte? Is she okay? What happened?"

He tapped my hand twice before removing it and grabbing the IV bag next to my bed. "She is fine. Do you know where you are?"

"Hospital?"

"Yes, Jake, you are in Rifle Medical Center, but do you know why?"

"No." I struggled to remember what had happened. I felt the pain in my head again and guessed, "Car accident?"

"No, Jake, you were not in a car accident. So you have no recollection of the event?"

Event? What is he saying? I tried hard to remember again. "Charlotte was upset. I was taking her to Rifle. We stopped for gas…"

"Yes, Jake, you are in the town of Rifle. At Rifle Medical Center."

"We stopped to get gas. I looked for my journal." Suddenly the memory returned to me. I tried to sit up. I pulled on both restraints, holding my arms in place. "Who did it? Who or what hit me?"

"Okay, Mr. Anderson. It's good you are getting your memory back. You took quite a hit to the head. Detective Ambers will be in to speak with you shortly, but for now, please try to get some rest. I will let the detective know you are awake now."

The nurse turned and walked out. I could hear him speaking, and as I turned my head, I saw a woman with long blonde hair and a white coat. I listened closely as the two conversed.

"Vitals are normal and stable. He is awake and seems to remember. I am going to alert the detective. He is asking for his niece."

"That's good to hear," said the lady in the white coat, and they both walked away.

I tried to process what happened, but my head ached, and my mind was everywhere. I remembered getting gas. I remembered looking for my journal. I remembered seeing Charlotte and the look on her face, and I recalled something, or someone hit me in the head, but not much more.

I squinted at the whiteboard on the wall across from the bed in which I lay. *June 12?* That could not be possible. "It was Sunday, June 9. How could it be June 12 already?" I lay back and stared at the ceiling. *June 12. Did I lose three days? What in the world happened to me?* Dazed and confused, I fought back the pain in my head as I closed my eyes and within minutes fell asleep.

When I awoke, Charlotte, the purple-haired girl with the heart tattoo, yellow dress, and high heels, sat next to me. Someone had opened the blinds, and now more light entered the room. As I looked at her, all I could see was a dark outline of her. I squinted and said, "Charlotte?"

"I am here, Uncle Jake."

"Jake Anderson?" The voice came from my left, and I did not recognize it. It was a deep male voice. I turned and saw a man wearing a brown tweed blazer and a black tie, standing beside my bed. He had bushy brown hair and a thick mustache. I noticed a shield on the left side of his waist attached to his belt buckle. I remembered the nurse had told me he would get the detective. But I could not remember what his name was. *Anderson, like me?*

Nothing came to mind when he finally spoke again.

"Mr. Anderson. I am Detective Ambers of the Denver Police Department. I am with the homicide unit. Do you mind if I ask you a couple of questions?"

"Homicide? What exactly happened? Why am I here?"

"Uncle Jake, remember? That bad guy hit you in the head."

I was lying on the ground, watching my car drive away and fearing for Charlotte's safety. Who hit me? It was all coming back to me now. I nodded in agreement as I once again made eye contact with Detective Ambers.

"Sir, the man who hit you in the head is wanted in connection with the murder of two young men in Denver. We believe he struck you in the head with a blunt instrument. A baseball bat, to be precise. It was at the scene lying next to you.

"I got hit in the head with a bat? And he stole my car?" None of it seemed possible, including the fact I was still alive.

"Yes, that is the charge against him, sir. I was hoping you could tell me as many details as you can remember. Did you see the suspect hit you in the head, sir?"

"I told you already. I saw him do it." Charlotte jumped into the conversation from across the bed.

"Yes, Ma'am, we have your statement on record, but I need to know what your uncle remembers."

Uncle? Uncle Jake? What on Earth? "What is..." I stopped myself. The LORD spoke to me and said, "Not now." So, I went along with Charlotte's story about her being my niece.

"Sir? You were saying?"

"Sorry, I said I don't remember. I mean, I remember watching my car drive off and fearing for the girl's life. I was in a lot of pain and dazed, though. I don't recall what happened. Sorry."

"So, you never had a good look at the suspect? No clothing, no identifying marks? Tattoos? Hair? Race?"

"I'm sorry, detective. All I know for certain is someone hit me in the head and stole my car."

A sudden realization hit me. I was in Colorado, and someone stole my car. I looked at Charlotte and back at the detective. "Is my car..." I looked back at Charlotte, "Is my car okay?"

"Oh yeah, it's fine. I took care of it," said Charlotte.

"What?"

"Your niece was extremely brave, sir." Detective Ambers flipped through the notepad he held. He read, "She grabbed the phone in the car and hid it at her side and called 911. The operator heard what transpired and called the state police. She and the suspect were both apprehended, and he is now in custody. If not for her quick thinking, this situation could have gone a much more serious route."

"You called 911? With my phone?"

She grinned and exclaimed, "Yep! I knew what to do. I saw him hit you, so I grabbed your phone and put it by my side so the operator could hear everything. The guy was dumb and kept answering my questions. I asked him if he was the guy that killed those two boys in Denver, and he said he was. But he had cut his hair and removed the piercings, but the skull tattoo on his cheek gave him away. "

Detective Ambers interrupted her, "Yes, your niece is quite the hero. We arrested her as we were unsure if she was involved, but we were certain she was telling the truth when she knew so much about you. So I have one more question, Mr. Anderson. Is Charlotte Taylor your niece?"

I looked at Charlotte and smiled. "Of course she is. Thank you for your bravery, dear." I could feel the sense of relief in Charlotte when I corroborated her story. I knew there would be time later to determine why she lied.

"Well, sir, I have two more questions for you, and I can let you go. The suspect we have in custody is David Smith of Denver, Colorado. He is charged with murdering two people, one count of aggravated robbery with a firearm, and if you wish to press charges, he will be charged with one count of felonious assault with a deadly weapon. He will be tried in Denver for the murders and robbery, and if you decide to press charges, you will have to be a witness in his trial here in Rifle. But the trial in Denver will take precedence because the assault on you took place after the murders.

"You don't have to answer now, but I understand you will drive through Denver on your way to Maryland." I glanced at Charlotte as he talked. She told him my story. "So if you decide to press charges, please stop by the precinct and ask for me. Here is my card." He handed me a card until he saw my hands were tied still. "But I will give it to your niece." He reached across me, and Charlotte grabbed the card.

I realized her hair was no longer purple. It was now a dark brown color. The detective continued, "Good luck with your travels, Mr. Anderson. I am a Christian myself, and I think you are doing a wonderful thing. If you are interested, while in Denver, stop by the North Denver First United Methodist Church. Google it for directions."

"I may do that, sir. Thank you and thank you for helping me get my car back. But that makes me wonder, why is this guy not being charged with stealing my car?"

Snickering while putting the notepad in his jacket, Detective Ambers answered my question, "Well, you see, since your niece was in the car, we could charge him with kidnapping too, but since you were at the scene when somebody took the car, he can argue you let him borrow it."

"What?" I yelled as I tried to sit up. Realizing I couldn't, I fell back. "He hit me in the head, but oh yeah, here, take my car."

"It's an unusual law; I know, sir. But trust me, this man will not see the outside ever again. We have eyewitnesses for the murders, so he is going to prison."

"Thank you, Detective."

"Thank Charlotte. I am sure you two will have plenty of time to catch up on what happened. I need to leave, and you probably need rest. Good day, sir." Detective Ambers turned and walked to the door.

I looked at Charlotte, who sat silently, no doubt waiting for me to fire questions at her.

"I am so glad you are awake."

"Well, thank you, niece," I said with a snide voice about me. "Care to explain?"

She laughed. "I think you need some rest first."

She was not wrong, and I took her up on the offer. I sighed deeply and shut my eyes. As I fell asleep, I questioned how long I would be in the hospital, and I wondered what Charlotte's story was and how she convinced everyone she was my niece. Before long, I fell asleep.

Chapter

12

My left eye opened. I tried to focus. I could see the shadow of someone leaning over me. My right eye opened, and light forced them to shut again as the figure moved back. She pushed the observation light away, and I heard a click as the room grew darker. I squinted, I winked a few times, and my brain engaged with the wakeful world around me.

"Good afternoon Mr. Anderson. I am Dr. Chavez. How are you feeling right now?"

"Where am I?" I asked myself as I tried to recall again what had happened.

"You're in Rifle, Colorado. In a hospital. Do you remember how you arrived here?"

Finally, it all came back to me, and I remembered everything from the gas station to the blow to the head and being in the hospital. I remembered the nurse coming to check on me and Detective Ambers. I remembered Charlotte, and I turned to see if she was beside me. She was not. I looked at the doctor. She was young, attractive, had pale skin and long blonde hair, along with bright blue eyes. She had a stethoscope around her neck, and I tried to read her name on her white coat. All I could see was the large MD. She was the doctor I had seen talking to the nurse earlier in the day.

"I remember now. I had to wake up."

"Yes, the meds we have you on will do that. Do you know what day it is?"

"Umm, I think it is Tuesday, but the last I remember, it was Sunday."

"That's correct sir, you were brought here by ambulance on Sunday, and you were in a coma until this morning. But that's a good thing because it allowed your body to heal from the severe concussion you suffered."

I tried to move my hands. They were still tied down.

"I think we can remove these now. I will have the nurse do that for you. We tied you down, Mr. Anderson because we wanted you to lie still while determining how serious your injuries were. Typically when someone gets hit in the head with a baseball bat, the results are not as good as they are with you, sir. Does your head hurt? Do you have any pain anywhere?"

"No, no pain anywhere."

"Good, can you wiggle your toes for me?"

Her hands were cold but soft as she grabbed my toes; I moved them as directed.

"Can you feel me touching your toes?"

"Yes."

"Good, can you tell me your name and address?"

"I am Jake Anderson, and I live in Baltimore, Maryland."

"Good, and can you tell me where you are?"

"Well, I guess I am in Rifle Medical Center in Rifle, Colorado."

"Good. Sir, you are doing well." She moved around to the other side of my bed, thus blocking the light coming from the window. She grabbed my wrist and looked at her watch. After fifteen seconds, she released my arm and explained what would happen next.

"You suffered a pretty severe concussion from the incident, and as a result, we kept you asleep yesterday. We allowed you to wake up today because no hematomas presented on your latest scan, and your brain activity was good. You did not suffer a fracture, which is a miracle. Your heart is good, you are responding to stimuli well. I must admit that I have not seen a case like yours. Never have I ever seen anyone take a blow to the head like you had and recover this quickly. You must be a healthy man.

"I like to think someone is looking out for me."

"I understand. I want you to spend the night here, and if all is still well in the morning, we can release you. Do you have any questions for me?"

"Yes, can I get something to eat?"

"That's a good sign also. I will make sure we get something for you. I will check on you again tomorrow, and hopefully, we can send you on your way."

"Thank you, doctor."

"You're welcome. Take care, Mr. Anderson."

As she left, the young nurse dressed in blue returned. "Hi Jake, I am Andrew, your nurse. I will be ending my shift soon, and Tina will be taking care of you this evening. I understand you want something to eat. What would you like?"

"McDonald's?"

Andrew laughed. "Well, you are welcome to have it once you leave. There is one a few blocks down. But for now, I can get you a cheeseburger from the cafeteria. Will that work?"

I tried to lift my hands again. "But can I get these released first so I can eat?"

Andrew reached down and untied the straps that had been holding my arms down. "Yes, sir. We only did that because we were not sure how severe your injury was. You were pretty lucky."

"So, I've been told. But I don't think luck has anything to do with it."

Andrew reached across me and untied the right side. "I understand, Mr. Anderson. I think it is pretty amazing what you are doing, and I have to admit, I don't know if I would have the courage to do it." He stood back up and looked at me. "Your niece told us all about it. She's proud of her uncle."

Someone walked into the room, and Andrew turned to see who. "Well, there she is. We were talking about you."

"How is he doing?" asked Charlotte.

"Really good. Dr. Chavez said he could go home tomorrow if all remained well. We want to keep him for monitoring tonight."

Charlotte walked around the bed and took the chair on the right side. I followed her with my eyes, the entire time wondering and asking God, *"Who is this girl?"* I tried to be friendly and take her to a friend's house since it was on the way, and now I find myself in a hospital with a head injury. I know I would have thought she was involved, but everyone is telling me she is the reason the police were able to capture the guy that hit me.

Even more, they are describing this guy as the one I saw on television who murdered those two teens in Denver. He must have tried to escape west, and I happened to be at the right place at the wrong time. I realized I had told Charlotte a lot about me and what I planned to do, but she silently listened and did not tell me much about herself. But here sat this girl by my side, pretending to be my niece and she had convinced the entire staff of the hospital and the police she cares deeply for me. *God, I am not sure how to process all of this. Please help.*

"I'll get a cheeseburger for you, Jake." Andrew turned and left the room, leaving me with Charlotte. As I turned to look at her, I could sense her anxiety. She fumbled her hands and feet and would occasionally look out the window. I waited for her to look me in the eye. When she did, I asked my questions.

"How did you do it?"

"Do what?" She asked as she grabbed her long hair and twirled it in her right hand.

I tried to see the purple, but all I saw was black with brown highlights. I didn't sense anxiety any longer, but I felt fear, hatred, and regret. I only hoped she would open and tell me the rest of the story. It was apparent to me she did not want to answer.

"I like your new hair color."

"Yeah, the purple got old quick. I needed a change." She continued to stare out the window of the hospital room.

"How old are you, Charlotte?" I realized I had not received an answer the first time I asked.

She turned and looked at me with a straight face. "Why does it matter?"

"Okay, Okay, no problem."

"Well, I am an adult if that is your concern."

"No concern here. Just curious was all." I paused. She was still glaring at me. "So, twenty? Nineteen?"

"Eighteen."

"Okay. We are getting somewhere." I stared at the whiteboard across from my bed. I had so many questions, but I didn't know where to start. I asked God for wisdom. I turned back to the stranger who had convinced people she was my niece. She was still staring outside into the vast void of the desert. I put my lips together as the thoughts formed in my mind. "Jane," I said it without even thinking. "Err, I mean, Charlotte."

She snapped to attention and welcomingly smiled at me. "It's okay. I understand. I have lost people close to me too."

But I had not told her about Jane. At least I didn't remember telling her about Jane and Timmy. "Did I tell you about my wife?"

"Well, no, not me directly." She fumbled in her chair and adjusted her position. "You kept saying their names when you woke up."

That, I remembered. I must have said more than I realized. I let it go.

"You said she and your son died in a car accident. You called the nurse Timmy once, too."

"Yeah, I am sure I did."

I wanted to change the subject as painful memories started to return. "So, Charlotte, let's start with how you convinced everyone you are my niece."

She smiled, looked to see if anyone was near, stood, walked to the door, and shut it before returning to the seat. "Well…" She reached into a pocket of the jacket she wore. Her hand returned in front of her, and I saw my phone. I knew it was my phone because I had a clear plastic case on it, and I could see the damage from when I dropped it a month earlier.

"My phone?"

Her smile multiplied. I sensed pride in the smile. "Yep, I hacked it. I had every intention of stealing as much information from it as I could when I noticed that dude come up behind you."

I didn't reply.

"Okay, I didn't hack it, and I would never steal from anyone. You checked your messages before you got gas, and I grabbed it when I saw that man hit you. It was still unlocked so I immediately dialed 911 because I figured he was going to take your car. "

"You're pretty smart there, kid."

"He had something in his hand, and I could tell he wanted to hit you. But he tripped, and he didn't get a full swing on you."

"It sure felt hard to me."

"Yes, but the doctors said he hit you full-on with the edge of the bat. You would be dead, but right before he swung, he tripped and hit you with the middle of the bat. That saved you. The doctor said so. You can ask her." She paused, waiting for me to speak, but when I did not, she continued. "So, he reached down and took your wallet, dropped the gas handle on the ground, and got in the car. You had left the keys in the ignition."

The memory of me leaving the keys returned. I questioned if I should take them but wanted to show a level of trust for Charlotte.

"He told me to get out when he saw me, but I yelled at him

and said, 'No, I want to help you. I know who you are.' He asked how I knew him, and I said I saw him on the TV and knew he was wanted. I recognized his tattoo." She pointed to her cheek with her right arm, and when she did, I not only knew she referred to the man I had also seen on television, but I noticed her tattoo again. I needed to ask her about her tattoo.

She continued, "He looked me up and down like a piece of meat and said, 'Okay, this could be fun.' I knew what he wanted, and he would not get it. But I had secretly called 911. It was sitting beside me. I hid it. I heard the operator come on, and I started talking."

She closed her eyes to remember. I was already impressed. This girl made a split-second decision that sounds like it ended up saving my life and helping the police to catch a criminal.

"So I said to him, you hit my uncle very hard. Is he dead? He told me to shut up. I said, but you left him at the Gas and Go, and you hit him in the head hard. He again told me to shut up. I said, but my uncle is Jake Anderson, and you tried to kill him. Are you the guy that killed those two kids in Denver? He said, 'You already know it is me.' I said back to him, well, where are we going? He said Los Angeles first and next Mexico. I asked if he planned to stay on the interstate, and he said no, he would take the back roads because there were too many cops on the interstate.

"So, I told him to make a turn, and I said, 'We are on 320 heading south.' I knew the police had heard that and that they would find him. I added to it when I said, 'You know they call this the last chance ditch' and pointed to a trench that ran along the road. He said he didn't care. I kept trying to give clues. So, I told the police, because they were listening, a church is up here on Village Drive. Can you drop me off there? He didn't respond, and I could tell I irritated him. That's when I saw it. We had been gone from the gas station only about fifteen minutes, and my plan worked because I saw a shadow of a helicopter and in the distance a roadblock. He screamed and stopped the car. He looked at me like it was my fault, and I shrugged and said I didn't do it. He jumped out of the car and ran. I sat there. Two cops pulled up behind us at a distance, one went after him, and the other came toward me. I heard the helicopter overhead. I grabbed your wallet, looked at your address, found your phone number on your phone, and quickly put it in my phone under Uncle Jake and waited for the police officer to arrive."

She looked at me asking with her expression if I had questions. Her quick thinking amazed me.

"He came at me with his gun drawn and told me to put my hands up and get out of the car. I started crying and did what he said. He put handcuffs on me and questioned me, and I kept saying Uncle Jake is hurt. I was taken to the police station, and they interviewed me. So, I took all that you told me in our drive to Rifle and used it. I knew about how you were traveling across the country, and I had memorized your address, and I knew your phone number. I had it on my phone, so they bought my story, gave me the keys to your car, and told me I could come to the hospital to visit you.

"Wow!" was all I could say. I believed every word, too. How could I not? "So, my car, it's okay?"

"You have a little less than a full tank of gas, but yeah it's fine."

"My wallet? What did you do with it?"

"Oh, that's a good one. The cops found it in the glove box because I stashed it there. They put it in a bag with the other belongings they found, including your phone. I have it locked up in the car. But umm...."

"Umm, what?" I was nervous.

"Well, I hope it's okay, but I used your credit card to get something to eat, and I got my hair dyed back to my natural color. I only spent a total of $85.50. I will find a way to pay you back. I have a few ways."

If I had the strength to come out of the bed and lunge at her, I probably would have. Instead, I sat back and remembered the words of Solomon. *Forgive her. She's a lost soul that needs your help.* The girl Solomon mentioned sat beside me. "How can I be mad at you for all you did for me? It's the least I could do. I owe you, not the other way around. Your hair looks nice, by the way." "Thanks, Uncle Jake," she smiled and shrugged her shoulders. "Well, I was an only child and never had a niece or nephew. I still can't believe you convinced them you were my niece."

Daylight gave way to dusk. Charlotte and I talked more. I finally asked about the tattoo on her arm. She hesitated to tell me about it but gave in. She purchased the tattoo when she was fifteen. The heart in the middle represented her mom, and the four small ones tied to the hub heart in the middle with zig-zag lines represented the four men who raped her mom one night. She resulted from that rape.

She told me she never knew which one was her father. Authorities never apprehended the four men, and no official charges were ever filed. Her mom had been a young college student, twenty years old, and had gone to a fraternity party where she was drugged and raped. As she told the story, the bitterness I felt in her voice was real and raw. She cried several times while she spoke of what had happened. She told me her mom was so ashamed that she never went to the police with her story. She simply lived with it and rarely spoke of it.

She went on to tell me how her mom tried to raise her to know Jesus and how they had gone to church when she was young. Her mom had sprained her ankle one day when Charlotte was nine, and the doctor had given her fifty OxyContin. Her mom became an addict as a result. She finished by saying she had not seen her mom for a year. She didn't know if she was still alive or not. I did the math, and it added up. During the opioid epidemic, Sean and I prepared a study for the "Journal of American Medicine," indicating overprescribing narcotics could lead to an epidemic. Charlotte would have been nine in 2010, and that is around the time it got hard to be approved for opioid use, but it was likely a doctor could have prescribed that many OxyContin. I now understood why Solomon had told me this girl was troubled and needed my help.

I tried to bring up God as a loving father, but she would not listen. She told me she had a hard time seeing anyone as a father. She said she didn't even like to talk to men, but something about me made her feel comfortable. The hour-long drive we had from Grand Junction to Rifle made her feel comfortable with me, and is why she called me Uncle Jake. It was a big step for her. I was glad to be a part of it. I felt so bad for her after hearing her story. I tried to get her to talk more as it seemed therapeutic for her.

"So, when did you find out what happened to your mom?"

She leaned in closer and rested her arms on the bed. "I don't know if it is true."

"What?" She spoke with such certainty, and I believed it was why she had the tattoo. "What do you mean?" I pointed at her arm, "What about this?"

"Oh, I got it for that reason. But my mom never told me the story. My grandma did. I think she was embarrassed when her Christian unwed daughter was pregnant, and she made up the story."

I was taken aback by what I heard. "Wow" was all I could say at first. "Well, what do you think happened?"

"I asked my mom about what Grandma told me. Mom laughed but would never say for sure. After I got the tattoo and showed her, she said grandma had lied."

"Really?"

"Keep in mind, though, pain killers ruined my mom at this point. She didn't know I knew, but I knew she got oxy on the street."

"How did you know that?"

"I had my ways." She paused for a moment, and I could see a tear forming in her left eye before she wiped it away. "Anyway,

91

mom told me that she had a boyfriend in college, and on the last day of school, she finally gave in and spent the night with him. She said that was when she got pregnant."

"Oh wow. Poor thing."

"Mom said she never told my dad of the pregnancy because she knew he would drop out of school and marry her, but she knew that success was on the horizon for this man."

"Whoa, there's a huge difference between being raped by four men and spending the night with a boyfriend."

"Yeah, and I am not sure who is telling the truth. My mom is a wonderful woman. Well, she was before she became a junkie. We are not as close now. But I still love her, and I don't care what the truth is. I never knew my dad, and I never will. I have come to accept that. I took a chance going to that church the other day, ya know. I don't like God anymore. I grew up without a dad, and what he let happen to my mom, I am not a huge fan. I went there hoping something would happen. I don't know. It was almost like I felt compelled to go there. It was strange."

The story I heard only became worse. I felt so bad for this beautiful young girl with so much life ahead of her. She didn't know how lucky she was. She already had ten more years more than my Timmy had. Additionally, she had already proved to be a knowledgeable person with how she convinced the police she was my niece. That had to take a lot of brainpower. She was also a quick thinker with how she dialed 911.

I prayed for God to provide wisdom. I knew God loved her greatly. I knew He could turn her life around, but how could I convince her that God was a loving father when she spent eighteen years without a father. I had been a pastor for twelve years and convinced many people to see God as a loving father, but this was the first time I had ever come across someone who grew up without one. Different situations always called for different solutions, and I did not know how to proceed. I had children in my congregation who came in with single mothers and even single fathers for various reasons. Still, I never had a chance to speak to them like the opportunity shaping before me. I prayed again for wisdom.

What happened next, I can't make up. It shook me to my core, and I still reflect on it often. In hindsight, if I had not asked the question, I may have left that hospital the following day and continued my journey. One question. One simple question.

"What is your mom's name?"

She now rested her chin on her arms on the side of my bed. Her head bobbed up and down as she opened her mouth to answer. "Regina Taylor, but her friends always called her Gina."

"Gina Taylor!" I said it with as much shock in my voice as I felt.

She pulled back from the bed and set her hands in her lap. She looked me in the eye and said, "Yeah, why?"

"Where did she go to college?"

"I don't know. Why?"

"You really don't know? Think, it is important." I was careful not to advise her. I wanted to shout *Did she go to Ohio State before transferring to UC Denver?* But at the same time, I wanted to be careful not to lead her to an answer.

"Well, let me think. I think Grandma did tell me that."

The anticipation in me caused an adrenaline rush. I was scared she would say Ohio State. I was nervous because Gina Taylor and I did indeed spend the night together, for the first time in our relationship, the last night we were together. She went home the following day, and I never heard from her again. I did the math quickly. Gina would be thirty-eight now, like me. Charlotte was eighteen. It worked. We were both twenty on that last day of school at Ohio State during our sophomore year. *Nah, it couldn't be.* I tried to reason with myself. I could feel myself starting to sweat. I waited. It seemed like hours, but it was more like three seconds before she answered my question.

"I'm pretty sure Grandma said she was at Ohio State when

93

that happened, but Mom always spoke of going to college in Colorado. I think she went to the University of Colorado in Denver, not Ohio State."

"Charlotte. This is very important. When is your birthday?" She glanced at her tattoo. "February 14. That was another reason for the hearts."

I've had hormone rushes before, but never like the one that hit me when she said February. She could have said any other month, and I would have probably caught the day, but she said February. I rolled onto my back, looked at the ceiling, and with a steady voice, asked, "Year? What year Charlotte."

"2001."

I panted. So much so that the monitor beeped loudly.

"Are you okay, Uncle Jake?"

The monitor alarm caught the attention of a nurse walking by my room. The door opened, and she walked up to silence the alarm. Suddenly, I felt the blood pressure cuff start to fill with air. I expected a high number. "It can't be," I spoke, but softly.

"Can't be what, Mr. Anderson?" asked the nurse. She paused for my reply, and I gave none. "You're fine, Mr. Anderson. Probably the pain medication is wearing off. Are you feeling any pain?" Again, I didn't respond. The pain I felt was not from my head. It was emotional. But great confusion mixed with it as well. "Mr. Anderson, are you okay?"

"He was fine a minute ago," Charlotte spoke up.

I turned to the nurse. She was new. I didn't recognize her. Seeing her was a great distraction. I was in immediate denial. "I am fine, thanks. I just...I don't know. Maybe it was like you said, the pain meds wearing off."

"Are you in pain?"

"No!" I shook my head and raised my eyebrows. I looked at Charlotte and back at the nurse. "No, I am fine, thanks." But, what I wanted was to get up and leave the hospital room. I wanted to ask where she parked my car, pull out my IV and all the monitors off me, and go.

"Your blood pressure was a little bit higher but still nothing to get excited over. I am sure if all remains well, you will be discharged in the morning. Do you need anything else? Ice? Water?"

There is no way. It's a coincidence. There are many Gina Taylors in this world. I tried to reason with myself. I could not be Charlotte's father. I remembered the days following that night. I wondered if maybe I had impregnated her, but she never said anything. But I am prophetic. *Yes, why didn't I think to ask you, Lord? Is Charlotte my daughter?*

God didn't answer, nor did I answer the nurse. Charlotte shook her head and waved her off, and the nurse left. Charlotte sat there watching me as I stared at the ceiling. Finally, I broke the silence and asked her, "Charlotte, I suddenly don't feel so good. Can I have maybe a half-hour or hour or so? I tell you what, get something to eat with my debit card. Be sure to keep the receipt and don't spend like $100 on a fancy restaurant." She laughed and nodded. Without saying a word, she stood up and walked out the door.

I closed my eyes as I prayed and asked God to speak. He remained silent. *How could it be? Was this the reason you were insistent on me coming out here? Is she my daughter? Did I get Gina pregnant? The timeline matches up too well. No, there is no way. There is no way. Well, there is a way, but how? How could I have not known?* The blood pressure cuff filled with air again and broke my concentration. I lay there, still as the air left the cuff. I heard a beep signaling the cycle was complete. I lay silent for a few minutes until I fell asleep.

Chapter

13

The lights were dim, the soft sound of machines whirring soothed me. But, it was this sound which eventually woke me. I noticed Charlotte was back in my room, sleeping in the recliner. I squinted to try to determine the time—10:35 p.m. I lay back, now fully awake, and remembered when I dated Jane.

She had visited me at the church where I pastored and heard what I considered the best sermon I had ever delivered. I called it "Inventorying Your Backpack." I spoke of how God provides us with gifts we put in our backpacks. Our backpacks are our lives, and God sows into our lives love, joy, peace, patience, and other fruits of the Spirit. But along the way, through our actions and sinful lives, we obtain boulders we eventually carry in our backpacks. We have boulders such as regret, fear, pain, loss, and distrust. God never intended these boulders to be a part of our backpacks, but we carry them anyway. As a result, we start to have heavy backpacks over time.

When we inventory our backpacks, we look at our past and present and see if anything holds us back. With the help of God, we can face fear and remove the rock we carry. We can tackle regret and leave it at the cross. We can meet the pain of loss and allow God to help us overcome our grief. We then find freedom and can move more fluidly in our lives and live as God intended. We break barriers, tackle hurdles, and tear down walls we have built up over time. We genuinely find the "fullest" life that Jesus spoke of in John chapter 10.

After the sermon, Jane and I had lunch, and she asked me if there were any boulders in my backpack. I had never told her about my night with Gina. She knew about my college sophomore year girlfriend because Jane became my junior year girlfriend five months into the school year. But when she had asked me this question, I had never told her about my rock of regret. I felt warm inside as she asked. I knew I could not rely on hesitation this time. I had to release this rock. I had to tell her what had happened.

She took it well. She said it would have surprised her not to have heard I had spent the night with Gina. She asked the question I never thought to ask.

"Did she get pregnant?"

"Well, no." I thought for a moment. I distinctly remember wondering if maybe she had. *No, she said she had protection. But what if?*

I let go of the rock over the next week but didn't realize I had picked up a new one—fear. For several years, I lived in fear that someday a child would come to my door and say, "Hi Dad!". I would forget about it for a time, but I would see a television program about a son finding his dad or a daughter finding a mom. I even saw a show once where twins, a boy and a girl, sought their dad. I often prayed God would tell me if I ever had a child, and I thought He said no. But now, it seems like I could have been wrong the entire time. The fear exited, and reality settled in. A big part of me wanted to wake up Charlotte and say, "I think I may be your dad." She answered the questions correctly, almost too correctly. Her mom was Gina, originally from Grand Junction. She went to Ohio State until her junior year and went to UC Denver after. She was my age, and Charlotte was born roughly nine months after that night. Her birthdate was February 14, 2001. Regret tried to creep back in, but I pushed it back. Fear lost its grip as I knew the consequences had to be faced. But sorrow came knocking with a battering ram as I reflected once again on Timmy. I saw his lifeless body lying on the gurney. Having to identify him and say yes that is my dead son still haunts me. It's a pain no one should have to endure.

Regret? Yes, my most enormous rock, but not from Gina. Regret rooted in need for a particular bag of roasted peanuts. I regret forgetting my wallet—guilt based on not putting everything back and going home. I stopped myself. I had been over this with my counselor many times. I needed to release fault. That young man made a choice, too. *Our lives are the products of the choices mixed with consequences,* is what he would tell me. He would always say that when the future came, I would date again and eventually remarry. But I first had to clean off the stuff stuck to me, he would say. He would simulate squirting me with a hose to remove all the "stuff."

Drowsiness set in again. I waited for the blood pressure cuff to fill with air again and slowly release when it squeezed my arm tight. I waited for the beep and slowly drifted off to sleep once again. I would not wake up again until morning.

They released me the next day. The doctors said I recovered well and I would be fine. The nurse quizzed me several times about what to do if specific concussion side effects took place. I have a photographic memory, so I repeated back to her what I learned the first time. Charlotte had driven my car through the half-circle patient pickup and drove about a mile past the hospital to a McDonald's, at which point I insisted I take over.

I sat in the driver's seat and immediately thought of the man who had stolen my car and hit me in the head before taking it. I prayed for him. The law dictated he would spend the rest of his life in jail and possibly face the death penalty. I knew Colorado considered abolishing the death penalty, but they had not done so yet.

Suddenly a thought came to mind. I exhaled and looked at Charlotte. She smiled back at me. I shook my head as if to say, *never mind.*

I pulled away and asked, "What's your mom's birthdate?"

"May 6, 1981, why?"

"Oh, just wondering. I was born in 1981, too."

I was not curious, though. That confirmed my suspicion. Sure, coincidence can happen. I am sure somewhere in the world there is a Jake Anderson born on March 31, 1981, and maybe even one originally from Ohio. But was there more than one Gina Taylor born in Grand Junction, Colorado, who went to Ohio State, and had a child born nine months after spending an evening with her boyfriend on May 6, 2000, her twentieth birthday? It was not likely.

My heart floated in my stomach. I knew it was adrenaline, but the feeling was both uncomfortable, and it invited fear. I was about to tell this young girl who disliked God that He brought her to me for a reason. I didn't know how she would accept it. I was not sure how closely she walked with The LORD, if even at all.

"So, am I taking you to Denver?"

"Sure, Uncle Jake. That is if you don't mind."

"Can I meet your mom?"

Her eyes widened, and she looked away. I could see her biting her bottom lip as she tapped her hand on her leg. I made her nervous.

"What's wrong, kiddo?"

I thought she was going to get whiplash with how quickly she snapped her head back at me. "Don't ever call me that."

"Oh! Sorry. I had no idea it was the wrong thing to say."

She looked at the ground before looking out the window. She didn't speak for another twenty minutes. I continually prayed, considered speaking up, but each time decided I would wait. Occasionally, I would catch a glimpse of her wanting to talk. She finally broke the silence.

"My mom used to tell me my dad would call me that if he was around."

"Oh! I can see why it would hit a nerve. I apologize, and I will not call you that again."

Another hour of complete silence passed. I took in the view of the Colorado scenery. We left the desert behind and were now in the mountainous region. Pine trees lined the road on both sides.

Occasionally, we would see a blue stream or a snow-capped mountain. Ski resorts were as numerous as golf courses in Maryland. As we approached Vail, I estimated we were getting closer to Denver. The air was undoubtedly getting thinner. The Vail Pass is over 10,000 feet in elevation. Even though it was June, we saw an occasional patch of snow on the side of the road. I couldn't imagine what this road must be like in January or February. I made a mental note never to find out either.

I wanted to meet Gina to know for sure, although Charlotte was not happy about me asking. But I had to know. She had told me her mom was an addict, which was most likely why she was so shy about it. She also did not know I knew her mom from the past. At least she didn't know yet.

"So..." I drew it out, "I guess that's a no for your mom?"

"She's in rehab, you idiot!"

I glanced at her and back at the road. I let the idiot comment slide. "I had no idea. But that's a good thing, right? I mean, it's going to help her."

"She overdosed two months ago. At home." Charlotte got choked up. "I came home from work, called 911, and the ambulance came. They gave her some kind of thing that saved her."

"Narcan?"

"Yeah, that's it. The paramedics took her to the hospital, and they arrested her, too. But they said if she went to rehab, she could avoid jail time."

I never understood why we as a society don't see the real issue with drug abuse. It's as much spiritual as anything else, but beyond that, sending someone to jail for an addiction is not correct. I was pleased she was offered rehab as an alternative.

"So, she took the rehab?"

"Yes, but reluctantly. She was mad at me for not letting her die." Charlotte's hand now covered her mouth. She raised it to wipe away her tears. She looked out to avoid me seeing her cry. I remained silent and gave her the few moments she needed.

As I drove, processing all she had said, I remembered the Cradle of Christ Church. "What about the church? You said you were there to find healing for your mom?"

She glared at me. The smirk, I thought, was much what Gina would have looked like if she had been angry. "I lied!"

"Ok, that's fine. I will listen if there is more you want to talk about?"

"No!" she said emphatically.

So Gina is in rehab? I still can't believe she became an addict. Spending twelve years as a pastor in a big city allowed me to hear many stories and see many lives destroyed. But I also saw many lives restored by the grace of God. I secretly hoped I could help Charlotte find freedom in The LORD, too. It would be nice to see Gina for two reasons—one to see if she was the Gina Taylor, I knew, and two so I could lay hands on her and pray for her. I am a firm believer in deliverance and healing, and I believe God gave me a gift to help those who suffer in this way. I have seen too many people change after prayer not to believe God still works miracles. It doesn't always work, but that never keeps me from trying with a willing participant. *Would she be ready? Will Charlotte let me meet her mom? How long is rehab?* The questions swirled in my mind like a commercial-grade Hobart bread dough mixing machine.

Suddenly, I remembered what the man on the trail said to me. Don't be worried about staying too long in Denver. *Well, I do have forty days.* I wondered if that meant I would spend a great deal of time there working with Charlotte and Gina? I felt anxious about it, but I trusted God at the same time.

A long silence ensued between us. It lasted for probably thirty miles. At one point, I thought I saw her start to fall asleep. We were now closer to Denver, and I contemplated telling her what I had discovered. A few more prayers and considering the consequences went through my mind. I decided it was time to break the news to her.

"Charlotte, I need to tell you something."

"I'm not listening."

"Okay, well, I am going to tell you anyway, so please do listen. I figured this out the other night in the hospital. When I was nineteen, I spent the night with my girlfriend in college. We had been dating for seven months. We had both said we would wait for marriage, but well, temptation knocked on the door, and we gave in."

"You had sex?" She chuckled as she said it.

I was shocked by the abruptness with which she asked me, but I nodded before continuing. "Well, that girl..." I paused. "Umm..." another pause. "Her name was Gina Taylor. The next day, she left for her hometown of Grand Junction, Colorado. I never saw her again."

Charlotte turned her head slowly. "I suppose the next thing you are going to tell me is this happened at Ohio State and that you think you are my..." Her eyes widened. Understanding creeped into her mind. She took a deep breath and yelled as loud as she could, "Stop the car!"

I didn't know what to do. I toggled between glancing at her and keeping an eye on the road. I didn't want to risk hitting an elk crossing the highway.

"Stop the car now!"

"But we are on the interstate, I can't pull..."

Charlotte grabbed the door handle and pushed open. I could see the blur of the road beneath her, and I felt the cabin pressure change. I eased up on the accelerator.

"I will jump out if you don't stop!"

I slammed on the breaks and pushed the hazard button. I eased to the side of the road. Thankfully a bare spot with no trees where I could safely pull off presented itself. Traffic was not heavy, but we were not the only vehicle on the road either. When I came to a complete stop, she opened her door wide and exited the car. I followed.

"Stop, no! Just leave. I don't want ever to see you again. Just leave."

"Charlotte, we don't know. It could be a huge coincidence. I mean, many people go to Ohio State, and many Gina Taylor's exist and also..."

"And how many of them get knocked up by their boyfriend who abandons them. Let me guess, it was on my mom's birthday too, right?"

I felt the rush of cars going by. The sun was hot, but the humidity was low. I was anxious and scared. Not only because I was on the side of the interstate but because I was on the side of the highway with an eighteen-year-old frantic girl who may have found out she had been traveling with her dad. To top it off, I was scared she was right. I wasn't ready for another child, especially an adult child. Flashes of Timmy being born, changing his first diaper, taking his first steps, and riding his bike all flashed through my mind, but this time it was not Timmy I saw. It was Charlotte. If it was true, if she was my daughter, not only did I miss that, but I caused this girl to grow up without a father, which is never suitable for a child.

"So what do we do now? DAD!" She said it with as much sarcasm as she could muster. Her right hand was on her hip, and her head cocked to the left. She showed a teenage attitude, and I was at a loss for words. "Well, don't just stand there, say something."

I lowered my head. Shame, guilt, regret, fear, and frustration all crept in. I heard the enemy whisper in my ear, *"Leave her, she won't love you."* I prayed for strength and protection for both of us. *God, if you got me into this, you can get me through this. Please help.*

"Charlotte, let's get back into the car. We will stop somewhere and get something to eat and talk this over. I can take you to Denver, and I can either leave you there, or I can..." I waved my hands above my head, "I don't know. I can help you out somehow."

"Help me?" She moved closer to me, so she was eight inches from me. She poked me in the chest as she looked up at me. "Help me? Where were you eighteen years ago? Where were you when I was eight and had heart surgery?" My eyes widened, and she read the expression. "Oh yeah, wanna see?" She proceeded to unbutton her shirt.

"No, don't!" I said as I stepped back, but she opened her shirt wide enough to show me a scar. She had open-heart surgery in the past. It could not be denied. She buttoned back up and continued yelling at me. She recounted many events in her life I had missed. She told me about living in Grand Junction and witnessing her dog get hit by a car. But what struck me the most was when she said the words, "When I was eight."

Leave her here. She will never respect you. You never knew her. This is not your fault. The enemy's voices returned, and once again, I prayed for God's armor. The voices subsided, and I was once again listening to Charlotte.

"And when mom twisted her ankle. You could have told the doctor no. You could have prevented her drug use. You could have saved her, but you were not here. I hate you. I hate you. I hate you." She pounded on my chest with each utterance of the word hate. She slowed and finally stopped before she collapsed. She fell to her knees at my feet, crying uncontrollably. I kneeled beside her and put my arm around her. I gave her a side hug.

"Let's get back in the car, Charlotte."

She nodded in agreement, rose to her feet by pushing off my shoulder, and held out her hand to help me stand up. Her hand was soft, wet, small, and gentle. *Is this the hand I helped create?* As I stood up, I turned and grabbed her and hugged her. She didn't resist but did not hug back.

"I'm sorry," she whispered gently. "I guess I had it all pent-up in me."

We walked back to the car with our arms around one another. I closed the door for her after she sat down, and I walked to my side of the vehicle. "Thank you," I said as I looked up and pointed to the sky. "Now, keep us safe."

Chapter

15

Calvin Coolidge, what on Earth was he thinking? Calvin Coolidge is the only president since Teddy Roosevelt to not have stayed at Denver's famous Brown Palace Hotel and Spa. It was also my home for my time in Denver while Charlotte visited with family and friends. Even though we were both certain now she was my daughter, we still had only known each other for over a week. And what a week it was—a concussion and hospital stay, a stolen car, and a local hero for helping police find a fugitive and suspected murderer, and of course, finding out you have a dad for the first time in your eighteen years of life. He also happened to be traveling across the country and, by chance, ran into you at a church that scorned you for your purple hair and visible tattoo. *I don't think even Alfred Hitchcock could come up with a story so compelling.* I sat in the chair by the hotel room window, looking out at the city and wondering why Calvin Coolidge never stayed at The Brown Palace.

It was our sixth day in Denver. When we arrived, the first thing I did was drive to a local retail store and purchase prepaid cards for Charlotte's phone, thus giving her the means to call or text anyone she needed. I told her it was my gift to her and she did not need to pay me back. All I had asked for in return was the courtesy of being told she was alive and well. She kept her word and once a day had sent me a text message saying all was well. An agreement was made between us that if she traveled with me, I would care for her, and any time she wanted, she was free to return to Denver, and I even agreed to pay for her airfare if necessary. Mixed emotions were my mantra for those few days. I desperately wanted to have Charlotte stay with me, but she was eighteen, and she already had a life in Colorado. I still couldn't believe the turn of events that had occurred.

I had spent many days in Denver, walking, praying, and contemplating. Convinced Charlotte was my daughter I never knew, I planned in my mind where we would live, how we would operate, and how we would make up for the lost time. I had put together a survey that I planned to ask her. I would ask her questions as we spent time together and never ask her to sit down and answer fifty questions. But I had questions, and I wanted answers.

Surveys are a great way to discover information about people. I talked on the phone with many influential people in social media and Internet-based companies about creating subtle surveys to mine information from people. People will quickly give up information about themselves for a game or take part in a fake holiday. National Taco Day and Son's Day, for example, are not actual events. But the amount of data programs collect about a person is staggering when these fake events go viral.

My conscience once gained the best of me, and I told people on social media not to participate in the games, surveys, and events I helped establish. Sean was outraged because he thought it was a conflict of interest. I assured him I faked my IP address and used a fake name every time I did it. But my best efforts did not stop the trend, and now so many unknowing people take part in these gold mines for data collectors.

My desire for data from Charlotte was different. She was my long-lost and, until a week ago, unknown daughter. I thought about Ralph and Marian. They had not seen their daughter for two years, and it destroyed them internally. I had not seen mine for eighteen years, but this past week in Denver had torn me up, too.

As I watched the traffic below, I contemplated the past. It had now been a year since the accident, and I recovered more. I missed Jane and Timmy each day. What would Jane say if she knew about Charlotte? Would she accept her, would she be mad? I had decided acceptance would reign in her, but Jane may not have wanted Charlotte to live with us. I didn't think I would like Charlotte living with us either, given she is older. A thought creeped in my mind: where would she sleep? I had a two-bedroom apartment in downtown Baltimore. Would I need to buy a home? Where would she work? Would she be interested in working for me? She seemed to be intelligent, and I was certain I could find a job for her at the company.

Blue lights and a loud "whoop, whoop" caught my attention. I watched as a police officer had pulled over a car on the street in front of me. Moments later, the officer administered a field sobriety test. Another officer pulled up and spoke into his radio. As the suspect walked a straight line, or shall I say, tried to walk a straight line, I caught a glimpse of a man walking a dog. They crossed to the opposite side of the street, where the officer placed handcuffs on the driver. The man and dog sat down at a park bench. I squinted to see if I could get a better look. I thought I was wrong, but how could I be? It was too recognizable. The man's dog was a beagle with a golf ball-sized black spot on its head, and the man wore an orange hoodie, blue jeans, an Angel's cap, and hiking boots.

"You must be kidding me!" I shouted aloud. "How on Earth can this be?"

Without even giving it a second thought, my feet moved toward the door. I quickly traversed the four flights, catching glimpses of the beautiful marble floors of the lobby area as I approached the main staircase. I hurried down the carpeted steps. I made my way past the sitting area, and jaunted toward the double golden trimmed doors of the arched doorway to the outside.

I stepped outside, and watched as one of the police cars drove away, and a tow truck connected the car left behind. For a moment, I felt sorry for the arrested lady. *What was her story?* I offered a prayer for her well-being. I hurried across the street and made my way toward the park bench, where the older gentleman and beagle sat.

"Zion?"

Zion walked toward me, as far as his leash would allow, and wagged his tail. I approached slowly and cautiously. "Hey there, little buddy, I thought I would never see you again." I bent down to pet him and looked up at the older gentleman smiling at me.

"Have we met?" he asked me. "I would say we have since you know the name of my dog."

"We did, sir." I stood up and walked to the bench. Zion let out a howl, and my heart rate increased slightly. It brought back memories of the ordeal at Cove Fort. I continued walking and sat down beside the man. "Yes, sir, we met on a trail in Utah."

"Oh yes, we did. Yes, I do remember. I see you are now in Denver. Welcome to our lovely city."

"Thank you, thank you," I said, as I formulated my thoughts. I didn't realize he was a Denver native, and I still had questions about how he suddenly disappeared that day. I still had the gold coin he had left behind, too. I quickly gave up the idea he may be an angel. If he had been one, he would have remembered me.

"If I remember correctly, young man, I told you it would be okay to stay a little longer in Denver. "

"Yes, you did. I wanted to ask you about that. How did you know? How did you know I was on a journey? I mean, who are you?" After I asked, I realized I still hung on to the angel theory.

The man laughed and looked around at the traffic and people

walking on the street. "See these people?"

I nodded as I looked around and sat down beside him on the bench.

"Most of them have heard of God. You would be hard-pressed to find one who truly believes He does not exist." He paused, looked down at Zion, who also looked at all of the people walking by. "But, ask one of them if they have a relationship with God, and maybe one out of every ten you ask will say yes."

I thought about it for a moment. I knew many famous polls had suggested only ten percent of Americans indicated they did not believe in God. But I also read a study by a reputable school in the Midwest, which suggested the number may be higher as some people remained afraid of the stigma of saying they don't believe in God. But it made sense for many more not to admit to a relationship with God. The sad truth in America was many people didn't know what it meant to have one. Those who knew what it meant often made it complicated or works-based when it was not difficult and not deed-based either.

"One in ten? Are you sure it's not more like one in fifteen or maybe even more?"

"Sure, I understand what you are saying, but I do believe you know what my point is."

The truth was I did not know what his point was, and he had dodged my question. But I wanted to know. "No, sir, I am not sure I understand."

"What got you through this past year? Was it your counselor? I am sure he was helpful to you. Was it your co-workers? Were you part of a support group? Was it your work? What helps a man overcome a tragedy like you experienced?"

"Sir, you are kind of creeping me out. I don't know you, and yet you know so much about me. Can I ask how this is?"

He laughed again as he continued to look around. "I do apologize, Jake, but we will get to that in time."

111

He knows my name, too. I don't remember telling him my name. He scared me more than his dog did when we first met. Regardless, I did start to understand his point. I let go for a moment that he knew about the accident. But what helped me through it?

"Well, the answer to how I got through it was obviously God. But how did you know?

"Yes, it was God. But more, it was your relationship with God that got you through. What if you didn't have a relationship with God? How would you be coping right now? It is, after all, because of God you are here in Denver and driving across the country, is it not?"

I was anxious, yet I felt comfortable in his presence. A big part of me wanted to walk down the street and seek help from the police officer. But what would I say? "Hey, I met this guy who knows all about me, and I met him on a trail in Utah."

"Jake, it's okay. I know you are not sure how I know all of this. As I said, we will get to that. But without this relationship, Jake, how would you cope? You met Ralph and Marian. Did they have a strong relationship with God? How are they dealing with their daughter's disappearance?

An angel, that's the only explanation. Hebrews 13:2.

"Jake, you have a great opportunity here, young man. God is with you, and He has anointed you for a time such as this. Make the most of it and grow from it. Let God guide you in your words and actions as you learn to trust Him."

A moment of silence, save the sound of traffic, was shared between us. I silently prayed when he spoke up again. "The name is Randall Davidson. You met my brother, Solomon, a couple of weeks ago in Beaver, Utah. I was visiting him when I found Zion here."

My mouth dropped. I realized how I must have looked, so I quickly closed it.

"Well, that certainly does explain a lot. But still, how did he, and now you, know so much about me?"

"Jake." He waited as if I knew the answer. "People these days claim they are so concerned with their privacy, and yet we carry these devices and use them, too." He held up a cell phone. "We have no privacy anymore. We willfully give it away in the name of entertainment, business, education, and keeping tabs on our favorite celebrities or sports athletes. Surely, you have heard of Facebook, right?"

"Well, yes. And Twitter and Instagram and the like." I knew them well because I built a business around the same concept. Data mining for marketing purposes, and Sean and I had jumped into this industry at the right time. "I understand. But still, I have taken great strides to protect my privacy."

He laughed. "Oh, Jake." He shook his head. "And yet, Solomon and I were able to find out so much about you."

The thought caused a knot to form in my stomach. But I knew he was right. No matter how much you try to keep your identity safe, there are public records, news stories, and so much more, and Jane and Timmy's death had made the local news. Many websites would have carried the story. Public records about their deaths were easy to find. But who would take the time to learn so much about the accident? The feeling of *you're creeping me out* came back to me again. I sat silent as I pondered all he had told me.

I watched as people of varying ages and lifestyles walked by. I glanced at Randall. He smiled and waited for me to speak. I stood up, stopped the first person who came by me, and said to him, "Excuse me, sir, do you have a relationship with God?"

"Get lost, moron!" He walked around me and continued on his way.

Laughing heartily, Randall asked, "That's one. If your theory is correct, fourteen more. Nine if my numbers are right."

I decided not to take any other chances. I sat again and laughed.

"So, Randall, I found this coin after you left. Did you drop it?" I reached into my pocket and pulled out the coin.

"Oh, my round tuit."

"Yeah, that's clever," I replied.

On the head's side of the gold coin was a cross with the word tuit beneath the cross in all lower case letters. On the backside was the inscription, I will get to know God when I get a round tuit.

"You keep it, Jake. Give it to the girl you met and use it as a conversation starter." I looked at him shockingly.

"And how did you..."

"Facebook, Jake. Facebook. You are gaining a following."

"I am what? But I haven't even been on Facebook since..."

Before I could finish my thought or press him for more information, I noticed Charlotte walking toward us. She caught my attention because she seemed to have been crying. I didn't see Randall stand up and walk away.

"Jake, can we talk?"

"Yeah, sure, but hold on." I wanted to introduce Charlotte to my new friend. But as I turned back, he was gone. I stood quickly. Partially angry, more so confused, I ran toward the intersection. I looked in both directions and across the street. Randall could be seen nowhere.

"Uncle Jake, please, it's really important."

How could it be this man and this dog had done it again? I spun around quickly to greet Charlotte, who had run up to me.

She threw her arms around me and whispered with a tear-filled voice, "My mom is dead."

114

Sorrow, grief, anguish, dolefulness. I was not clear how to adequately express the emotions Charlotte felt. We had gone back to my hotel room where we talked, cried, and shared our grief.

Charlotte had been at her mom's home when the phone rang. A doctor from the rehabilitation center said her mother suffered cardiac arrest at 9:45 a.m. and was rushed to the hospital. Charlotte walked a mile and a half to the hospital, but her mother was deceased when she arrived. The cause of death was officially cardiac arrest, but the belief was that drug use factored into her heart issues. Charlotte told me she would go from heroin to meth and sometimes cocaine when she could find it. Her body broke down, and her heart gave out.

I knew all too well the agonizing task of having to say goodbye to someone you loved. As a pastor, I performed over one hundred funerals in twelve years, and each involved a family trying to deal with their loss. Some were sudden; some came expectedly. I had families that buried their 100-year-old mother and a family that buried newborn twins five days apart. I learned what to say and what not to say in those moments, but this was difficult. The last funeral I had spoken at was Jane's. I had passed on twelve funerals after her death, and it was also one of the reasons I had stepped down as a pastor. I thought I was ready to face death again but hearing the news was like ripping a scab off a healed wound. I prayed, I cried, I sat silent, and I listened to Charlotte talk. I searched for the right words, but I could not find any.

The reason I had not heard from Charlotte all day finally made more sense to me. The hospital social worker had arranged for the funeral home to work with Charlotte. Gina did not have life insurance and had spent her savings on drugs. Charlotte had quit her job, and there were no family members willing to help.

"They are going to cremate her and put her ashes in the trash."

I assured her even though I was not familiar with the state of Colorado's law on cremation for families that could not afford a funeral service, I knew for a fact they would not throw her ashes in the trash. I knew what I had to do. I prayed over it to be sure it was the right thing to do and felt for certain it was. I was about to speak up when Charlotte spoke.

"Dad, what am I going to do?"

Tears welled up in my eyes. I wiped them away, hoping she would not see, but I was too late. She had called me dad. It was a name I had not heard for over a year.

"You called me dad."

"Well, you are my dad. Unless you are going to abandon me, too?"

"No, no, no, honey, I am honored. I haven't heard it for a long time. You can call me that." I sniffled and laughed. "You called me dad. Oh and yes, what are you going to do? I glanced at my watch. It was 9:10 p.m. Let's get some sleep and call the funeral home tomorrow and tell them a family member came forward and will pay for the funeral."

"Geez, how much you got, man?"

I was shocked by the crass way she asked me.

"Sorry, I mean, no. You don't have to. I mean, maybe pay for an urn?"

"No, Charlotte, I have the means to pay for her funeral. We will arrange it in the morning. Okay? But right now, let's get some sleep. You take my bed, and I will sleep on the couch."

Charlotte didn't argue with me, and I would not have allowed her to anyway. She had been through a great deal, and she needed rest. I unfolded the sofa bed before turning off the lights. I lay staring at the ceiling fan whirling above my head and processed the day.

I thought long about what Randall had said to me. It was my relationship with God that had helped me through the past year. I was not sure what Charlotte's relationship with God was, and I needed to find out. It would be what would get her through the coming days, weeks, and months. I would be there for her, but she would need God more than anything.

Losing a loved one is hard enough. But knowing the deceased is in heaven eases the pain. Knowing you will go to heaven someday and see them again also reduces the pain. Someone like Charlotte may live another seventy years or more, three and a half times the life she has already had. That's a long time and a lot of life to live without her mom. She now had me, but we had only recently met. She would always have memories of her mom, but I understood the last two years of those memories were not good.

We needed each other, but she needed God more. Sure, salvation and acceptance of Christ's gift through His sacrifice was enough to get her to heaven to see her loved ones again, provided her mom was a Christian. I stopped myself. *Yes, Gina was a Christian. We had long talks.*

But it was the strength God could provide, a force you cannot explain from where it comes. It was the joy He bestows. It is all of the fruits of the Spirit, and it's the gifts He delivers. It's the daily knowledge that the creator of the universe is your friend. These things helped me through the last year, and I knew

Charlotte would need to get through this next year and the many more to come.

I thought about my mom and dad. It had been ten years since I lost Dad to cancer and seventeen since I lost Mom to a stroke. They both were still missed, but I get by knowing God's strength, His joy, and His peace are all on me because I have a strong relationship with Him. What I used to take to my earthly father, I now take to my heavenly Father. I can now share the stories I would share with my earthly mother with the God of heaven.

I needed to find out what Charlotte's relationship with God was, but I also needed to tread lightly in helping her establish or strengthen it. Too many well-meaning Christians have driven people further from God instead of closer to Him by demanding they have a relationship with Him. I asked God to help me with the task before me. I knew it would not be easy, but I was confident I could do something. As Randall had said to do, I decided I would trust God to lead me.

My mind suddenly went back to what both Solomon and Randall had said. They both focused on telling me about a relationship with God. *Was I missing something? Was there more to it?* I decided not to let my mind wander. I took it to God and asked if I missed something. What wisdom or knowledge had my years as a pastor suppressed? What did God want me to understand?

With my eyes feeling heavy and my thoughts slowing down, I was almost asleep. However, I rolled over and grabbed my phone. I opened a web browser and searched "facebook.com: Jake Anderson near Interstate Seventy." The first result amazed me, so I pushed the link. The page loaded and I read "The Pop-Up Pastor." A picture of me in my red Ford was in the background and an image of me in the parking lot at Cradle of Christ church was the profile picture. I remembered her taking the picture, but I didn't realize she used it to make a Facebook page. I scrolled down and saw a video post with 775 comments. The local news had interviewed her about the incident in Rifle where she helped authorities find David Smith. She explained how she remained calm and called 911 so the police could apprehend David.

It was surreal. If I had not seen my picture, I would not have believed it. Charlotte had made the page because I didn't. I looked for page creation information that would help me know how long it existed. Only three days earlier, while we were in Denver, she established it. I didn't want to draw attention to myself, so I was not happy. I wanted God to have all of the glory for this journey. I wished she would have asked me first before she made the page.

I kept looking around. The page already had 8,235 followers. Fascination came over me as I had well-known clients who didn't have as many followers on their Facebook pages in a month, let alone a few days. I debated with myself. I would have to pray about it. Solomon's words of wisdom rang in my head. It's not about how many people know you. *It's about how you let God impact people through your actions.*

I was about to set the phone down when my finger clicked on Charlotte's name as she was the video post's author. Her page came up, and I saw a picture of Charlotte with her arm around a woman. At the bottom, it said, I love you, Mom. I double-tapped the image to expand it. It was without a doubt Charlotte, but the woman with her was not the Gina Taylor I knew in college.

Chapter

17

As a resident assistant in a college dorm, one must put aside friendships to be effective. One evening, I witnessed a close friend who lived two doors down from me get sick in his trash can. Usually, this would not have been an issue. The problem surfaced because he vomited in a trash can that sat in the hallway across from his room for three days. I had asked him twice to remove the can or I would have to write him up. He laughed at me and said I would not do it. When I witnessed him getting sick, I wrote up the incident report.

He was notified of the indictment the next day and received a $25 fine payable to the school. He also removed the obnoxious trash can that morning. I heard a knock at my door in the evening, and when I opened it, my friend stood there leaning against the door frame.

"You wrote me up!"

I told him I had given him two warnings, and he ignored them both. I reminded him I was not even obligated to provide him with one. He pushed me away from the door, stepped in, and slammed it behind him. He smiled at me as he locked it. Yes, I was a little nervous.

He asked me if I knew how it felt to get a piece of paper saying he had been fined, knowing a friend caused it.

I felt terrible for him, but I also felt justified in doing what I had done. I explained I would suggest the school waive the fine, but the incident would be on his permanent record. He was not pleased with my response, and he punched me hard in the stomach.

I had bent over in intense pain that lasted for almost thirty minutes. I even considered calling 911 because of the pain's intensity. As I reflected on that day all those years ago, I believed the pain I felt in my stomach because of my recent discovery was probably much worse than I had experienced at the hands of a friend. No one had punched me in the stomach, but I had to confront the young lady lying in my hotel room bed. I had learned to love her as the daughter I believed she was.

Physical pain differs greatly from emotional pain, but emotional pain is often worse depending on the person's pain tolerance. I certainly felt the sting in my stomach. I tried to reason in my mind most of the night until exhaustion finally took over, and I slept. I estimated it had been around three o'clock in the morning before I eventually fell asleep. It was now 7:44 a.m., and I contemplated my next move.

With thoughts of *that's not her mom*, and *indeed there is an explanation* running through my mind, I replayed the events of the last week. Charlotte's birthday was February 14, which I could see from Facebook, but I could not verify the year. The date lined up. Her profile said she had lived in both Grand Junction and Denver. I saw pictures of her at Mean Jean's in Rifle as well. The images of her getting the heart tattoo had been a few years earlier. Everything she had told me proved to be accurate, but the picture, with the caption "I love you, Mom" did not match—unless that woman was Gina Taylor, but not the Gina Taylor I knew. My mind was all over the place. I wanted Charlotte to be my daughter, but I also felt a sense of relief in knowing perhaps she was not. She had already admitted to telling me several lies. Was this another one to add to the growing list?

I sat on the edge of the still unfolded sleeper sofa staring at the picture I had found when Charlotte spoke up.

"Good morning Uncle Jake. I mean, Dad."

I didn't reply. I was nervous, but I had to know. I stood up and slowly walked to the edge of the bed. I laid the phone down so she could see it and said, "Is this your mom?"

She lay silent for a moment. She pushed the phone away before speaking, "That's cruel, Jake. You know my mom just died. I don't know who it is."

I knew she was lying. I would have bet my life savings that she had. I was convinced.

"Okay, so let's go to the funeral home and pay for the funeral. Get ready. I will drive us."

"Well, if you still want to pay for it, I thought maybe you could write me a check or Venmo me the money."

"Venmo?" I was starting to get irritated, and my voice did not hide it. "You have a Venmo account?" I waited for an answer.

"Sure, should I also send enough to pay for your college, too?"

"Uncle Jake, why are you so angry?" She sat up in the bed.

I paced to the other side of the room and walked back. I was praying, asking for guidance. Solomon's voice popped into my head, "Give her grace. She is a troubled soul." I wasn't sure how he worded it due to my mixed emotions, but I knew God had placed that thought in my mind. I sat down on the edge of the bed. I calmed my voice.

"Charlotte, this is serious. Is this your mom?" I grabbed the phone and held it up again.

"I thought you said you were not on Facebook."

"No, I said I had not been on in a long time because I don't like how they operate. But my account is still active. I am the pop-up pastor now, too. Right?"

She laughed. "Yeah, do you know where St. Clairsville, Ohio is? Some guy from there called you that. His name was Brad McLellan or something. Isn't that a neat idea? You needed that page. Here let me see, and I will show you how to update it."

"I know how to update a Facebook page. Stop avoiding my question." The anger rose again. "Is this, or is this not your mom in this picture?"

"Uncle Jake, come on. She died yesterday. Why are you doing this?

I stood back up and paced one more time. I came back, and she now sat on the edge of the bed. She was crying. I sat down and put my arm around her. I pulled her in for a hug and whispered in her ear, "I love you, my sweet daughter."

She pushed me away. "Yes, that is my mom, and yes, she died, but not yesterday."

I was not expecting that. But at least I knew this was not the Gina Taylor I knew, which meant Charlotte was not my daughter. The pain was mixed with anger and loss, confusion, and deceit.

"Okay, thank you for being honest with me. I think you know now this means you are not my daughter. This is not the Gina Taylor I knew in college."

"Patricia!" she shouted at me as she lay back on the bed.

"What?"

"Patricia Taylor, age forty, died of a drug overdose two months ago. That part is true. She was an addict. But her name is Patricia, and she is two years older than you. My mom was indeed raped by four men when in college, and that is how I came to be. My birthday is February 14, 2000. I was born several months before you spent the night with your girlfriend. I never knew my father, and well, I thought I had found one, but I guess now you don't care." She rolled over to her stomach and cried uncontrollably. She smacked her hands on the bed, screaming, "I'm sorry. I am so sorry, Uncle Jake."

It was worse than being punched in the stomach. I walked

over to the window and looked out. I secretly hoped I would see Randall and Zion sitting there again. I needed advice. I closed my eyes and prayed. In the background, I heard Charlotte's cries waning. *What do I do, Lord?* I was silent, listening for that still small voice.

She needs your love.

I knew the voice, and I had learned to trust it because I knew it was God.

I looked over at Charlotte and called her name. No reply.

I called out again, "Charlotte?"

Still no reply. I walked to the bed, sat down, and said, "Okay first, thank you for your honesty. I am not letting this end this way. Sit up, and let's talk. Let's see where we go from here. I am here for you. I love you like a daughter, even though it is not likely you are my biological daughter."

With a muffled voice, I heard, "I'm not your daughter, you're not my uncle, and I want to crawl under a rock and die right now."

"Charlotte, please sit up. Let's talk."

The pit in my stomach subsided. But now, the questions had come in. How did she know about Gina? How did she know about that night? How on Earth did she figure this all out? Was my privacy not as secure as I thought? I grabbed my phone and opened a browser. I typed in Jake Anderson near Gina Taylor.

My LinkedIn Profile came up with information about Morris and Anderson, but nothing more. I reminded myself I should probably make sure I didn't have too much personal information on the social media site. The third item in the list was a Facebook page, The Pop-Up Pastor, Jake Anderson. I had to admit, the sound of it appealed to me. I clicked on the page. 10,532 followers. My eyes widened as I saw how it had increased so much overnight.

"Hey Charlotte, we have 10,532 followers on the Facebook page you created."

She rolled over and sat up. "I was hoping for 12,000 by

now." She laughed. "So…"

She looked at the phone. "Are you mad at me?"

"For the page? No, not mad, but I am not sure if I want to keep it."

"Well, I meant for the other thing."

"I am certainly not mad. But I do wonder how on Earth you knew about Gina to convince me that I may have a child." I stood up and walked. "I mean, that is some crazy stuff. You knew things only I knew, or so I thought. How in the world did you get that on me? I am sure it's not on the Internet."

It hit me. I walked to the end table next to the fold-out sofa. There I found my journal. I picked it up but immediately remembered what I had written. Seeing Joe Smith and talking about Gina caused me to write some memories in the journal near the beginning. I looked back at her, and she put her head down in shame.

I opened the journal to the entry from Salt Lake City. I read what I had written. Joe knew Gina and went to high school with her. I wrote the date of the last day of school my sophomore year at Ohio State and simply noted it was a good night and Gina's birthday.

"Charlotte, did you read my journal?"

"Umm, well."

I walked over with it in my hand. My anger rose again, but I quelled it quickly. "Charlotte? We need honesty in the future, okay? No more lies, no more deception. If we are going to salvage anything from this, you have to be honest with me. Did you read my journal?"

I could see her head nod twice.

I dropped the open journal on the bed. My sorrow showed. I was not so much upset she had read my journal as much as I was upset when I now realized no chance remained that she was my daughter. Even with the morning's events, I still had a small glimmer of hope that she was. I wanted her to be my daughter. I needed her to be my daughter.

I knew she would never replace Jane and Timmy in my life, but I did have hopes for a parent-child relationship that I had come to accept I would never have in my life. I assumed by the time I was finally ready to start dating again, if I ever did, I would be too old to have children, and marrying a woman with children already would be fine, but I didn't expect any child to see me as a dad. Having Charlotte come to my life as an adult child was exciting, and now I had to decide, along with her, if we still wanted that to happen.

The silence between us was a thick heavy fog that settled in both of our brains. It was an awkward silence and one without movement on either of our parts. I honestly had never seen a human being sit as entirely still and silent as I witnessed with Charlotte. I finally broke the monotony and sat on the bed. I knew I had to be the adult. I knew I had to be the one to give the grace. Many conflicting thoughts tore at me. I could leave and never see her again, write about the experience in my journal and move on. I could offer to take her with me for the rest of the trip. I could unofficially adopt her as my child. She desperately wanted a dad, and I needed the companionship we had established. I felt betrayed, and I felt loss. It was the sting of losing Jane and Timmy all over again. It was worse than being punched in the stomach. Acetaminophen could not cure it.

I had contemplated this moment during the night. I ran many scenarios in my mind, and I knew what I wanted and would accept. But would she buy it? I also feared rejection, so I was hesitant to ask her. I wanted to adopt her unofficially. In the Bible, in Romans chapter 8, Paul mentions God adopts us into His family. That was the kind of adoption I wanted for her—a permanent one.

"Charlotte, what are you feeling? What are you thinking?"

"Embarrassed," she said softly.

"Wait. Hold on." My thoughts quickly turned to the side of

the road between Rifle and Denver. "That little stunt you pulled on the highway. What was that? You knew you had conned me. You knew you were not my daughter, yet you still yelled at me as you had met your birth father for the first time. How did you pull it off? Those were some real and raw feelings there."

"I told you, I had it all pent up. When you bit and accepted, and man, you knew I was your daughter, all that anger I had built up over the years, it all poured out. I practiced those statements for a lifetime, and I finally had a chance to let them out. I needed to tell my dad how I felt, and well, you were him."

"And the Oscar goes to...," I beat my legs simulating a drumroll, "Charlotte Taylor for her role in 'The Pop Up Pastor'"

I looked at her. She looked at me. We both laughed.

"Shut up, that's not funny."

I reached over and hugged her again. She didn't push me away nor resist this time.

"I don't know what to think, Charlotte. You fooled me, but I needed to be fooled. You clearly want to have a dad in your life, especially after losing your mom. I get why you did it, and you are so incredibly crafty in your approach, too—tremendous wisdom in such a young lady. You are probably still reeling. Along comes this guy from Maryland on a crazy mission from God, and he happens to have a journal that speaks of a girl with your last name." I shook my head. "I got to hand it to you, that is movie material there, girl."

"You think so?"

"Definitely! I don't know how to make a movie or who would ever be interested in making one. I always wondered if I made this journey across America if I could write a book and explain it someday, but I never anticipated this type of drama unfolding."

The silence returned along with her catatonic state. We still had to decide what we were going to do. I needed more information from her. *Who is her family now, where has she been living for the last two months? Is she truly eighteen?* I had many questions. I wanted so badly to be able to get into her mind, swim through her brain, and see what was inside.

"Get dressed, let's go eat, and we can go walk in Cheesman Park and decide what we are going to do. Is that okay with you?"

"Sure, Dad." She smiled.

I smiled, too. I grabbed my journal, walked across the room, and sat on the sofa. She went to the bathroom for a shower, and I read through my diary to make sure there were no more hidden surprises. I did not find any, but I wondered how much she knew about me. It explained how she knew about Jane and Timmy. I did not believe I spoke of them when I woke up. I reasoned in my mind that I would have to be careful with her until I knew I could trust her. She had lied a few times, and she had shown herself to have great intelligence and wit. I wondered for a moment how her life might have been different if I had been her dad for real. I was relieved, but at the same time, disappointed to find out I was not. *But what if she had grown up under my care?*

For one thing, she would not have lived her life in Colorado. *How would that come into play, too?* All of these questions raced through my mind. I reflected on how I felt when Timmy was born. I knew my life was going to change, and I was unprepared. Those same feelings surfaced again, but the right word to explain my feelings and emotions this time was prepared but anxious.

Trusting God was the only way I planned to go forward.

Chapter

18

Being so high above sea level, the air in Denver, they say, is thinner. A golf ball will travel farther when hit because there is less drag from the air. I always liked golf but never played well. I also did not have any clubs, so I could not put the theory to the test. However, what I did put to the test was physical exhilaration. The thin air can make walking a challenge for someone who is out of shape. Traversing the circular path at Cheesman Park several times wore out my legs. I had to find a park bench and sit as Charlotte made one more trek.

We discussed her family history, her mom, and her mom's death during the first two laps. Lap three comprised of her uncle's bursts of anger and his inability to cope with his sister's death. By lap four, my legs ached, and my feet screamed for me to stop, but I wanted to go further into the conversation I had started once before regarding Jane and Timmy. Knowing it was important for Charlotte to know the entire truth, including how I forgot my wallet, and of course, the roasted peanuts. I felt she needed to know the entire story, so I pushed through the pain. Some may say we commiserated on our family loss issues.

During our walk, Charlotte explained how she reached out to her uncle, who lived in Grand Junction after her mother had passed. He offered to let her stay with his family, but he verbally abused her. She had been driving her mother's car, which had broken down two days before I met her at church and was left with no transportation. When she moved from Denver to Grand Junction, she had quit her job, too. She had no job, no car, no mother, and now no place to live because she could not stay with her uncle any longer. As if the difficulties she faced were not enough, the attorney she and her uncle hired to handle the execution of her mother's estate threatened to declare Charlotte an unfit executor since he had not heard from Charlotte for so long. Hearing of the miraculous that took place at Cradle of Christ Church, she visited one day, hoping God would reach down to her and bring the healing and comfort she so desired.

As a child, Charlotte heard the story of Paul touching aprons, napkins, and handkerchiefs and how these items, when taken to the sick, brought healing. She thought if she took a piece of a blouse belonging to her mother to the non-denominational church, she might receive a miracle. Explaining that the Bible's miracle was true, but she needed to be careful in putting her faith in a piece of cloth instead of God did not resonate with her. I thought it best to table the subject for another time.

Stretching my legs outward and oscillating between pulling my toes toward me as much as I could and pushing them out as far as they would go, I felt some relief. All remained well when I heard a loud shout. I knew the voice. It was Charlotte.

Catching a glimpse of a man running after her, as she ran toward me, I jumped up, forgot about the jelly feeling in my legs, and ran toward her.

"Help, Jake, help!" she cried out as she ran.

Seeing me run toward the two of them, the man stopped, measured me up and down, and turned, strolling in the opposite direction. He looked back once to see if I would chase him and kept walking when he realized I would not pursue.

Looking around her to get a better view, I engaged her in conversation. "Who was that, and what did he want? Did he hurt you?"

"No. I am okay. He's some jerk I used to go to school with. It's not a big deal. He didn't know I was back in town."

"Had you not seen him before today? He has not been bothering you, has he?"

"No, I happened to run into him. He scared me, though. He said he knew my mom and that she was a bad person. He asked where she was."

Embracing her and scanning the area around us as I did, I assured her it would be okay. I told her we should get going, and I meant not from the park. I suggested we leave for Kansas as soon as possible, but we had to deal with the attorney first.

A bright green and blue sign sitting at the road's edge informed us we had arrived at the lawyer's office. I greeted the receptionist with a smile and asked for an audience with the attorney. I indicated I was a relative of Charlotte's and wanted to help her with the estate. After waiting in the well-decorated lobby, I was guided back to his office, with Charlotte in tow.

Sixty minutes ticked off the clock, but it was time well spent. Signing the necessary paperwork and providing my contact information was all Charlotte and I were required to do. I paid him in advance for his work and informed him I would be willing to discuss any matters regarding the estate with him. According to Colorado law, he indicated I could do this as long as Charlotte signed a waiver and was present when any phone conversations took place. He estimated the estate could be closed within two weeks now that Charlotte had signed much of the paperwork.

As the only remaining next of kin and the estate's executor, she would receive whatever monetary amount may exist when the estate was closed. An estimate on Patricia's house deemed it worth less than the amount owed, so it was not likely Charlotte would be a benefactor of the sale. Few that they were, personal belongings would be auctioned off, which may increase the inheritance.

Closing a final chapter in a loved one's life is difficult. Charlotte was emotional after the meeting and spoke little as we drove away from Denver. She shared the story of how her mom had hurt her knee. Loving to jump as a child, Patricia purchased a trampoline for her daughter. After many years of jumping on the trampoline, the floor gave out. While the two enjoyed a day of jumping, Patricia's foot went through the floor, which caused her other leg to twist, tearing both her MCL and ACL simultaneously. These two critical ligaments in her knee caused her pain and made it impossible for her to walk without surgery to repair them.

Two surgeries later, her mom took OxyContin, a highly addictive prescription narcotic, twice a day and one time a day after a week. This went on for five months. When the prescription ran out and no more refills were available, she started looking for relief in other ways. Eventually, the drug use led to her heart giving out. I couldn't help but be thankful it was not Gina, but I also felt a little less of a connection to Charlotte because it wasn't. However, the emotional connection the two of us had established compensated for the lack of bloodline relations.

"Timmy always wanted a trampoline, but Jane always said it was a shortcut to knee surgery for me, so we never purchased one."

"Timmy sounds like he was quite the character."

"He was great. I think you would have liked him."

"I don't know about you, Uncle Jake, but this day has made me hungry."

"I don't know about Uncle Jake anymore, Charlotte. After what you told me about your uncle, I am not sure I want the title."

"Well, I shouldn't call you dad."

"Why not?"

She did not answer.

A giant blue sign with a sunflower carefully placed on the left with the words Welcome to Kansas let us know, not only had we been driving for two and a half hours, but we were in for some flat, boring highway ahead.

"The sunflower state, did you know that?"

"Yeah, they taught us in school. We had to know the state flower for Colorado and all the neighboring states. So I know all about the Sunflower state, the cowboy or equality state, the Beehive State, The Land Of Enchantment ...," pausing, she caught her breath, "Do you want Arizona, Oklahoma, and Nebraska, too?"

"Wow. How many states border Colorado?"

"Seven."

"Hmm, I guess I didn't know Oklahoma did. Must be the panhandle."

"You are correct, sir. Would you like to know facts about Oklahoma?"

"Actually, I would prefer to know where you would like to eat."

"Well, let's stop in Kanorado since we are right here."

I had seen the same sign she had seen, and I was delighted to be stopping. Both my gas tank and stomach were almost empty.

Standing outside the car while I pumped gas at the Kanorado Co-Op Oil filling station, Charlotte scanned the area. I smiled when I saw what she had done. Seeing someone clobbered with a baseball bat probably shook her to her core, and she did not want to witness it again, at least not from the passenger seat. I finished pumping, took my receipt, and hopped back in the car.

Food at the King's Café was home cooked and delicious, the staff was friendly and inviting. During our stay, a man and a woman who seemed to be in their late twenties or early thirties, and a boy and girl, probably around the age of five or six, occasionally glanced at us while we shared our dessert nachos. The woman would place her hand by her mouth to block what she said to her husband. She was on the inside of the booth, with the young girl sitting on the outside. He was on the outside, with the young boy on the inside. Charlotte paid no attention, but I tried to catch what they were saying. She spoke softly, but he spoke up in a normal tone. "Well, go ask them." I heard it plain as day.

She looked at Charlotte before looking at me, and when she saw me looking at her, the redness filling her cheeks was unmistakable. Part of me wanted to greet them and engage them in a conversation. But with her embarrassment so new, I stayed seated.

The man did not feel the same. After wiping his face, he set his napkin down and pushed along the table before exiting the booth and walking over.

"Excuse me," he looked directly at me. "But, by chance, would your name be Jake Anderson?"

The smile on Charlotte's face would have brightened any of my darkest days. However, I did not feel the same glee she did. I wanted to know how someone in a small town in Kansas knew of me, a quiet and reserved man from Maryland. The warmth of my face let me know right away I now matched his wife in the color of my cheeks. I had no choice but to be truthful.

"Yes, I am Jake Anderson, and you are?"

"My name is Bill. We live in Goodland, Kansas, and well, my wife is a big fan of you and Charlotte."

I didn't know the girl could smile so much, but with hearing her name, she widened even more. As I studied her, I knew why she smiled, and I knew how they knew us. "Let me guess. You saw the Facebook page?"

"Yes, my wife loves what you are doing and loves the story."

"Story?" My gaze and question were directed solely at Charlotte.

"Well, Dad here doesn't know about all I have put on there yet. I have not had a chance to catch him up, but I am so glad you took time to recognize us."

My eyes caught a glimpse of the woman picking up the young girl and placing her back in the booth. She screamed her displeasure but immediately went back to coloring. Approaching Charlotte first, she held out her hand. "Linda, nice to meet you, Charlotte."

Charlotte graciously returned the gesture, and Linda shook my hand as well. "The pleasure is mine, Linda, Jake Anderson."

"So, where are you headed next? What day are you on?" She turned to look at Charlotte again. "Catch any more criminals?"

Charlotte laughed. "No, and I hope we don't have to. We are still trying to get to know each other, you know, it's been eighteen years and all, so...."

"I think this is such a fantastic story of redemption and love." Turning her eyes to mine once again, she added, "You should write a book about this. It would be a bestseller for sure."

I was speechless, and that was mainly because of my confusion. Anger? No, it was more like wonder. Well, it was a mixture of both. I was angry that Charlotte put information about us on Facebook but in complete awe at how it had gone viral. *God, are you behind this?* The answer I received was one I was used to by now. Nothing. He did not answer. While Linda engaged Charlotte in conversation, I silently asked God. *Please let me know what is going on.* Again, no reply.

"So, how did you get this much time off work, Jake? If you don't mind me asking."

I didn't mind him asking, but I also did not want to say, *well, you know, I am half owner of the company.* "My boss is also a long-time friend, and he understood."

"Wow, that's great. Well, hey, I see you are still eating, and it was rude for us to interrupt, so I think we should let you get back at it. Linda?"

"Yeah, hold on." She held her hand up to her husband. "The last four digits are 4702. Text me anytime."

"Okay I will."

Did Charlotte take a stranger's phone number? I shook my head.

Linda and Bill walked back to their booth as the waitress arrived with their dinner. This time they both sat on the outside, and the kids sat on the inside. Linda would occasionally look over, and when our eyes met, she would smile instead of blush. Looking at my watch, I recognized it would be dark soon, and I knew I would need to arrange for the night's lodging. Having planned to spend most nights in a tent at a campground, I asked Charlotte how she felt about camping. Thankfully, she was on board with it. Ironically, I had two air mattresses if one was ever punctured or would not stay inflated, and my tent was large enough to accommodate both beds. The only outstanding issue was finding a campground that could accommodate us. After finishing our meals, I suggested to my copilot it may be an excellent time to find a location for the night. We both said goodbye to Bill and Linda, and Charlotte said she would text. I knew she probably never would.

Reaching the car, I took my seat, and before I started it, I asked Charlotte to explain.

"Why did you start that Facebook Page? What were you hoping to get out of it?"

"We are celebrities, Jake."

"Oh, so now, it is Jake, but in there, you called me dad."

"I had to play the part."

I looked at her. My eyes said explain more. I knew she was a bright girl and would pick up on the cue. She did.

"Okay, well, where do I begin?"

For the next ten minutes, we sat in the parking lot of the King's Café while Charlotte explained the Facebook page. She started it in Denver, during the time we were apart. She explained how she grew up without a dad. She indicated she had hitchhiked to Grand Junction to go to Cradle of Christ Church. I stopped her and asked if she had lied about living with her uncle.

"Oh no, that is true. The hitchhiking makes for a better social media story. If you had asked, I would have shown you where my mom's car is now. It's at a junkyard." I shook my head.

According to Charlotte in the post, she went to the church according to God's direction, and upon seeing me, explained I was the one about whom she dreamt. We sat in the back pew together and talked during the entire service. When the sermon was over, we went outside and discussed how it might be possible we were related. It seemed a little far-fetched in my mind, but many were buying into it.

I couldn't believe what I heard. This girl was so creative, and had I not known the truth, I would have accepted the entire story. She said I was taking a journey across America to visit various churches and help people. I stopped her and asked if she had mentioned Timmy and Jane. She had not.

She went into detail about the incident in Rifle where I was hit with a baseball bat by a murderer and how she led the police to catch him. This became the explanation for the video on the page. Hearing it again amazed me even more. She made herself out to be a hero, and in my mind, she was one of the greatest.

"To kind of wrap this up so we can get on the road, I let everyone know you are my dad and God brought us together, and I am traveling with you across the country."

"But how did you get it to go viral?"

"Oh, well, the national news picked up the story out of Denver, and when I put the video on the page, it helped people share it. Well, there is that, and I have a large following on Instagram and YouTube."

I was intrigued. "How big of a following, and what do you do?"

"Last I checked, I had about ninety thousand subscribers on YouTube and about sixty-five thousand followers on Instagram. You can check me out. I am @CTaylor4Hearts, and I tell people about my life. About my heart surgery, about my mom's addiction. That's what really shot me up. Do you know how many people are addicted to drugs in this country? People share stories with me, and I share stories with them. It's like a vlog for the brokenhearted."

It was brilliant. The marketing tactics were superb. I still had mixed feelings about my trip being so public, but it became apparent people caught on and followed.

"So, you said God brought us together. Do you still believe it, or was it only for the story?"

She spoke, but we were both distracted by Bill and Linda walking to their car. I waited a short time for her to reply.

"Charlotte?"

"Yeah, I am here. I don't know Jake, Dad, I mean. I still have a tough time seeing God as a loving father, you know? I mean, mom taught me all about Jesus. How he died on the cross and when we believe we go to heaven. She even said someday I would have a relationship with God. I guess I am no longer mad at him, but I don't quite get the concept of a father like most people do. Ya know what I mean?"

Know what she meant? Yes, I knew what she meant, and I had dealt with others in her situation. I dealt with adults who had been molested by their dads when they were children. I dealt with adults who never knew their dad, and some were in their forties. One was also an atheist, and I believe because he never knew his dad. I dealt with children struggling with divorce and with dads who left for no reason. I was thankful to know my dad so intimately growing up, so could I relate? No. But did I understand what she meant?

"I get it. I really do."

She nodded before looking at her phone and punching in some letters. "Umm, it looks like unless you want to squat in an open range cow pasture for the night, our best bet for camping is about two hours away."

"Really, that far?"

"Yep, some ranch in Saline. The only option."

Poor planning on my part was not something new to me. It was a significant character flaw and one I had tried for years to overcome. I was tired, and it would be dark in another two hours, but I was not too fond of the idea of trespassing on someone's cow pasture. Well, trespassing had nothing to do with it. I refused to sleep in a cow pasture. So, I asked Charlotte to navigate, and we were on our way to the C2T Ranch on the Saline River.

Three hours later, with little daylight remaining, we pitched the tent and filled the air mattresses. Sleep was all I could think of, but someone had other plans for me. I could see Charlotte typing super-fast as the light from her phone lit up her face. She looked angelic. While biting her bottom lip, her eyes would occasionally roll up as if she were pondering what to say next.

"Who are you texting?"

"No, typing a post. I am letting our fans know we are in Kansas now."

"Our fans?" I knew what she meant, but there was still a part of me that valued my privacy, and I was still not a "fan" as she put it, of the Facebook page. If I had rolled my eyes any higher, they might have taken me to orbit. I prayed silently, seeking God's wisdom, and of course, He replied, *let her be.*

Curiosity piqued. "How many followers do we have now?"

After shifting her eyes, her mouth dropped, and she looked at me. Her face still aglow from the white background, she announced. "85,302."

To say I was not amazed would have been a lie. I was surprised anyone could gather so many followers on any Facebook page without a national brand name or a successful company. Her established social media following must have followed her to Facebook. God said to let her be, so I let her be. I was thankful she did not mention Timmy or Jane on the page. I was not happy that she had lied about being my daughter. *It makes a good story.*

"Your phone is ringing."

A wandering mind is supposed to be a sign of creativity, but in my case, I had moved past the Facebook page and had begun planning the next day's adventures in Kansas.

"Jake, your phone."

I continued to ignore her. I didn't care who it was, and I knew my voicemail was not full. I would hear it in the morning.

"Ralph Adams?"

Hearing his name redirected my focus. I rolled off the air mattress. "Hello, this is Jake."

An excited and boisterous voice spoke from miles away. "We got her, Jake. We got her. Sara is coming home."

Chapter

19

Knowing my traveling companion who read my intimate journal did not read all of it was somewhat relieving. I also accepted she could still be lying and saying she did not read it. Oscar-winning performances like the one along the interstate seemed to be something she was perfect at, after all. However, she did seem genuinely surprised and interested in the story of Sara Adams.

We were driving to our next destination, Salina, Kansas, and the Kansas Wesleyan University campus. I was fascinated with universities associated with mainline denominations for a long time, and KWU was a college campus I wanted to visit. I was not sure what I was looking for, if anything, but I knew it was a destination, for it was one place God had placed on my heart.

"Sara had been in Tehran and while in a marketplace one day, she saw a man she said 'Looked American' so she moved close to him and whispered in his ear she was an American that had been kidnapped and could he help."

"So, a random dude that looks American was in a foreign country, and she ran into him?"

"Well, this 'random dude' as you say it happened to be a CIA agent, too."

"Oh, well, that makes it all the more convenient for her."

"I sense a bit of unbelief in your voice, young lady."

"No, it's not that. I am sorry, go on."

I did indeed continue but remained unclear why Charlotte suddenly acted this way. I made a mental note of it and continued with my story.

"The agent knew of a missing person from the Boston area, and though it was not his assignment, he called it in. That occurred about three weeks ago. Ralph tells me the government assembled a team, and two days ago they stormed the building where she had been held prisoner and rescued her."

"Anyone get killed?"

"Remarkably, no. The man who took her, Sadiq, did not put up a fight at all and surrendered to the agents. Since he is a citizen of Egypt and was on a student visa in the United States, I don't know what will happen. But they asked Sara if she was there against her will, and she said yes. She arrives in Boston today. Ralph and Marian are there now to pick her up."

"Well, I am sure she will have to have counseling and medical treatment."

"Oh, no doubt about it. But the funny thing is Ralph never mentioned the baby. Sara was supposed to have had a baby boy."

"Well, maybe they sold the baby. I heard they do that there."

I couldn't help but look at her. "They do that there. How do you know?"

"I don't know. I saw it on the Internet somewhere."

We both laughed, knowing that when it is on the Internet, there is no factual guarantee. "Well, if she did have a baby, I hope he is okay."

For the next thirty minutes, I tried to imagine the incredible joy Ralph and Marian were experiencing. I recalled my conversation with Ralph the night I stayed with them. He tried to explain to me what it was like to lose a child. He said to imagine a toothache, or a backache, or even a headache. The pain can be intense, and you want it to go away when it is happening. You know you can take various medicines to make the pain go away or change your position. You can lay down or stand to find comfort. Losing a child is not like that. The pain never goes away. Knowing my grief of losing my wife and child, I tried to remind him his daughter was not gone. He believed there remained no hope of ever seeing her again.

"Acetaminophen doesn't make this pain go away," he reminded me.

"Yes, I understand."

I was angry at him for giving up on seeing his daughter. I had no chance in this lifetime of ever seeing my son and wife again. My last memory of my son was not good. His face had been lacerated and bruised, and I barely recognized him. My wife had wasted and atrophied over the forty days, and here was a man who could see his daughter again someday. I knew the pain of loss, but he did not know the pain of permanent loss, and I knew he would not. I always believed Sara would return.

Gratefulness and happiness flooded my body as I replayed the conversation in my mind. Tears formed in my eyes, and I felt them run down my cheek. I never had an adult child, and I never knew what it was like to see your child drive a car, graduate high school, and go to college. They knew that, and now they could build a life with her again. I couldn't do the same.

I looked over at Charlotte, who was once again typing in Facebook. Adoption was never something we would have a legal option for, given her age, but I had adopted her in my mind. She was now my daughter, and I was her father. For a moment, I remembered the verse Ephesians 1:5, which says God adopted us through Jesus. Adoption! That thought kept resonating in my mind. I unofficially adopted Charlotte.

"So, young lady."

"Yes?"

"Are you sure you want to go through with this? I mean, do you have any reservations at all? I know we will never have paperwork, but how do you feel about being adopted as my daughter? How does it sound to you to have someone you can call father?" As soon as I said it, I imagined myself not saying it. I used the word "father," and I knew Charlotte still struggled with it. She would only call me dad. Oh, how I wished I could not have said what I had said.

There were no words. She simply looked at me. I didn't push the issue, but now my stomach was in knots. I allowed fear to grip me again because I didn't want to lose her. I tried to reason with myself. *She didn't answer, but that doesn't mean no. Give her time.* I gripped the steering wheel a little tighter—an entire gamut of emotions coursed through my mind. I was angry at myself for pushing the idea and anxious for her reply. I was happy to live the moment with her, and fearful of going through the pain of loss again.

God? Can you help me here? No reply. Glimpsing movement, I turned to see if she would speak up. Instead, what I saw was a scared young girl curling up into the fetal position. She wrapped her arms around her legs to hold them in place as she placed them on the seat. Tears formed in the corner of her eyes as she closed them. Her jaw rested between her knees. Within moments, I could see she had fallen asleep.

I found joy in her restfulness but knowing I had asked the wrong question caused me to dig my fingernails deeper into the steering wheel until I felt pain. I eased up, but this did not ease my stomach. I focused on my driving and waited for her timing regarding our talk.

What I expected to be a boring drive soon proved otherwise. Parked alongside the interstate heading east was a long line of motorcycles. Their parking had no pattern. Many bikers still blocked the right-hand lane of the interstate while most rested on the berm. I slowed significantly as I approached, and the change in speed woke Charlotte. One motorcyclist had stepped into the interstate and waved her arms, indicating she wanted me to stop.

"They will jump us and steal our money if we stop."

"Charlotte!"

"What, they will. They are probably two percenters."

"Charlotte Taylor, stop judging people by their choice of clothing and what they drive." I focused on the biker in front of me, who walked to my window. I first noticed the black leather vest and Harley Davidson bandana she wore. On her left side were sewn letters: SJMC. I rolled it down, but not before instructing Charlotte. "Let me do the talking, okay?"

She nodded.

"Sorry to stop you, sir, but do you mind sitting here with your flashers on?"

"Sure, but can I ask why?" I pushed the button for the lights.

She talked, but I had trouble hearing her as she pointed ahead of us and looked at a row of bikes. "Up there, one of our guys hit a cow. I don't know how he did it, but he did. I think he's hurt. We already called 911, but I don't want anyone barreling through here. We didn't think it would be good to block the entire road with our bikes, but a car may work." She leaned back down to my window. "I know I am asking a lot of you fine folks, but if you don't mind."

"How do you hit a cow?" Charlotte couldn't contain herself.

"I guess you are not from around here. In Kansas, we have open-range pastures, and that means some farmers don't have fences. It's rare, but these critters will occasionally wander onto the highway. With it being a Black Angus and with the time of day, I guess he didn't see it in time."

"Is the cow okay?" Charlotte asked.

"Well, it took off running pretty quickly, and we haven't seen it. But John is down. I think he may have a concussion. He likes to lead, and he was a good fifty feet ahead of me."

"Well, the important thing is you called 911, right?"

"Yes, sir. Would either of you know any first aid?"

"I do!" replied Charlotte.

Before I could say anything, Charlotte left the car and navigated the maze of motorcycles. "Charlotte, wait!" It was too late. She kept walking. I opened my door and followed the female biker to the scene. Charlotte checked the unconscious man's pulse and listened by his mouth for breathing. The motorcycle was ten feet from him. Another biker picked it up, and I could see a scratch on the gas tank as he lifted it.

"Did anyone see if he was ever conscious?"

"He rolled around a couple of times and kind of stopped and laid there on his back. He moaned once, that's all."

The faint sound of a siren pierced the night, and as I looked up, I saw red lights approaching from the east. "Help is coming, Charlotte. Do nothing," I said to her.

"I am making sure he is alive. I know what I am doing. Trust me. I have had to do this before."

I backed off and watched.

"Pulse is 137. That's a little high." He is not sweating, but just in case, we should see if he has any broken ankles." She lifted his pant legs, but black boots covered his ankles. She grabbed the right while looking for an expression on his face. Seeing none, she grabbed the left. "His ankles don't seem swollen. I need something to prop his legs up."

"Here!" a fourth biker handed her a blanket rolled up like a log. She placed it underneath the man's legs, propping them up.

"That's in case he is in shock."

After this, the sirens became deafening as an ambulance, a state trooper, and a fire truck all arrived simultaneously. They each drove across the median and stopped at the scene. Paramedics immediately jumped out and ran to us. Charlotte backed up and reported the vitals to them.

"Pulse is 137, he is breathing, and I propped his legs up in case he is in shock."

"Thank you very much. You did well. We will take it from here."

Charlotte walked over to me and started crying profusely. I embraced her and told her I was proud of her for acting so fast. "I tried, Dad. I tried."

"Tried what?"

"I tried to save her. But, they were too late. I tried to save mom."

I knew she relived the night her mom had passed. We had discussed it at the park in Denver, but not in great detail. She told me she tried to give her mom CPR but could not revive her. I tried to console her, and she gathered her emotions while watching the paramedics work.

The female biker who stopped me explained to the officer they typically did not ride this late at night, but they were on a poker run, and it had started late. She said the victim had looked back, probably to see how far ahead he was, and he must not have seen the cow crossing the interstate.

While the officer interviewed other bikers, the original female biker asked where we were from, and I said Baltimore. She advised we were a long way from home, and I agreed. I didn't get into the details of our excursion.

Ten minutes passed, and the paramedics put the victim into the ambulance before rushing away. Several of the remaining bikers thanked Charlotte and me for stopping and asked if there was anything we needed. I said a good night's rest, and they told us a hotel was hard to find near our location. I informed them we intended to travel to the campground, and they asked if they could escort us. I agreed. Returning to the car, we drove and allowed traffic to flow again.

"That was something, huh?"

Charlotte didn't say anything. She looked straight ahead and forced a fake smile.

Something was troubling her, and I did not know what it was, but I intended to find out.

The motorcycle gang all gave us a thumbs-up as they continued past the campground, and we pulled off the exit. It took another fifteen minutes to arrive at our destination. The office was ready to close for the evening, but our site was paid for and provided. Charlotte fell asleep as soon as the mattresses allowed. I didn't set the alarm and decided the sun would be our alarm clock.

Chapter

20

Maybe it was the purple sign with white letters that indicated I was on a college campus. But it could have been the number of trees and white cement sidewalks. I was unsure what it was, but Kansas Wesleyan University reminded me of Capital University in Bexley, Ohio. Capital was also a school affiliated with a mainline denomination, the Lutheran Church, but KWU was much more prominent in space, the number of buildings, and enrollment.

As we drove along West Clafin Avenue and past Wesley Hall, I noticed a sign in the yard congratulating the nursing program for being accredited. I made a left onto Santa Fe Avenue and looked for a place to park. I was not sure if the church would be open to the public or if anyone would be inside, but I wanted to see the interior of the campus United Methodist Church. Parallel parking was never easy for me, but with the size of the Fiesta, I found the task to be relatively simple. Charlotte finally broke the silence she had taken on when I asked that terrible question the night before.

"What are we doing?"

"Well, I wanted to see if I can catch a glimpse of the inside of this church. This campus reminds me of a campus near my hometown, and I wanted to see if it's similar inside this building. I won't be long, but you are welcome to come with me if you want."

"If it is, all the same, I think I will hang out here."

I nodded.

From the front, the church looked like many buildings I had seen in Philadelphia, Pennsylvania. Knowing the approximate build date, I believed the architecture seemed appropriate. There were seven ionic-style columns. The door in the center was white with an older style architecture around it. I walked up the steps to the door and tried to open it. It was locked. I fully expected it would be. Long gone were the days when churches could leave their doors open day and night for weary travelers to visit and pray. Feeling the blood flowing again in my legs, facilitated by walking, was lovely. I took a seat on the steps, taking a moment to pray.

I closed my eyes and spoke silently to God. I thanked him for His provisions, His blessings, and for helping me get as far on this journey as I had now come. The birds sang a sweet song of worship to the King, and the gentle, warm breeze brushed against my cheeks. My mouth moved, but no words came out as I sat still by myself.

"Can I join you in prayer?"

I jumped. My eyes opened and slowly adjusted to the influx of light. Before me was a tall man wearing black slacks and a tweed jacket. Carrying several books in his right hand, he wore glasses and had a full beard. His brown and gray hair thinned near the top of his long face.

"Sure." I pushed myself up to stand.

"No, don't get up. Let me come sit."

I fell back to the cement, and he sat on my left side. He held out his hand and introduced himself to me. "I am Reverend Pete. I am one of the pastors here."

"I am Jake Anderson, and I am passing through here. Your campus reminded me of a place near my hometown in Ohio, and I wanted to come by and see your church."

"Oh, well, I can certainly let you in and see it if you would like."

"No, No, it's fine. I can't stay long, and I wanted to pray a little, so all is well."

"Well, Jake from Ohio. If I may ask, is there something I can pray for as well?"

"I am from Baltimore now. I grew up in Ohio. But, yeah, there is this young girl with me, and I am not sure how committed she is."

He leaned back. His face showed I had better give a better explanation.

"Oh my goodness, I am so sorry. I have a bad habit of often thinking people can read my mind or something. I start talking, knowing what I mean, but I don't explain it well."

He laughed, "Oh, I understand. So, is this girl your daughter?"

"Well, yes, I adopted her. I mean, it's a long and complicated story. She is nineteen, and I met her a few weeks ago and I sort of adopted her. Oh my goodness, I am all over the place." I debated where I should begin. "Well, how much time do you have?"

"I am fine, but it sounded like you were the one in a hurry."

"Yes, I am, but I am not. I am several days into a forty-day journey. I know it sounds strange. Anyway, I stopped here because I wanted to see your beautiful campus. Before I got here though, I met this young lady in need of help, and I took her in, and we agreed to an adoption of sorts. I will be her dad, and she will be my daughter. She needed a dad, and I needed a daughter." The look on the reverend's face was priceless. I knew the look. Someone comes to you with anxiety all over them and tries to explain a story quickly, and it seems too implausible, so you listen. "I am not making any sense. Anyway, I don't know if this young girl is committed to this or if I should…"

"Should what?"

Not even the realization her mom was not the Gina Taylor I knew could have topped the gut-wrenching feeling I had when I saw Charlotte in front of me. I closed my mouth and wondered how much she had heard. Maybe I was not committed. Perhaps the whole thing was a mistake. I should have known she would not stay in the car. It was a hot day.

"Hi, Charlotte. This is…"

"Hi, Reverend. What were you going to say, Jake? Don't you know if I am committed? Maybe you are the one not committed. I mean, why not? Every man I have ever known has abandoned me. Why wouldn't I believe you would do that, too?"

"Maybe we can all go inside and…"

Charlotte started running toward the car but ran past Santa Fe and continued to West Clafin. I interrupted the reverend and chased after her.

"Wait! Please hear me out."

"I've heard enough. Leave. I will find my way back to Denver."

My longer legs allowed me to not only catch her but get in front of her. She tried to move around me, and I grabbed her and pulled her back. I wanted to hug her, but she pulled away and turned and walked toward where she had run. I followed but not too closely. "Can we get in the car and talk?"

"I have nothing to say, but I also don't have any idea where I am, so I will go to the car, but I think you should drop me off at a truck stop or something. I can find my way home."

"Where is home?"

She turned, pointed her finger at me. "Anywhere you are not!"

I stopped. I was stunned and upset. How had it escalated to this level so fast? The amount of loss I felt in the moment became too much. I watched as she rounded the corner and prayed she went back to the car. I walked again, and as I reached the corner, a sense of relief overcame me as I saw her sitting in the passenger seat. Reverend Pete stood on the opposite corner. I avoided him as I crossed the street diagonally toward my vehicle.

"Have a great day," I heard him say.

Opening the door and sitting, I turned the keys, pulled out, and drove back to the interstate. We were both crying, but neither spoke. I pulled myself together and waited until we were off campus before trying to speak but no words would form. When we were up to speed on the interstate, I finally broke the silence.

"I am not going to abandon you."

"You said I am not committed!" She was emotional. No knife could have cut me as profoundly as hearing those words.

"I didn't say that. I asked myself if you were. I mean, this is a drastic change for both of us. I want to be sure we have both thought it through. I don't plan to live in Denver. My job is in Baltimore. Do you want to live on the East Coast?"

"I needed a dad my whole life. I should have known when I finally found someone who could be that person he would not believe in me."

The knife pierced deeper into my heart. Sadness and torment flooded my soul. *Was I not committed?* I wanted to believe I was.

"I have never known what it is like to have a dad. I will never know. I think maybe I should go home."

"But where to Charlotte? Your mom has passed, and you don't have brothers or sisters. You don't like your uncle. The house you lived in belongs to someone else now. Is there anyone else?"

"I hate you! I hate you," she said, pounding both fists on the dashboard as hard as she could as she continued to yell. "I hate you!"

"You hate me?"

"Why did you leave me, Mom? Why? I hate you for leaving me all alone. Why did you have to be an addict? Why did you have to take those drugs? Why did you leave me? Why? Why?" Her voice became unrecognizable as she continued to shout.

In a fitting display of nature imitating our lives, the darkness of the skies opened up, and rain poured. I slowed the vehicle and put on my hazard lights as I continued to drive.

Manhattan. I recognized the voice in my mind. It was not an audible voice, but I realized it. *Is that you, Lord?* Manhattan again came to mind. I pulled off the next exit, and when at the stop sign, I grabbed my phone. I typed in Manhattan, thinking I would see a picture of the Freedom Tower appear, but instead was a map of Manhattan, Kansas, and below was an advertisement for the Four Points Sheraton Hotel. I knew we would stay there for the night. I hadn't considered even stopping here, but God redirected my steps, as He so often had done on this trip. The home of Kansas State University was to be our home for the night.

Separate rooms with little conversation was the modus operandi for the rest of the evening. I texted Charlotte at ten o'clock before I fell asleep and asked if she needed anything. She said she was fine, but she also apologized for her behavior earlier. I told her it was understandable and I had forgiven it all. I asked if she would forgive me, too. She said she had. I reminded her she could always talk to me about anything. I didn't use the term father, but I let her know I was a person she could trust, could rely on, and would always do whatever I could to help her be happy and safe. She thanked me, and that was the last I heard from her until morning.

I lay in bed and prayed, "God, I don't know what will happen, but I trust you. If she decides to leave and go back to Colorado, please be with her. If you want to make this work for us, help me be the father she never knew. Make me more like you, oh Lord, for you are holy and pleasing. Help me be to her the father you are to me. Lord, you know I am not trying to replace Timmy and Jane but thank you for bringing Charlotte into my life. I needed her as much as she needed me. Amen.

My mind wandered from Jane and Timmy to the day in June a year earlier and to Beaver, Utah. I considered how Sean was doing and if he needed my help. I tried to calculate how much I had spent on gas and hotel rooms. My mind raced in all directions until I let it calm, and I heard The LORD speak to me. *She is going to leave you, son.* I tried to ignore it, but in my heart, I knew it was true. I felt unprepared.

Chapter

21

Never in my life to that point had I ever considered a plane crash. Never had I ever worried about a plane not making its destination. It was an anxiety that kept many people from ever flying, but I never considered it. Turbulence never bothered me, and rough landings never kept me from boarding a plane. I had no fear that I would not make my destination. As I watched the Boeing 787 Dreamliner take flight bound for Denver, with Charlotte aboard, that fear of failure mixed with great sadness in my heart.

Earlier that morning, I met her for breakfast, and she broke the news to me. She had asked her uncle if he would pick her up in Denver if she could get there. She had checked her bank account that morning, and the money from the estate settlement was not there yet. But she had heard from the attorney that she would be receiving $1,793. She asked me if she could borrow $307 for a plane ticket and that with Venmo, I would get my money back.

I held back the tears with great restraint as I told her I would buy her a plane ticket and she didn't need to worry about paying me back. She explained she loved the idea of having me as her father, but her life and her home were in Colorado. She had not decided if she would stay in Denver or live with her uncle in Grand Junction. She would determine that upon arrival. But she felt she could not continue this journey with me any longer.

She had urged me to continue to write about my journey on the Facebook page.

"People want to know when the pastor is going to pop-up in their town," she said. "All 108,925 of them."

The number boggled my mind. But I assured her I would continue to write. I asked how she wanted me to handle her departure to the cult-following we had. Shockingly, she directed me to tell them the truth.

"Tell them I am not your daughter, that we discovered this and I returned home."

"But don't you think this will harm the following? This is all you, Charlotte. This is not about me."

"No, Jake. It's not about either of us. Maybe you should read it. It's all about God."

Embarrassed I had not yet looked at the page since I accidentally clicked on her profile, I promised Charlotte I would review it all later in the evening. I had planned to stay in Manhattan for a few days, but I did not tell her it was to recover from the depression I felt, knowing she wanted to leave.

"They will accept it, Jake. They know you did this because of God and know I was someone you happened upon along the way. Trust me. They will continue to follow and share your posts, and God will get the glory."

It was the first time I had ever heard her mention God and glory within the same breath. I was happy. I knew she was growing closer to God as we discussed Him often when we would camp for the night. I recalled the night I gave her the gold coin Randall had left behind. She had fallen right into the trap when she said, "I will see God as a father when I get around to it." So I gave her a round-tuit. She thought it was the funniest thing she had ever heard, and she adored the coin and carried it with her every day after.

When I returned to the hotel, I wrote in my journal how much I missed her already and wondered how I would continue this journey without her. As expected, a stint of depression gripped me with talons so strong, not even the most potent lion could have broken free. The day following her departure, I lay in bed the entire day. I put the Do Not Disturb sign on the door and only arose to use the facilities. I ordered room service around three o'clock but ate nothing else for the rest of the day.

As evening approached, I finally sat up and looked out the window as I often did on business trips. In Ephesians chapter six, the Apostle Paul mentions putting on the armor of God for protection against the various ways the enemy can enter our minds and harm our bodies. An activity I often began, especially in hotel rooms, putting on God's armor was an activity I did not do that night. I regretted it later, too. Sadness and despair over the previous day's events had entered my mind. The enemy talked, and although I knew how to combat them, I failed to do so.

Go home now. The journey is over. I knew the voice was not God, but I also knew it was right. *What was the point any longer?* I decided I would pack up and begin the drive to Baltimore in the morning. Eighteen hours if I did not stop. Why would I stop? I had nothing to stop for any longer. Leaving at six o'clock would put me at home by midnight. The trip was over. I wondered how God would feel about my decision, but I reconciled in my mind that He loves me and would accept what I decided.

Oh, how often we reason in our minds that God will accept our decisions. He does. But it is not always what He wants for us. God has given us a choice, and we can certainly do whatever we wish with these choices. We can stay, or we can stray. We can surrender, or we can control. Moses told the Israelites before them was life and death. He encouraged them to choose life so they would live long in the land God had given them. My decision was not a decision of life and death, but it was a decision of obedience to what God had called me to do. I was ready, more ready than ever, to abandon what He had called me to do. Leaving the trip became my only option.

"When you quit, you will never know what you could have been." My dad spoke these words to me when I wanted to end my marriage with Jane after one year. Giving up on Jane would have been the easy way out. Two people fall in love and sometimes quickly. They grow closer and fall deeply in love, but when they must live together and see the other is different than what they are accustomed to, marriages sometimes fail. Too often, couples never know what they could have been because they chase the fulfillment and false belief that someone else may fill the void they feel in their lives.

As a pastor, I always tried to remind those who would listen that we all have a void. But it is not put there by God so that we will love Him. The void is put there by the enemy that convinces us that we have it. I often repeated this phrase several times. The enemy puts the void there. God never created us with a vacuum. Many pastors and teachers teach this void is born in us and that only God can fill it. It's a lovely way of saying only God can give you fulfillment, but when you start by suggesting God created something less than perfect, you diminish the beauty of God's creation. God did not make the void. The enemy convinced us we had it.

Filling the void, I struggled with my decision. My knowledge of God being able to fill the void was second according to my understanding of how it formed, and that was where I fell short of God's glory. My priorities had become misaligned. The knowledge of the purpose of my journey came back to my mind. I realized I shifted my focus, and I needed to realign my thoughts. Recognizing this, I fell to my knees and prayed at the side of my bed.

"God, I am lost. I don't know if it is because she left or

because I still feel the pain of loss from my family. Was I trying to fill this void in my life with her instead of you? I was so confident, Lord, you ordained this trip for me finding her. I was to help her, and you helped me, too. Father, help me see the error of my ways. Speak to my heart as I pray silently now. Set my priorities to yours. Change my will to be your will."

There are moments in our lives when we know God is speaking. Many struggle to hear His voice, but once you listen to it, it becomes as clear as your closest friend. God was speaking to me. I had laid it all out before Him. In my heart, I approached Him with no hindrances and sought His guidance. I desired His wisdom and wanted His love to shower me. I remained on my knees with my hands folded on the bed in front of me. I gently rested my head. My mind started wandering. My stomach ached. I spoke silently, this time asking God to clear my mind and ease my pain. He did.

I saw a vision of an angel descending from Heaven. He twirled in a stream of white light as he fell and landed before me. I was in a grassy meadow, and darkness surrounded me, but I saw light within the small area where the angel landed. It seemed as if the sun shined a spotlight only where I stood. I smiled, and the angel spoke.

"The LORD, the God of heaven, He is the Holy One. He has heard your cries. Listen carefully and do not stray. Focus on my words, for they come from The Most High, God and Creator."

I bowed my head and said, "Speak to me. Your servant is listening."

"Thus, saith The LORD. I have called you for a time such as this. I have set before you people in need of healing. With your words and with the touch of your hands, I have healed them. I have worked through you for my glory. But I know your pain. I suffered your pain, too, when I watched my son die. Do not think I endured the pain because I knew I would see Him again when I raised Him from the dead, for I knew the pain of loss as you do now. But I knew my pain was for a purpose. Your pain, though it is much to bear, is for a purpose as well. My son died so others may live. Your son and your wife died, not for this reason, but so you would show others, my love. The actions of many caused the death of your family. Not one, but many. It is for the actions of these many that I allowed my son to die."

With an outstretched hand, the angel reached over and lifted my chin. I felt the warmth of his fingers as he directed my head upward. "Do you understand these words?"

"Yes, I understand. My family has been taken not because of my actions but because of the actions of others. My actions, too, have caused distress and grief for others in my life, but my actions have also brought healing and restoration through God's work in me."

"Yes, you are receiving the wisdom of God for your understanding. Do you know why God sent you on this journey?"

"Yes. I do. He sent me, not for my healing but the healing of others. My healing will be complete when through me, I have allowed God to work."

"Yes, you are receiving the wisdom of God for your understanding. Do you know why you met the people God sent you on this journey?"

"Yes, I do. God sent me so others would know He loves them without condition. It is not for the actions they perform that He loves them, but for the fact that He alone is God. I met the people so God could show His love through me, and this was not for me, but it was for them. My healing will be complete when I have allowed God to show His love through me."

"Go forth now, Jake. The decision is now and always has been your own. God loves you not because you obeyed. He will not stop loving you if you return home. He will love you always because He is God."

The angel twirled again and disappeared from my sight. The vision ended, and when I opened my eyes, I saw the many colors of the comforter on my bed. *Was I dreaming, or was it a waking vision?* It didn't matter; it was real either way.

Pushing off the edge of the bed, I stood and looked around. Streetlights and moonlight shone through my window. Turning back and sitting, I pondered what had happened in the vision. My mind took me back to the night I first heard God speak about making this journey. I realized it was not about me but was God's way of healing me. My obedience did not build up God's love in me, but my compliance allowed God to work through me to bless others. If I had chosen not to be obedient, He would have used someone else. God wanted to show the people I met that He loves them.

As I apologized for not understanding, I replayed the Angel's voice in my mind. *You are receiving the wisdom of God for your understanding.* It was not so I could meet Charlotte or Ralph and Marian. It was not to encounter Solomon or Randall, or even so I could fill up my journal. I was on this journey because I obeyed the leading of God, and He used me to help others understand His love.

I remembered Solomon's words to me. I had written them down. I fumbled through my journal pages until I found it. "**It's not about how many people you will reach. It's not about how many people will know your name. It's about how many people you will allow God to impact through your actions as you speak the name of Jesus, our Lord.**" I had highlighted it so I would never forget it. It's not about me and never has been. When I accepted this, I felt healed. For the first time in over a year, I felt whole and restored.

Before setting my phone down for the night, I followed up on the promise I had made to Charlotte the previous day. I wanted to look at the Facebook page she had created. As my tired and weary eyes scanned the posts, I saw the one made by the man from Ohio. He called me the pop-up pastor because I popped up in various little towns. The concept caught on, and many people posted—

visit us, come to my church, come pray over my child, and more. The number of followers, now over 130,000, seemed to multiply. I went back to the latest post to see if Charlotte had said anything about her departure. She had not.

A quick flip of my index finger sent the posts scrolling by before stopping on a picture of a young man wearing a ball cap, sitting on what I assumed was his mother's knee, and holding a sign. The caption read "Visit me Jake." It was written with a crayon and in large bold letters. Beneath the picture were the words: "Mr. Anderson, this is my son James. He keeps saying there are creatures in our home, and he can't sleep. We have taken him to churches, but we always get the same reply 'Pray for protection.' We have done this many times to no avail. We hope that if you can stop by the small town of Meriden, KS, we would be grateful. PM me for directions."

But God, what do they think I can do for them? I only asked the questions, and immediately in my mind, I knew. This family needed to know how much God loves them. The download I received was overwhelming. I wrote it in my journal. *They are looking for answers in churches, but not all solutions are in the building. I dwell in the hearts of believers, and there is my protection.*

But God, I asked, *what about the creatures. Spiders or demons? What are we talking about here?*

I AM who I AM, and I am greater than anything I have created, and all I have created is not as great as I AM.

I repeated it to myself several times. I wrote it down, and after again hearing the angel's voice say I received wisdom for my understanding, I realized it didn't matter what the young boy saw in his home. God is greater. If one could have seen me, they would have seen the light bulb above my head. I was confident. "This family needs to know your love, and the rest will flow." Moments earlier, I planned an eighteen-hour trip to Baltimore, and now I was planning a short jaunt to Meriden, Kansas.

Chapter

22

Small towns and large cities, I had seen them all in the last few weeks. But this town was unique. A quick Google search indicated the population to be around a thousand. Still, this town had four churches, a coffee shop, a post office, a metals processing plant, an elementary, junior high, and senior high school, a sports bar, and so much more. But the surrounding farmland, for as far as one could see, is what made it so unique. One could suggest farmers built a small town in the middle of their land one day. They probably would be correct. The map showed nothing but farmland. It did start to make sense, however. If you want to live in a secluded town, you need to have everything in town because it is at least twenty miles from the nearest city.

Arriving at the home indicated in the private message, I was greeted by James' mother who waited for me on the front lawn. She must have recognized my car because as I approached, she leaped up and ran inside. She came back out holding hands with ten-year-old James.

Sally, the mom, was five foot five with short, blond hair and blue eyes. She wore a pair of jean shorts and a white tank top. She had a heart tattoo on her right leg, which caught my attention as it reminded me of Charlotte. Their house was a small brick ranch-style, probably two bedrooms. A gold Pontiac Sunfire sat in the gravel driveway, and I pulled up behind it.

A shorter man with coal-black hair and deep brown eyes with bushy eyebrows stepped onto the porch. He wore a Kansas Jayhawks basketball jersey and blue cotton shorts. I caught a glimpse of his bare feet as he walked toward a chair and sat.

I exited the car, and I immediately extended my hand to Sally, who returned the handshake and declared her son was the one about whom she had written. He snuggled up next to his mom's left leg and turned his head so I could not see his eyes. *Shy, I see.*

"Hello, Sally, is it? I am Jake."

"Yes, I am Sally, this is James, and that is Fred, my husband."

Fred waved to me and nodded.

"Well, first, thanks for coming. I know you are busy."

Everyone always said *I know you are busy,* but I never let myself get to the point of burnout. I knew I could not visit everyone following the Pop-Up Pastor Facebook page, so busy had nothing to do with it.

"No, I am glad I could come by." I looked at the young man. "So, what kinds of creatures are you seeing, little fella?"

"He won't talk to strangers." My head turned to the sound. Fred had spoken up to provide some information. "He's been taught that way."

"Very good. Very good. Okay, well, can one of you explain what he may be seeing?"

Trying to push James away as he grasped harder and mumbled something inaudible, Sally looked at her husband and back at me. "Well, he says he sees black people with red eyes."

"Black as in shadows?"

"Well, yeah, I guess. James said they are all black except for their red eyes."

"Okay, Okay. Well, has he seen any horror movies lately?"

165

"We don't let him watch them. But Fred and I are huge fans."

My first thought was, are you sure he is not watching when you don't realize? But I didn't ask the question. However, the question did not need asking as The Holy Spirit spoke to my spirit and told me what to say.

"So, you watch horror movies in this home?"

"What's that got to do with it?" I didn't mean to, but I ignored Fred's question. I thought it had a lot to do with it, but again The Holy Spirit spoke.

"Can I ask you, folks, if you believe in God?"

"Yes, we both do," she pushed James away again. He quickly returned and grasped her leg harder this time. "Ouch, that hurt."

"Okay, that's very good. That's foundational. If I ask any questions you don't want to answer, don't feel like you must. I am not trying to pry into your personal lives here. I am trying to understand what is going on. Are we good?"

Sally and Fred both nodded in agreement.

"Okay good. So, when did he start seeing these creatures?"

"About a month ago?" She looked at her husband, and he agreed.

"Did anything you can think of that may be relevant happen a month ago?"

Irrelevant Jake. Remind them of God's love. The thought in my head was strong and concise. "Never mind that question. It's not important." I paused and put my hands together in front of me. I looked up at the sky to gather my thoughts. "So, you both believe in God. Do you know God loves you?"

Sally pursed her lips together. She looked at Fred, and he simply raised both hands as if to say, I don't know. "Well, I want to believe, but you see, we both used to curse a lot, and I had a gambling addiction, and Fred, well, he used to drink. But we are trying to quit. Fred only drinks about once a week now, and I haven't gambled for close to two years; and when was the last time we cursed Fred? Six, seven months ago?"

"About that, yeah."

Help me, God, speak to me so I may. I looked at Sally and Fred and smiled. "Can I tell you both something?"

"That's why you're here."

I looked at Fred and smiled. "God loves you both beyond measure. I hear many people say because of their past, they don't think God loves them. They feel many times like they must perform so God will love them. Do you know where that comes from?"

Sally shook her head, Fred remained stoic.

"It comes from us being human. When you two fell in love, there was a reason. Maybe Fred did something you enjoyed. Perhaps he bought you flowers or took you out to eat.

She blushed. "He did."

"You probably did things for him that made him feel loved. Maybe you gave him a back rub, or maybe it was the way you kissed him. You both made each other feel incredible love for one another, am I right?"

They looked at each other. It was the first time I had seen Fred smile since I had arrived.

"You see, we learn to love one another because of what we do for one another, or at least it is what we think. The truth, however, is love doesn't work that way. Love is not based on works; love is a creation of God that exists, and we experience. We don't earn it, and we can't create it. We cannot go to the store and buy five ounces of God's love. It's always with us, in us, and part of us. We decide whether or not we want to use it. The Bible says love is patient and love is kind, and love doesn't boast and it sees no wrong."

"1 Corinthians 13," Sally said.

"Yes! You got it, but we interpret it as 'If I love, I must be patient and I must be kind.' Am I right?"

She nodded.

"But love simply exists and is patient and kind because God

created it that way. 1 Corinthians 13 has nothing to do with how we need to operate. It has everything to do with what God created and that He exists in our lives. Does that make sense?

"I actually follow what you are saying."

I glanced at Fred to see if he followed. "Go on."

"Great. So, God's love does not consider our past. No one can earn God's love, and you cannot lose it. The same guy who wrote 1 Corinthians 13 also told us nothing could separate us from the love of God. Nothing and one thing he mentioned in Romans chapter 8 were that demons could not divide us. Angels can't, and people can't. Nothing in creation can separate us from God's love. Cursing, gambling, and drinking cannot separate us from God's love. Do you see what I am saying?

"Yes!"

"So, if love exists, and nothing can separate us from God's love, we should have no worries. We should not be concerned with black creatures with red eyes because they can't harm us."

"Well, what do we do about them? How do we remove them?"

"We just love. Love will conquer them. When we love, we fill ourselves with something God created for us, and they will simply move on because you are not letting them in."

"Hmm." Fred stood up, walked down the two steps of the porch, and came near to us. "Sir, I want to thank you. I know I sat on that porch trying to act tough. The truth is I figured you were another phony preacher who would tell us to pray, and you would put your hands on us and then leave feeling like you changed the world. Now, sir, don't get me wrong. The Bible is clear that laying on hands is useful when properly used. But what you said penetrated my heart, man." He pounded his chest with his palm. "That was deep. I have heard no one speak of God's love like that. The whole thing with 1 Corinthians and God's love has always existed and..." He started shaking his head. "Wow, powerful stuff."

"Well, thank you, but it came to me from The Holy Spirit. I

have never thought of it that way before either. You two are the first I ever have spoken to like this."

"Really?"

"Yes, ma'am."

"Okay, well, it's all good. I like it, but what does it have to do with what the little guy is seeing? I get you are saying they will move on, but when? This boy is scared."

"Well, I asked the question of myself, too. But God was clear to me on this. When you arrive, speak of my love. You see, God's love is mighty. I didn't ask this, and I am not asking now, but I would guess that the two of you have had some marital issues." I stopped and raised my hand when they both looked at one another. "I don't want any details. It could be because of what your son is seeing. But God wanted you to hear this message so you can work on your relationship with one another and on your relationships with God. Hold on." I ran back to the car and grabbed a pen and paper.

"Look at this." I drew a triangle on the blank page. "This is you, Sally. This is you, Fred" I drew their names at the bottom of the triangle. One name in each corner. "You two have a relationship with one another." I drew a line with arrows on both ends between the two names along the bottom. "See, you both have your relationships with God." I drew the same line with arrows between each name and the top of the triangle. I wrote in God at the peak of the triangle. "This is by design. So, if things in your marriage turn upside down," I turned the paper over, "God is strong enough to support the marriage, and is why He is at the point." If we had Fred up here and the marriage turned upside down, Fred would not be strong enough to support the weight. No offense, Fred, it's God's job. The same if Sally was up here. But God is strong enough to support this triangle if it turns upside down."

Fred and Sally looked at one another and smiled.

"I've never heard of it that way, but it does make sense. So, if

I am not wrong, what you are saying is if we work on our own relationships with God and use His love and understand His love as you explained, we can be stronger with God and in turn that makes us..."

"Stronger together," they both spoke in unison.

"Yes!"

"I am impressed. I thought you would waltz in here in your fancy clothes, and I see you don't have them. No offense. Why you're just in a plain ole' pair of khaki shorts and a Maryland Terrapins T-shirt. I figured you would just say your prayers and leave."

Fred extended his hand, but not for a handshake. He also grabbed his wife's hand as well, and she raised her right to my left. We all held hands. "Can you pray for our son now? I trust you now, my friend."

Without even thinking, I closed my eyes and prayed, "Lord, God, we thank you for the lesson you provided. God, we appreciate your love and adore how much you love us. Without measure, without condition, and simply because you are who you are. Father, as I speak, I hear your voice, saying what James has seen is now gone. What he has seen will not return. For your love has entered into this home, and you have changed the lives of all here today. Glorious God of heaven, make your presence known in this home. In Jesus' name, we pray, Amen." I opened my eyes to see James standing in the center of all three of us. He had released his mother's leg and looked up at me directly into my eyes.

"They don't like you. They said they had to leave because of you, and they don't like you."

"Who said that, buddy?"

"The black men with red eyes. They said they had to leave because of him."

James pointed at me. A chill came over my whole body as I listened. "But that's okay because the white men with wings said they will make sure they don't come back."

"White men with wings? Where do you see them?" asked Sally.

"They are all around our house, Mommy, I see them." He pointed from left to right in front of the house and continued around until he made a full circle. "Jesus sent them, Mommy. The one you and Dad, talk about? He said he sent the white people with wings, and they won't be leaving now."

I wanted to shout *Praise the LORD,* but I remained silent. Instead, I took in the smiles on Fred and Sally's faces as they stepped together, hugged, and told each other they loved one another.

"Thank you so much for responding to my post and for coming here," Sally said, as she hugged me.

"Jake, it's been a real pleasure, sir. Where you off to next?"

"Oh, I don't know. I guess I will probably look at the Facebook page and see what God has in store for me."

Squinting her eyes and looking around and trying to see in the car, Sally spoke, "Where is the girl? Your daughter? Is she not with you?"

It's not about her. It's about the people before you, Jake. "Oh, she will be back. She went to visit some family. All is well." I was angry at myself for saying it. I had lied because she was not coming back. I should have told them the truth.

"Oh, good. I hope she enjoys her time away. Would you like to come in for some lunch?"

"Oh, I would love to, ma'am, but I think I need to get back on the road. I feel like Kansas City is calling me."

"Be careful there. It's not like Meriden, that's for sure."

"Thanks, Fred. I appreciate the heads up."

"God bless you both, and remember, work on your relationship with God. It's not about what you have done. It's about who God is and what He did in the form of Jesus on the cross."

171

"Yes, thank you. I think we will be much better off now. Especially since we have," Fred paused and looked around his house, "angels all around us."

"Yes, you do. I am glad I came by. God bless, and I will talk to you all on Facebook."

"And we will spread the word about you, too. Thank you again."

After getting gas and food in Topeka, I got back on the road heading toward Kansas City. What a change of events had occurred in the last few days. I was ready to throw in the towel and go home entirely, and now I had taught a couple and myself a new way of looking at God's love. "Wow, God, thank you for the message. I never thought of love like this before, but I will use it again for sure."

When we realize God's love exists as much as He does, we learn ways to administer it that share the beauty of His creation. I made a mental note to journal what The Holy Spirit had provided.

Seeing the sign that indicated Kansas City was sixty miles ahead, I couldn't help myself. I started singing the Wilbert Harrison song. "Going to Kansas City, Kansas City, here I come." I laughed so hard tears formed in my eyes. I wiped them dry in time to see I had missed a call from Charlotte.

Thirty-eight years. That is how long it took me to realize that Kansas City was in Kansas and Missouri. I realized it as I entered Kansas City, and unlike Dorothy from *The Wizard of Oz*, I was still in Kansas. After crossing the border into Missouri, I was once again in Kansas City. I had to speak to a local on the street to get an explanation.

The irony of this is that I had once visited Kansas City, Missouri. Immediately out of college and in the year before starting the business with Sean, I worked for a national association for groundwater scientists. They had their annual convention in Kansas City, Missouri. It was one of the worst experiences of my life, but at least I knew of all the best restaurants in town. Mario's Italian Restaurant was no exception.

Known for their great lunch specials is secondary to their setting. One may feel like they stepped into an old Western Saloon. There is even a claw foot bathtub in the restrooms. Spittoons and saloon-style entries aside, I was grateful to be able to eat some excellent Kansas City pizza.

I did not see her approach me from behind, so I was unsure

how long she had been behind me. Feeling someone observed me, I wanted to turn around, but I also wanted to keep a low profile with the Facebook page going viral. Finally, she approached from my right, and I recognized her right away.

"Aren't you that guy I met on the highway?"

She did not wear her black vest with numerous patches nor her Harley Davidson bandanna, but I have always had a knack for remembering faces. Her hair was let down and not pulled up as it had been when we met. She wore business attire, so I may have thought she was a stranger if I had not recognized her facial features.

"Yes, I was the one who stopped after your friend hit the cow. How is he doing?"

"May I?"

"Certainly. Please sit."

"John is fine. He spent the night in the hospital, and he did pass out, but it turns out it was not from the accident. He has diabetes, and his sugar went low, which is most likely why he crashed. We think he never actually hit the cow but probably scared it. He doesn't remember."

"Well, that's good he was not seriously hurt."

"Yep, not a scratch. He spent the night in the hospital for the low blood sugar, but his bike was the only thing scratched. He was lucky."

"Well, I am happy to hear."

She looked around me to the empty seat to my left. I sat at the bar. "Where's your friend? Was she your daughter?"

I paused as I gathered my thoughts. *Get up and leave. You don't need this right now.* I suppressed those thoughts, "Charlotte is in Denver. It's a long story, but yes, she is my daughter."

"That's cool. I don't mean to pry into your matters. I wanted to let you know we all appreciated what she did. To help a stranger takes a special person in this day and age."

"Yeah, Charlotte is a special girl for sure."

We sat and stared forward for twenty seconds until my pizza arrived.

"Need another Diet Pepsi?" asked the waitress.

"Please."

"Anything for you?"

"No, thank you. I need to get back to work."

I watched as the waitress walked away and wondered if I should engage my new friend in conversation. I could not think of anything to say.

"Look, I don't mean to be a crazy person, but can you pray for me?"

I looked at her. This marked the second time on this journey someone asked me to pray for them out of the blue. I knew my Bible was not with me, so I didn't know how she knew who I was. I reasoned it was from Facebook, but I did not bring it up.

"Of course, I will. What's going on?"

"Well, it's my mom and dad." She choked up as she wiped a tear from her eye.

"They don't appreciate my lifestyle. They say I am going to hell."

I tried to determine what it could be. *Abortion? Drug use? Paganism?* I stopped my random thoughts and let her tell me.

"I am a lesbian. I have been for several years. I have a successful career as a real estate agent in Kansas City, but my girlfriend, well, she is the one that got me into the Smokin' Joe's Motorcycle Club."

Before answering her, I flashed back to the night of the accident. I had seen SJMC on her vest and did not understand what it meant. Now it made sense. My silence triggered her, and she thought I was judgmental.

"I know. I should have known. I am sure you don't approve either."

She stood up to walk away, and I grabbed her arm. "What's your name, if I may ask?"

"Sheila."

"Sheila, don't take my silence as judgment. I tried to understand what SJMC meant. I had been wondering since the night we met. Anyway, I don't pass judgment on you. I am sorry your parents are. I can probably explain why they are. Do you have a couple of minutes?

She sat back down but glanced all around her. It seemed she tried to determine if she knew anyone, but Mario's had seen busier days.

"Your parents love you deeply. I am guessing they raised you in a church?"

She acknowledged my accuracy.

"They probably feel that anyone who claims to be a homosexual is probably not saved. Maybe I am wrong, but either way, they feel you are violating what God wants for your life."

She nodded again. She laughed slightly.

"I am not judging you. The Bible tells us to love our neighbors as ourselves, and in the last few weeks especially, I have learned to love myself more, which means that I love you even more. Now, this love is not romantic. It's more of a…"

"I know, like a Philia love."

I smiled. I was shocked Sheila had used the term Philia, but she used it correctly.

"I went to Bible College. I studied Greek."

"Fantastic. Okay, then you know what I mean. God loves you, too, but with agape love."

"I tried to tell them, but they won't accept it."

"Well, I am sure they won't accept it because of what the Bible says. You went to Bible College. How do you reconcile your lifestyle to what the Bible says?" Her expression spoke volumes to me. "Again, I am not judging. I am asking how you reconcile it."

"I get it. I know precisely what Romans 1 and Leviticus 19, among other passages, say. Believe me when I say I struggle. But it's almost like an addiction. I don't want to do this, but I do. You know, like what Paul says in Romans 7."

"Yes, I get that. I thought the same thing, and we all have struggles. Many people struggle with sexual addiction in many forms. I am not saying it is not real. I know your feelings are strong, and you feel you can't overcome them. I know the human condition. I am human, too."

"But you are not gay."

"No, but I am a sinner in need of God's grace. It's just my sins are not as political as your sin, and that is what I tried to get at. Your parents realize the political aspect of your lifestyle, and they care so deeply for you, so they may fear for your life or may fear you are beyond being saved."

"Are you suggesting salvation is not an option for the LGBTQ community?"

"No, No, No, not at all. I hope I didn't make it sound that way. Let me try to explain what I meant."

God, give me the words, please. "Salvation, as you know, comes to us when we confess with our mouths and believe in our hearts that Jesus is Lord. Right?"

"Yes, that's what the Bible teaches."

"Yes, it does. Now the Bible does say that liars won't see the gates of heaven and that a man lying with a man is an abomination, and it also teaches us that calling your brother a fool is like murder." She nodded in agreement. "Jesus said he didn't come to abolish the law but to fulfill it. So, we can't throw out all we read in Leviticus 19, can we?"

She spoke, but I interrupted. "Please, let me finish. I am not judging you."

"Okay."

"Where we often have a disconnect is when we try to reconcile the Old Testament with the New Testament. We see all the laws, and we see all of the dos and don'ts. We think we must do what we can to be righteous. But remember what the prophet said and what Paul reiterated. The righteous shall live by faith. You with me?"

"Yes," she stopped crying and listened intently.

"Living by faith does not mean we have to tackle our issues alone. Living by faith means taking my entire broken self to God and saying, 'Here I am, Lord. I am broken and in need of your help.' But we as humans have this 'I can fix me' mentality, and we try to fix ourselves, but we fail. If we would stop looking at one another as broken vessels and stop isolating those broken people, we would have a better society. But instead, to make ourselves feel better about what we fear, that God would reject us, we isolate those we see as more visibly broken. It takes the onus off our broken and sinful lives and places it on others. In many ways, it makes us feel like, 'Well, someone else is worse than me, so God surely will save me,' but again, this is a works-based mentality."

"I do understand what you are saying. I have a hard time thinking my parents are broken and are isolating me because of their brokenness."

"Sure, we don't want to think of our parents as anything other than superheroes. But they are human, too. They need Jesus, too."

"Yeah, but how does that help me with my struggles?"

"I can't help you with your struggles. You can't help yourself with your struggles. A counselor can help you cope with your struggles. We sometimes use drugs to alleviate the pain of our struggles. But only God can truly fix the brokenness inside us. Only God can fix our struggles."

"Okay I am a Christian. But I am still struggling. Trust me. I know each time I take part I am grieving the Holy Spirit."

"Yes, and if the Holy Spirit were a human, we would all be in trouble. Again, you don't realize it, but you are still trying to fix yourself by saying, 'I am a Christian.' You see it as a fix. I did my part. I accepted Christ. Boom! It should be fixed. Wait! Why am I not fixed? Being a Christian is the foundation. Spending time with God in prayer is the solution."

She looked at the clock on the wall. "I need to go. I have to show a house soon. I appreciate your words, and I will think about them."

"Do me a favor, don't think about them. Take them to God. I know you have probably heard this before, and I know you understand this, but ask yourself and ask God, can your relationship with Him grow stronger. If the answer is yes, and if you are honest, it will be yes, then say God, I want to have a stronger and healthier relationship with you."

"I will, thanks."

I watched as she walked away, pushed open the saloon doors, and exited. I prayed for Sheila and asked God to work with her to help her understand what I meant.

As I sat and processed what transpired, I caught a glimpse of the television in the corner. Activists had blown up a family planning clinic in a city in Oklahoma. I shook my head at the tragedy. The news report did not indicate if anyone had died because of the bombing. The damage to the building, however, had been extensive. My thoughts raced, and anger rose. I was angry with both sides. I am against abortion as a choice, but I also despise violence in the name of righteousness. It was not what God intended for us. I closed my eyes and prayed silently. God, how can I convince people to come to you instead of acting out in their aggression and self-righteousness? How can I help them see you will change us if we focus on you and spend time with you? What can I do?

I opened my eyes. The world seemed darker. I felt I carried the weight of a lesbian who did not grasp what I tried to teach. I also handled the load of a girl who grew up without a dad and would not see God as a loving father who deeply loved her. *God, I can't carry it all.*

I never asked you to carry it.

I smiled. He was right. Of course, he was right. He was always right. After paying my bill, I walked three blocks before I arrived at St. Luke's hospital. I sat outside and enjoyed the sun while praying for the many people in the hospital as God would bring them to mind. I never knew if my prayers made a difference for anyone, but it did not stop me from doing it.

When I walked back to my car, I had to open both doors to escape the trapped heat. I sat down and looked at the Pop-Up Pastor Facebook page. I saw myself sitting in the front of the hospital with my eyes closed. The caption read: The Pop-Up Pastor praying for people in St. Luke's. I smiled.

"To you be the glory forever and ever, amen."

Chapter

24

Sweat formed on my forehead as I walked briskly past the Neighbors Credit Union Building on Mexico Street in St. Peters, Missouri. Any stranger walking past the blue metal-roofed building may have mistaken it for a church as I had at first. Drive-through window bays presented themselves to me and I knew it was a bank. I saw my destination; a white tent ironically measuring forty feet by seventy feet. It was the summer home of an organization known as the Mosaic Temple Ministry or MTM. Admittedly, the tent's dimensions piqued my interest at first, but it was the type of service they offered here that spoke volumes to my inquiring mind. It was Sunday and my last day in Missouri.

Still reeling from the sting of Charlotte leaving, I did not journal much during my time in Kansas City and even had a bout of depression that lasted a few days. But God, in His incredible grace and mercy, carried me through the valley. After three attempts to call her back after the missed call, I realized she either did not want to speak with me or did not have any time remaining on her phone. Before I walked to the MTM, I logged into her account and purchased another 300 minutes. An email or text would have likely informed her of the gift I provided, but she still did not return my call. I hoped she was safe and happy.

Meeting only in the warmer months between May and September, the MTM group rented space for their enormous tent. It served the community daily with various worship services, Bible studies, and counseling services. Resembling, but not meeting the exact specifications of the tent of meeting in Exodus, the founders of the church, three former pastors from the city, wanted to embrace the Old Testament gathering and the freedom of the early church in the book of Acts.

From their website, I learned of their beliefs: "We want to teach the Christian community that the church is not a four-wall building, nor a tent, but is where the Spirit of God resides in the people who know and trust Him daily in their lives. We have a tent simply for protection from the elements, but this is not the church. The church is in you."

Intrigued by their website and eager to learn more, I made my way to their summer location. No ushers greeted me, and no one handed me a bulletin. I accepted the fact that I was alone in the tent. I stepped into the shade provided under the canvas and found some relief from the summer sun. However, the humidity that built up under the structure was like that of a greenhouse. Even though the tent was white on the outside, it held the heat well.

As I moved toward the center to an area with several seats, the cross breeze blowing through the open and tied back, sides brought some needed relief to my warm body. Walking from a different direction, I saw an older man dressed in blue jeans and an orange oxford-style shirt. He wore an Angel's ball cap, and though he looked familiar, I shook it off. A little beagle with a black spot between its eyes was not with him, but without a doubt, the man walking toward me was Randall. I continued my walk to the front of the seating area, where the familiar man stood waiting.

"Well, hello, young man. Fancy meeting you here."

"Randall."

"Yes, please have a seat." He pointed to the row of chairs behind me. Before me, where one may have expected to see an altar, sat a six-foot folding table adorned with a bright red tablecloth. A brass cross decorated the middle, along with an older, large altar Bible. A chair remained pushed in beneath the table on the side opposite me. It was a simple church if even a church was a good name for it.

"Seems we are both alone these days."

"I was going to ask where Zion was. Is he okay?" I took a seat in the front row.

"Oh, yes, that old fellow. I had to give him away." Sitting down beside me, he slapped his knees. "I travel a lot in my line of work, and caring for a dog was not something I could continue to do."

"So, do you still live in Denver?"

"I make my home in many places. Denver is one of them. But, now let me ask you, how are you doing without your traveling companion?"

"Oh, well, umm, she is visiting friends and family."

"Family? She is not a fan of her uncle, and in fact, I believe he disowned her after his sister died. She never knew her father, and she never had brothers and sisters. Patricia's mom went home to the Lord, so I don't imagine she has a lot of family. Have you checked on her?"

Embarrassed and ashamed, I confessed to him. "She called me a few days back on my way to KC. I tried calling a few times, but she wouldn't answer, and I did buy more minutes for her phone, but I have not successfully checked to see if she was okay. I am trusting God."

"And is that working for you?"

"Trusting God or not checking on her?"

"Well, both actually?"

"It's hard. I grew fond of that young lady. I needed her as much as she needed me, and she went back to what? As you stated,

183

she doesn't have much family." I realized what I had said, "How do you know she doesn't have a lot of family?"

"I watch the news in Denver. I have ways of finding out information, as I told you in the past."

I looked at him. Yes, he had told me before, but I still had suspicions about this man—doubts about his identity.

"She is fine. Keep trusting. You will hear from her again."

"How do you know? And who are you, Randall? You seem to know a lot and know when to show up and disappear. Are you..." Stopping myself for fear how it may sound, I stood up and turned around when a commotion behind me filled my ears. A young lady had come in and sat in the back row of chairs behind us. Eyes closed and head tilted back, she prayed silently.

"I guess you could say I work for a powerful entity."

I sat back down. "Are you CIA? FBI? Homeland? Who do you work for?"

"Oh, I don't work for the government, but who I work for is important."

"Hmm. I don't mean to be rude, but you are an interesting person."

"Let's say my job is to know things and to help. When you need help, I may show up. If I sense you need a friend, you may see me."

"Okay that's creepy if you think about it. But I will bite. Are you going to tell me how you...," I used air quotes, "just know?"

"You seem to be a man who wants a lot of information. Must be your data scientist nature."

Sensing a longing to talk to the lady behind us and knowing Randall would not give me the answers I desired, I excused myself and walked back a few rows. "Can I pray with you?"

"Are you the pastor?"

"No, ma'am, but I am a pastor. I am not sure who the pastor is of this church." I looked around again, still confused why no one was in attendance. The website had indicated they were in attendance nearly twenty-four hours a day. This must have been the 'nearly' time of day.

"Is it that man?"

At least I knew someone else could see him. However, it didn't discredit him from being an angel, but it also did not cease my wonder. "No, that man is Randall. He seems to pop up everywhere. I don't know for sure who he is."

"Well, I need someone to pray for me. I need help badly. I don't know what else to do. I have prayed. I have begged, I have pleaded, and I can't lose him. I can't lose my son."

"What's wrong with your son?"

Instead of answering, she threw her head into her hands and cried. She sat up again, looked around me at Randall, and grabbed my hand. "Will you pray?"

"Certainly, ma'am, what's your name?"

"I am Diane, and my son is Devon. He is eight years old. We were at my sister's house over in Bellevue. She has one of those two-story homes built in the early 1900s. You know when St. Peters was still a young farm town." I nodded in agreement. "Well, Devon and Deshaun, my nephew, played upstairs. Devon sat on the windowsill with an open window. Deshaun insists he didn't push him, but Devon fell, He landed face-first on the ground, and now he is at Mercy in St. Louis, and the doctors don't know if he is going to make it." She started crying again. "Sir, I have gone to church my whole life. I have prayed, and I try hard not to sin. I am not perfect, but I am a good woman. I don't know why God won't listen to me and heal my son. I know He can. I know Paul did it. I know the story of the boy that fell out of the window, so I know God can do it. But He won't. Sir, why won't He heal my son?"

I turned back to see if Randall had any thoughts. He sat in front but not looking at us. "Diane, I am going to pray for you, and I want to explain something to you, okay?"

"Yes, pastor, please pray for my Devon. Pray God will heal

him. I know He can."

"Yes, He can. Let's pray." I grabbed her hands and she squeezed so hard I opened my eyes. She strained and stiffened her body in anxiousness. "God, I pray for your servant Diane. I pray you will heal her body of anxiety. Ease the fear that has gripped her and is eating at her. I pray, Father, that you will pour your spirit upon her at this moment and heal her."

"For Devon, not for me."

I opened my eyes again. Diane did not, and her body was still locked up tight with anxiety. *Now, Father, while I watch, release her, I pray.* As I continued to pray aloud, her shoulders slouched, and her grip lessened. She no longer clenched her teeth. "Father, I pray for her son Devon. I pray, Father, you will heal this young man. Father, Diane has devoted her life to you, but we know, Lord, it is your will for us to all know you and accept you as the God you are. Lord, in our grief and times of sorrow, remind us that we are your children and you love us. Heal our broken hearts and restore us to your glory. We ask this of you in Jesus' name, amen.

"Will he pray for Devon? Where did he go?"

It would have been more of a surprise to see Randall still sitting there than it was to see him gone. "He had to leave."

"But I need someone to pray for Devon."

I squeezed her hand and looked her in the eye. "God will heal your son, or He won't, but trying to win God's favor by telling of what you have done in your life is not going to change His mind. Asking pastors to pray for your son is not going to change God's mind."

"But He owes me. My son didn't do anything wrong either. He's only eight. He's just a little boy."

"No, I am sure he is a wonderful child."

"Eight, he turned eight while he was in the hospital. He's been there five weeks now. He turned eight last week."

Eight. Timmy's age. You can get relief from a toothache or a sore back, but the pain of losing a child does not go away quickly.

"I am not sure if this will help, but if you read the gospels, there were countless people healed."

"Yes, Jesus can heal Devon."

"Yes, He can, but will He? That is another question altogether." I didn't mean to make her cry. I knew the pain. "The Bible recounts the story of a woman walking in a crowd of people. She wanted only to get near him so she could find healing. She touched the edge of his cloak, and He felt the power go out from Him. Those people in that crowd all wanted to be healed. But He only healed one lady. Jesus could have healed every single one of them, but He chose not to. Do you know why?"

"She was close to Him, she prayed?"

"No, not at all. I would venture to guess most of those people prayed more than she did. Most of them probably traveled daily with him, and yet God chose to heal one lady. Do you know why?"

"Devon, I can't lose him. I can't lose him."

Her oblivious attitude about my teaching did not bother me. I continued to speak.

"There is another story where a man was by a pool, and he had had a disability for thirty years. All he wanted was healing. But someone always made it into the pool of healing waters before him. Jesus shows up and heals him on the spot, not by putting him in the water but by speaking it aloud. But not the others that were around the pool. Do you know why?"

"If I knew why, I would do what that man did so Jesus would heal my son."

"I know you would. I know all too well. I would have done anything to keep my son alive, too, but I lost him a year ago when he was eight."

"I can't lose Devon."

"I am not sure if you will or not, but God is sovereign. He can heal whom he wants when He wants and how He wants, and sometimes, He doesn't heal."

"Why, pastor? Why? He can heal everyone. Why won't He?"

"We would have to have the mind of God to know exactly why, but I can tell you this. In the midst of pain and suffering, In your distress over your son, God wants one thing of you right now. He wants you to rely on Him. I mean fully rely on Him."

"I am. That's why I am here. I went to all of the churches, and everyone I met prayed with me. But Devon still hasn't woken up yet. Why?"

"God wants you to ask Him why. Have you asked God why?"

"I think so. I don't know. I mean, I have prayed my whole life, but I never really felt like I was worthy enough to ask Him anything."

"This is difficult to explain and even more difficult if you have lived your life with different teachings. God will either heal your son, or He will not. But it is independent of who you are as a person, what you have done in your life, and what you will do. God doesn't heal based on conditions. Our God is not like that. He heals for reasons beyond our understanding, and He does not heal for reasons beyond our understanding. I know it doesn't make it easier, but it is the truth, regardless of what you have learned. You said your son is in St. Louis. Right?"

"Yes, at Mercy. I came home to get some rest. My husband is with him. My husband told me the same thing you did. We need to trust God and have our own relationships with Him whether Devon lives or not. That made me mad."

"Well, I am sorry, but your husband is correct. Do you know what it means to have a relationship with God?"

"Go to church, pay your tithe, be a good person?"

"Not really. You see, all those things are a result of a relationship with God. Having a relationship with God is like one with your husband, son, or sister. Someone you talk to every day. Someone you cry to when your son is in the hospital. Someone with whom you share all of your concerns."

"Yeah, that's what my husband said, too. I guess I can try.

What do I do? Talk to him like I am talking to you?"

"Yes! That is what you do. I promise you that He will work with you and bring you along. He has ways we don't understand. You will start to grow closer to Him the moment you choose to. He has told us that we will find Him when we seek Him with our whole heart. Do you think you can do that?"

"Will it help Devon?"

I tried hard not to roll my eyes. Every part of my being wanted to shake the woman, but God spoke and told me to give her grace. "The act of you getting closer to God is going to help you. Your prayers for Devon, my prayers for Devon, everyone who is praying for Devon will help Devon. He may not be healed, but it will help. Do what your husband says and try to build that relationship with God. God will do the rest, and He will get you through this difficult time. Psalm 34 says that He is near the brokenhearted, which means He is with you, too."

She sat back in her chair and looked over my shoulder. I sensed someone walking up behind me, and I heard the footsteps to confirm it. Feeling the hand upon my shoulder, I turned to see Randall. He returned.

"Go to the hospital, Jake. Go to St. Louis."

I nodded in agreement. "Okay. I will. Thanks again for being in the right place at the right time."

"I always am."

He continued walking toward the entrance of the tent, where I had stepped in. "Ma'am, can you give me the address for the hospital and what your son's last name is so I can visit and pray with him? I am on my way to St. Louis today."

We exchanged information, including phone numbers, and I said a final prayer for her. I could visibly see she was calmer, and The Holy Spirit witnessed to my spirit that she would be fine. I knew a stronger relationship with God was on the horizon for this woman.

Randall had disappeared again, and in futile attempts to find him, I had walked around the entire perimeter of the tent. The MTM seemed to be a fantastic way of spreading the gospel, but I would have to learn more about them from their website. I liked the concept, but for no one to be present during the day didn't sit well with me.

I reasoned with myself it was poor timing. Or was it? I got to speak to a woman about strengthening her relationship with God. While walking back to my car, I checked on the Facebook page. 195,982 page likes greeted my view. I appreciated what Charlotte had done with this page. I wondered how she was doing and desired to reach out to her, but I allowed the thought to pass. I knew I needed to let her go and pray for her as she came to mind.

Scrolling through the page, a lady in Pocahontas, Illinois, caught my attention. She said she was living with a man she no longer knew. Her husband of sixty-eight years had dementia, and it was too much for her to handle. She asked for prayer, and though she did not ask for a visit, I typed a message to see if she was open to one. But first, I had to stop in St. Louis to visit Devon.

The day's heat caused sweat to develop on my face again, and I could feel my skin burning. None of this would have bothered me if my passenger side tires had not both been flat when I returned to my car. Someone purposely slashed them.

Chapter

25

Ted, the tow truck driver and the garage owner who towed my car, offered to dial the police for me. I thought of filing a report, but I refused. I was a stranger in a strange town, and I considered it a random act of violence, though I was sure the enemy tried to stop me. Ted's business gave me a discount on new tires when I explained why driving across the country brought me to his city. He told me he was a Christian and tried to help out other Christians when he could. I asked if he had heard of the MTM, and he said he had. Imagine my surprise when he told me they did not meet on Sundays. He said they believed the church was not about a building and not about Sunday mornings, so they left the tent open, but no one would be there. I later found this indicated on their website, and I reasoned that God had blinded me to it to meet Diane.

I paid Ted and continued to St. Louis. It was early evening, and I was hungry, so I stopped for dinner before proceeding to the hospital. When I arrived, I was directed to the Pediatric ICU unit on the fourth floor but had to wait for a nurse to admit me. With my delays in St. Peters, Diane arrived before me and was in the room with her son. The nurse informed the family of my arrival, and Devon's dad came to greet me.

The muscular African American man greeted me by name. "You must be Jake. I am Dominic."

"Nice to meet you, sir."

"Can we sit and talk for a moment?"

We walked past a young lady sleeping on a sofa and sat across from one another in two chairs in the corner of the waiting room. "How is Devon doing?"

"Well, that's why I wanted to talk to you." He heaved a deep sigh. "He will not make it."

"Oh, I am so sorry to hear."

"Yeah, me, too. I wish it weren't the case. I don't know how much Diane told you, but he was hurt badly. Somehow, he didn't break his neck, but it did severe damage when he hit his head on the ground. He is in a medically induced coma. The doctors are telling us there is no brain activity at all." Speaking the words caused him to tear up, and he wiped his eyes with his sleeves. "Diane won't accept it. She insists God will heal him."

"And how do you feel about that?"

"Well, I am so glad you came. I believe in miracles, but where do you draw the line between faith and reality?"

I had asked myself the same question many times. "Yeah, I know what you mean. You want to believe, but the doctors are professionals. But I always say faith is my reality, and God is my sovereign Lord. So, my faith is in His hands."

"Man, I like that. That's wisdom."

"God is good, Dominic. All the time. He is good to us."

"Diane told me what you told her, man. Thank you."

"Well, praise God. I only spoke what I heard."

"I tried telling her something similar. That God isn't required to heal him because we have been faithful in our church. God set this world in motion, and we live in it. I mean, it's not beyond His power to heal, but it's not a requirement. Know what I mean?"

"Yes, I do, and all we can do is pray and ask for the miracle. I have seen miracles happen. I have seen tumors shrink, blood sugar levels return to normal, and pneumonia leave a person by praying. I believe in miracles, and I believe God heals. But I also believe God is sovereign, and if He chooses not to heal, we have to learn to lean on Him for our healing."

He started crying again and tried to wipe away the tears. I handed him a tissue, which he accepted with gratitude and used to dry his eyes. Twice he started to talk but was at a loss for words.

"Can we pray now?"

"Sure, let's do it."

"Father, we love you for who you are. We adore the creation you have given us to live in. We respect you for great power and might and how your ways are beyond our ways and your thoughts are greater than our thoughts. Father, we lift to you, young Devon. We lift him up and ask you to heal his broken body. We ask you to restore brain function to him. We ask you to give Dominic and Diane the miracle they have hoped for and the miracle they desire. Father, if it is your will, let this young man recover right now. Hear our prayers. Hear our prayers, Almighty."

"Thank you, Jesus."

"Hear our prayers and answer them as we lift them to you in the name of your Son, our Lord, and Savior, Jesus Christ, Amen."

"Amen. Thank you so much. I can't tell you enough how much I appreciate you stopping by. What church are you with again?"

"Well, that's a long story." I moved up to the edge of the chair and leaned my elbows on my knees. "I am from the Baltimore, Maryland area, and I was a pastor for twelve years in a Methodist Church, but I stepped down earlier this year."

"Oh, sorry. Wait, did you say Baltimore? As in the Orioles of Baltimore?"

"Yes, that's the city."

"Okay, I won't hold that against you. You here on business?"

I wanted to stand up and shout *I am on a mission from God* but controlled myself instead. "I am traveling across the country along Interstate 70. I started in Cove Fort Utah and will finish soon in Baltimore."

His eyes widened, and his brows raised. "Really? For pleasure?"

"It's a long story, as I said, but let's say I am following God's lead. I am trying to visit various cities and meet people along the way. It's a bit of a healing process for me, too. I am also rediscovering my relationship with God."

"Wait a minute. I heard about this." He snapped his fingers twice. "It was on the news the other night. What was it they called you?"

I waited for his response. Not mentioning Facebook, I couldn't imagine that he referred to me. I had not watched the news in weeks, so I was unaware of any other media coverage.

"The Pop-Up Pastor, that's what they called you. Are you that guy?"

I nodded. With amazement at the status that followed me, I could only nod. "Well, I didn't know I was on the news, but yes. I am curious. Was it only local?"

"Yeah, man, they said you were traveling across the country, and you would likely travel through St. Louis in a day or two. That was two days ago. They said you had a large Facebook following."

"Well, the story is even crazier how the Facebook thing came about, but yes, that is me."

"Wow, man, it's so cool to meet you."

"I appreciate it, I really do, but you know, and I know it is not about me. Right?"

"Oh yeah, sorry, man. I know it is about God. But I needed this distraction, you know? I am considering my son is already gone, so meeting someone on the news; well, that's cool."

"Again, I appreciate it, but my focus is you. I don't want the celebrity status I am receiving in the media."

"Man, I appreciate your prayers. I don't mean to intrude, but is there a way I can contact you to keep you posted on how he is doing and what we decide?"

We exchanged numbers. I wanted to tell him about my loss as well. I knew the pain this man endured. He was ready to accept the loss of his son, so he was ahead of the curve. But I also knew the pain and suffering that would be waiting for him if his son did not recover. I encouraged him to continue to help Diane if Devon did pass. He agreed she would need him, and they would all need a lot of prayers with their older daughter.

When I returned to my car, I was grateful to see my new tires still intact. I sat down in the driver's seat and was about to pull away when the gravity of the situation struck me like a bolt of lightning. Memories of my eight-year-old son's lifeless body lying in a hospital bed came back to me. Many people I had met on this journey knew the pain of loss, and I came alongside them during their time of grief. I held it together, and God prevented me from breaking down, but it all changed as I sat there.

"Why God? Why so young? I don't understand, but I don't need to understand. You are God. You are sovereign, and I respect all you do. Though you slay me, still my lips will praise you always."

I shed many tears for both Timmy and Devon. For Jane and Diane and Dominic, too. For myself. Over the eight years I had with him, I rejoiced and prayed Diane and Dominic would do the same.

"Will you heal him?"

I received no reply.

"Please heal him."

This time I sensed God speak to me and say *my grace is sufficient for you and will be for them.*

Within minutes, I was on Interstate 70 once again. As I drove, I prayed for Charlotte and prayed for her protection. A familiar feeling came over me, and I had learned to respect it. I knew she was in trouble, but I also knew it was out of my hands and in the hands of the Almighty.

Chapter

26

The drive to Pocahontas from St. Louis was less than forty-five minutes. Martha sat in a rocker on her front porch when I pulled into her long gravel driveway that wound through the woods. She greeted me with a smile and handed me a glass of fresh sweet tea when I stepped up to her porch. I accepted and took a seat beside her to begin our meeting.

"Thank you for coming by, but you didn't have to. I am sure you are a busy man."

She spoke slowly and with a broken tone. At eighty-seven years old, her body looked frail and showed signs of slowing down. With her short white hair, pointed glasses, and age spots on her arms, she reminded me of my grandmother.

"Oh, I don't mind at all. I enjoy meeting new people. It's why I am traveling the country after all."

"Well, my daughter said I should talk to you. You talked to her. I don't know how all that Internet stuff works. When I was young, you wanted to talk to someone you visited or mailed a letter. I didn't even have a telephone until I got married in 1951."

"It's fine. I do understand what you are saying. Technology

can be difficult."

"So, forgive me, young man, but why are we meeting?"

Her comment caught me off guard. "Well," I paused, "Your daughter wanted me to pray for your husband, who is suffering from dementia?"

"Oh dear me. Yes, I do remember."

She attempted to stand, sat back down, and raised her hand to me. I stood up, grabbed her, and she used it for support while she stood up.

"Thank you, young man. Let's go inside."

Instantly the smell of freshly baked apple pie filled the air as she opened the door. She crossed through the kitchen, past a small two-person dinette, where the steamy pie sat. On the counter on the opposite side was a pitcher with iced tea. Condensation formed on the outside of the glass pitcher and started puddling beneath the container.

She walked slow but steady, reaching for objects as she walked to steady her gait. As she approached a green recliner, I could see the bald head of a man sitting in the chair.

"Dennis, the preacher is here."

"Who? You're a teacher?"

"No, Dennis, the preacher is here. Shirley told us about him."

"Shirley's here?"

"He doesn't hear so well. You will have to speak loud for him to hear you."

"What did you say?"

"Nothing, dear. He wants to pray for you."

"Oh, okay, if you say."

I walked up to the older gentleman, and I kneeled. Martha continued across the room and sat on a similar green recliner. She backed up to it and slowly set herself down.

Silently I prayed for the right words to say. I still was not clear why Martha's daughter had agreed for me to visit. I thought I had been texting with Martha the entire time, but Martha informed me

Shirley had been. Did I miss something? I replayed the conversation in my mind. Dennis, I knew, had dementia, but I was not sure what the desire was beyond that.

"Dennis, this is Jake."

"Are you from the church?"

Speaking loudly, I answered him, "No, sir. I am a friend."

"You were in the war? We won that war, you know."

"Dennis served in Korea. He talks about it all the time."

"No, I was not in the war. But I thank you for your service."

"Martha, is there a specific need you want me to pray for?"

"Yes, I remember now why I asked Shirley to contact you. I hate to ask this but look at him. He doesn't even get up to use the bathroom as he should. We have a nurse that comes in and stays the night with us and another spends most of the day here. He has no life. Half the time, he doesn't even remember who I am."

"You were in the war, you say? Which side were you on?

"Just ignore him. He does this all the time. Dennis, this is Jake. He wants to pray for you."

"I don't want to pray for him."

"No, Dennis, he will." She waved her arm at him, and with a softer voice, said, "Forget it." She looked at me again. "Where was I?"

"You were telling me about the home health care you have."

"Oh yes. So I hate to ask this, but can you pray God will take him home? I know he will be so much better if He does. I hate to see him like this."

I was not sure what to do. In my years as a pastor, no one ever asked me to pray for God to take someone because they were older. I prayed many times for those with cancer to let go and go home and even prayed for a man who had multiple heart attacks but still lived. His quality of life had diminished, and he feared the next heart attack. He had asked me to ask God to take him. I avoided meeting with him and always said I would pray for him.

Feeling ill-prepared for this type of situation, I connected with God silently, seeking His counsel.

Remind them of the fifth commandment. Seek what more may be in store.

"Do you know why Dennis has lived such a long life?"

She shook her head as she stared at her husband.

"Exodus chapter 20 tells us the Ten Commandments, and in verse 12, the fifth commandment is to honor your mother and father so you may live long in the land The LORD your God has given you. So, this has two meanings. Dennis here probably did honor his mother and father, so God gave him a long life in return. This doesn't mean children who don't honor their parents will die young, but it is a reward from God to live long."

"But look at him."

Dennis had fallen asleep with his mouth open. Drool ran down his chin. Seeing a cloth on the opposite arm of the chair, I reached across, grabbed it, and without fear or loss of dignity, wiped his chin and set the cloth back in place.

"I know. You are probably wondering what kind of life this is."

She nodded.

"But the second part of the commandment is for your children. Do you have any other children other than Shirley?"

"Oh yes. I have Jeff and John, too. Dennis Jr. died in a car accident twenty years ago."

"Oh, I am sorry to hear about the accident." Although I promised myself I would not let the circumstances of others influence me, I failed this time. Hearing "a car accident" caused tears to form in my eyes. I gathered myself. "Do any of them live close?"

"Shirley is in Chicago. John is in Terre Haute, and Jeff lives closest in Effingham."

I was unsure how far Effingham was from Pocahontas, but I knew Chicago was close to four hours away, and Terre Haute was at least two hours. "Do any of them ever come to visit? Do they help you out?"

"Jeff comes by two or three times a week. He cuts the grass and tries to talk to Dennis, but they all get so frustrated. I am frustrated."

"Martha, with your permission, I am going to ask God to help you and your three children, and oh, what about grandchildren? Any close?"

"Jeff Jr is close, but I have not seen him for years. Logan and Lisa live in Chicago, too, and John never had kids."

"Okay. With your permission, I am going to ask God to help you see His wisdom. I am going to ask Him to help you understand what He understands. You see, there is a reason Dennis still lives, and God is asking you to seek Him out to find out what the reason is. Can I do that?"

"Yes, please do."

I had to adjust myself to sit on the floor. The pain in my knees became unbearable. I prayed for fifteen minutes, asking for God to pour out wisdom on Martha. I asked for God to have mercy on Dennis, but I could not ask Him to take his life. I never accepted the concept of asking God to take a person's life, no matter the circumstance. In this case, I could not even speak to Dennis and tell him to let go. He didn't know what I said.

My parents passed at a younger age, and I lived in Baltimore when my grandparents aged and passed. Even in my congregation, I had not experienced another human being lose their mind. Dennis was my first.

While praying, my phone vibrated in my back pocket. I tried to ignore it, but someone tried with great anticipation to reach me. I helped Martha back to her feet as Dennis snored. Martha shushed him, and this caused us both to laugh. She walked me to the door and thanked me for the prayers. She offered to give me the pie she had baked, but I told her I would drive to Indiana and could not eat it. It did smell great, however. I left her and Dennis behind and continued praying silently as I walked to my car. When I opened the door, the vibration started again, and I grabbed my phone. I first saw seven missed calls, and the same person making the eighth attempt. It was Charlotte.

"Hello?"

"I need help. I need help badly. I screwed up."

She was frantic and sniveling. I heard the roar of traffic in the background and wondered if she had car trouble.

"Are you okay? Where are you?"

"I need help. Can you come get me?"

"Wait, where are you? Tell me where you are and what's going on."

The phone transferred to the car, and her crying and frantic voice filled the cabin.

"I need help. I am in Denver, at a Salvation Army, but I can't stay here. He's after me. Logan is after me."

"Okay calm down. Who is Logan, and why is he after you?"

"I turned him in. He knows, and now he is after me. I can't stay here. Please come get me."

"Charlotte, I am in Illinois. I am, I don't know. Probably twelve hours at least from you. Can you get to the airport?"

"I am scared. I should never have left. I messed up. I am really, really sorry. I want to come home. Please, can you get me to where you are? Can I come to Indiana?

Indiana. Yes, great idea. "I will buy you a ticket if you can get to the airport. I will fly you into Terre Haute or Indianapolis. I will call you back when I have a ticket ready for you. Please tell me, are you safe? Do I need to call the police?"

"They said I would be safe here. I will see if someone can get me to the airport. I will call the detective. He should be able to help me. He has been helping me."

"Detective Ambers?"

"No, Johnson. Long story. Please, I will pay you back somehow. Please get me out of Denver. I am sorry I left you. I was so stupid. I want to come to be with you if you will still have me."

"Of course, I will have you. I will call you back. Be safe, and I will get back to you shortly."

I had reached the end of the long gravel driveway, and I opened a website. The next fight from Denver to Indianapolis was in twelve hours, and one seat remained, but only in first class. I paid more than I expected, but I would have given my entire savings to fly her back to me. I made the purchase and called her back.

She had calmed down, and I could tell she was inside. I explained the details to her—the when, where, and how. When I hung up, I said a prayer and drove to the interstate. Indianapolis was only three hours away. I couldn't wait to see her.

Flying into Indianapolis for a connecting flight to Kansas City, Missouri, was the only time I had been to the biggest city in Indiana. I had seen the speedway from the sky and someday wanted to visit the racetrack, but it would have to wait longer. Sitting in the airport, knowing flight 824 would not depart for several hours, I called Charlotte back.

Being well-equipped to help the poor, needy, homeless, and many more, the Salvation Army is an incredible organization and one I often support. While lying in a bed in one of their homeless shelters in Denver, Charlotte explained her situation.

While we were at Cheesman Park, a man appeared to have chased her, and when I stood up, he turned away. Being told this man knew Charlotte from high school, I thought little of it. It was Charlotte's ex-boyfriend. Secretly, she had been texting him, and he had promised a new life for her if she returned to Denver. He was now working and wanted to support her and start a life with her. Like a worm wiggling on the end of a hook and appearing to be a tasty meal, she took the bait, and the predator reeled her in. I knew the word was harsh, but I also knew it was perfect for this man. His intentions were not to start a life with her but to tap into the inheritance he expected would come her way.

Although I regretted doubting her commitment, I now believe the experience would serve only to strengthen our relationship. When one does not experience concepts and ideas that come to mind, they may wonder what could have been. She wanted to avoid the infamous 'What If' scenario in her life. She would not doubt or question any longer. She had returned to her old life and found her old life had nothing to offer.

Logan met her in Denver, not her uncle. Driving past a home with Sold printed on top of the realtor yard signage, he explained he could purchase this home, and it was where they would live with his new job. The next day, he convinced her to open a checking account with him and transfer the money from her mom's estate. He had promised to set up his direct deposit to this account and told her to freely use what she needed, as long as she told him what she spent so he could keep a running balance. She bought into it without question, and they opened the joint account. Since they used the same bank that housed the estate account, the transfer would be seamless.

After two days of living in Logan's car, Charlotte questioned him because the house was not ready. Anger and rage showed his true character, and she became scared and discerned a con was in the works. Handing her a $100 bill he had received as a tip from his job, she felt more at ease and discarded her fears.

On the third day, she used the $100 to take a taxi and follow him on his way to work. After the fifth stop, she pieced it all together and realized Logan's new job was being a drug mule and he dropped off the product to dealers around the city. Being a child of a drug addict, this did not sit well with her, and she hired the cab driver to take her across the city to the police precinct of Detective Ambers. She had kept his card in her possession the entire time. She gave the cab driver what she assumed was drug money and told him to keep the change. She then went inside looking for her police officer friend.

Detective Ambers found another detective from the Denver drug task force to take her statement and arranged for her to stay at a woman's shelter where she would be protected. The result of this became her first phone call to me—the one I missed, but she was too embarrassed to answer when I called back. Later that day, the attorney contacted her and let her know the estate was closed and she could access the money in the account. She called the bank and made the transfer to her new account. I had received an email from the attorney as well but ignored it. The money belonged to Charlotte, and I thought nothing of it.

At the woman's shelter, Charlotte gained permission to utilize a laptop. She logged into the bank's website to arrange for a withdrawal, but she was too late. Logan had already emptied the account. She spoke with a social worker who explained she had no means of retrieving the money he took because he was a legal holder of the account.

After five more days, the drug detective visited the woman's shelter to inform Charlotte a confidential informant had let him know Logan was looking for her and her life was in danger. The detective placed her into protective custody at a safe house on the south side of the city. Scared and anxious, she agreed to go, but during a change in shift, when no one watched, she left the home and made her way to a Salvation Army shelter.

Because I was not flying and was only picking up a passenger, I had to stay outside the boarding and arrival area, watching the digital flight board. Flight 824 had departed and would arrive on time. Minutes seemed to take hours as I waited. Many thoughts traversed my mind. Had he harmed her, would she have any luggage? When was the last time she had eaten? I stood up and started pacing. Each time I went a little further than before.

I could have answered anyone's question about arrivals and departures. I hoped someone would ask.

After several hours of a grueling wait, I took a last glance at the board. Her flight had arrived and deplaned. At any moment, Charlotte would be walking through the doors, and I would be waiting.

"Charlotte!" It wasn't her. It was another young lady that looked like her. With each person who walked through the large glass doors, I waited in anticipation of finding my daughter. Finally, I caught a glimpse of long brown hair bobbing up and down in a crowd. Briskly I moved to the door, as far as permitted. Yes, it was her. I backed up to not clog the area as the crowd filtered from the secure site to the public space. She walked past me as I tapped her on the shoulder. She jumped and turned.

She hugged me so tightly and whispered, "Thank you so much for letting me come home. I am so sorry I left."

We both cried and embraced one another. I pulled back. "I missed you so much."

"Dad. Can I call you dad? I really need a dad right now."

"Oh, my dear! You can call me anything you want, but yes, dad works well for me. Welcome back."

She followed my lead as we walked amidst the sea of people. "Are you hungry?"

"Yes, very. They tried to give me peanuts and water on the plane, but I haven't eaten for almost twenty-four hours."

"Let's get something. Chika-Fil-A? McDonald's?"

"I don't have any money. I don't have any way to pay you back either."

"Young lady," I said, placing my hands on her shoulders, "I have adopted you into my family. What I have, is yours. What I can give, I give to you. Where I live, you may live as long as you want. I never expect you to pay me for anything."

She looked down. "Thank you. I don't deserve this."

"Deserve?" I stood beside her again, and we continued walking. "Deserve has nothing to do with it. I am doing all of this because I love you. I have chosen you, and I love you, and nothing is ever going to separate you from my love for you."

"I love you too, Dad." She grabbed me and hugged me as she cried again. "I need to tell you something."

"Ok, I am listening."

"I was being stubborn and didn't want to call you. I told myself there was no way you would ever take me back and figured I had to get on with my life. But I read something in the Bible. Do you know what I read?"

"No idea, but whatever it was, I am glad you read it."

"I read Luke 15. The whole thing."

I recognized it. The story of the prodigal son rested in that chapter.

"You know, Jake, I mean Dad, I think I finally understand what it means when you refer to God as a father. I was lost. I mistreated you. But you still let me come home like the kid in that story. His dad, I mean father, let him come home, too."

I was speechless. I tried to fight back the tears that formed.

"So, where's my fattened calf, bud?"

I burst with laughter. "At McDonald's. Let's go."

I never felt like I floated out of my body, but I did when I heard those words. I seemed to have drifted off the ground. All I ever wanted for this girl was the best I could provide, and for her to say she now saw God as a good father was one of the most incredible things I have ever heard in my life. My entire journey until that point proved to be eventful and full of good and bad days. I had seen a lot of pain and had pain inflicted on me, too. I promised God forty days, and I still had a long way to go, but I could have easily ended the trip at that moment. I wanted to heal. I found it. She could not replace Jane and Timmy but hearing her say she understood God better because of my actions meant the world to me. I felt a sense of tremendous healing.

Charlotte and I did our traditional camping that evening at a state park in Indiana. We enjoyed a crackling fire and comfortable chairs. She had been reading the Bible more while staying at the woman's shelter and the Salvation Army. A list of questions lay on her lap, and I answered to the best of my ability.

Abraham, Isaac, and Jacob questions topped the list. How old was each when they died? Why did Abraham leave his home in the first place? Who was his dad? Why didn't Laban let Jacob marry Rachel, and my favorite was, "Wait, Isaac's servant put a ring in Rebecca's nose?"

From there, she continued asking questions about the epistles. I asked her why she skipped the Gospels. Much of it she had learned from her mother and from paying attention in Sunday school.

Big words often tripped her up, too.

"What is a prince a..." She reread it, underlining it with her finger, "A prince a palp..."

"A principality?"

"Yeah, is that like a big city or something?"

I chuckled at the irony. I had once thought the same thing years ago. "No, a principality is a high-ranking demon. Right under Satan in rank. It is believed that principalities rule certain regions. Now some principalities are good angels, too."

"So, what is the difference between a demon and an angel?"

"Great question. The only difference is in who the spirit serves. Demons serve Satan, and angels serve God."

"Well, I know atheists who don't serve God, but I still call them human."

"Yes, but you don't call them Christians, do you?"

"Awe, good point. So are there demons with us right now?"

I was amazed by her line of questioning.

"Are they with us right now? Well, I pray daily for God to equip me with His armor."

"Hey, that's where that word came from." She looked at the notes on her lap. "From Ephesians chapter 6."

"Yes, that is what I am referring to. There are many beliefs about what this armor is, what it does and how it protects us."

"What do you believe?"

A baseball player would call this the dream pitch. She put the ball carefully over the middle of the plate, and all I had to do was swing, and a home run would follow. I prayed quickly, asking for the right words.

"I believe we are spiritual beings. God created us as spiritual beings because He created us in His image. In His likeness."

"Genesis 3?"

"Very good. It's actually in chapter 1, but I am impressed you got close."

She smiled, tilted her head to the left, and greeted it with her left shoulder.

"Because we are spiritual beings, we are subject to spiritual laws, too. Okay, let me back up for a second."

I grabbed a Pepsi can that sat in the cup holder of my chair. It was half full. I held it out and dropped it, knowing gravity would take it to the ground. It sat up and did not spill.

"Gravity is a physical law, and the law of gravity binds all physical objects. Correct?"

She nodded in agreement.

"But spiritual beings are not physical, so they are not bound by gravity."

"So that's why angels can fly?"

"Hmm, I never thought of it that way before, but yes, that is why angels can fly. They are spiritual."

"Well, if God created us as spiritual beings, why can't we fly?"

"You see, we are also physical. We have a body, a soul, and a spirit." The body is physical, the spirit is spiritual, and the soul is the essence of who we are. It isn't elementary. Let's stick to the spiritual part for right now."

"Okay, I think I follow."

"Okay, so our physical bodies are affected by physical laws, like gravity. Our spiritual bodies are affected by spiritual laws, like faith, grace, and love."

She cocked her head, raised an eyebrow, and looked at me quizzically.

"Bear with me. When Satan fell from heaven because he wanted to be like God, the Bible tells us he took one-third of the angels with him."

"Wait, so there are two times as many angels as demons."

"You are smart! These angels and demons are spiritual beings and can affect us spiritually. So, let's say you are angry a lot. That can be from something physical affecting your body, but it can also be from a demon which has found a way to afflict you and cause you to have anger issues legally."

"Legally afflict me?"

"Yes, let me give you a physical example. You are driving down the road, and you see a speed limit sign that says SPEED LIMIT 55, and you purposely drive seventy. If the police officer

211

observes you doing this, she can give you a ticket."

"Of course, I deserved it."

"Yes. So let's say you have been engaging in a sinful act for most of your life. Let's say you continually tell lies. That breaks one of God's laws, and as a result, the demons have something against you. They plead with God that they are permitted to afflict you. The police officer can plead with the judge you deserve to pay a fine, these demons say to the judge, she is a liar, and I should be permitted to afflict her. The human judge allows you to be charged, and you must pay a two hundred dollar fine. The God of heaven says, 'I will allow you to afflict Charlotte because she continually lies.' So, this demon causes you to have anger issues."

"So, if I lie, I will be angry?"

As I finished my sentence, I realized it may not have been a good idea to use anger as the affliction. I knew I had to redirect, so I again went to God, asking for advice on how to proceed.

"No, that's not exactly what I am saying. I guess I meant if you do something physically against the law, you can be physically charged, but you may also end up with something bad. For example, if you continually run into a brick wall headfirst, that's not illegal, but you may have a sore head as a result. You could even die. The results of physical actions are physical. The results of spiritual actions are spiritual."

I sat back for a moment and thought deep on the subject. I knew I could find a better way of explaining. Suddenly, I remembered something from my past. It would be an excellent way to see if she also had this experience in her past.

"When I was thirteen, I played with a Ouija board."

"Those things are cool but also a little creepy. I played with one, too." I received my answer.

"Okay, did you know even though a toy company created a physical device when your spiritual body asks spirits to speak to you, you are opening a portal? A portal to the demonic. You invite the demonic into your spiritual life, which can cause anger, depression, addiction, and many other things much more than sinful acts like lying. I want to be clear."

"So, sin can cause me harm, and inviting spirits to guide me can cause me harm?"

"Yes, and if we don't renounce that sin, the effect can last a lifetime. When I played with one, I let demons in my life. I had to renounce the action, and when I did, I changed. The affliction in my life ended."

"What do you mean renounce?"

"When you renounce something, you break all ties with it. You say I no longer want any part of what I had. If someone renounces their United States citizenship to live in Canada, for example, they break all ties with our country. Make sense?"

"Yeah, I think I get it. So, if I do demon things, I should renounce it?"

"Yes, but let's deal with the sins first. We all sin. Romans 3:23 says that we all sin and fall short of God's glory. That means we all will sin in our lives. No one can save themselves from it. But Jesus, He never sinned. So, when He died on the cross, He paid my penalty for sin."

"Yes, the cross is our cure. He cured us of our ailments, and now sin doesn't affect us, right?"

Cure? I had never considered the cross a cure. But it made so much sense. I wondered where she had heard this before because it was profound. *The cross is a cure.* I tucked that one away for later use.

"Fascinating concept calling it a cure. I like that. But yes, we are not affected by the penalty of sin, but we can still be affected by sin. I will try to get to the point for you. Our physical and spiritual bodies are tied together so wholly with our souls and only God can separate them. He understands where this separation can occur. As far as we are concerned, like Jesus is God and God is a Spirit, we are a spirit, body, and soul. We cannot separate one from the other. So, what we do with our physical bodies can affect our spirit, and what we allow into our hearts can affect our bodies, too. Does that make sense?

"Wait, did you say Jesus is God?"

"Yes, I did. God became a man in the form of Jesus."

"But I thought Jesus was born of the Virgin Mary and conceived by The Holy Spirit."

I recognized the Apostle's Creed. "Yes, conceived by God. God is His father."

"Right, so how can He be God? Oh, wait. I get it. Because God is His father, is He God? Maybe I don't get it."

"Let me put it to you this way. I am one person. Right?

"Yes"

"Ok, but I am a husband. I am a son, and I am a father."

"Oh, I get it. You are one person, but you are all three. So God can be God the Father, God the Son, and God the Holy Spirit."

"I don't think I could have said it better."

"Yes, it does. But what about..."

I watched as her eyes shifted to the ground beside me. They continued to widen, and she pointed. No words, she simply pointed. I thought at first a stranger visited us, but as I looked over the side of my chair, I saw a gray and black creature walk up beside me. The raccoon sat back on its haunches, reached out with its sticky black paws, and put one on each side of the Pepsi can. I glanced at Charlotte, who glanced at me. We both watched in wonder as the raccoon lifted the can, opened its mouth, and drank the beverage I had moments earlier used as an illustration of gravity.

He set the can back down gracefully as quickly as he began, leaned forward on his front legs, and turned back. As he disappeared into the darkness, Charlotte stood up. "Of all the times for me to not be videoing something. My fans would have loved that."

"Did you see that? I mean, did you see that?"

"Yes, but I don't believe it," she replied. "And I highly doubt anyone will."

I believed it, and I knew others would. While in college, I had camped at Pokagon State Park, across the border from Toledo, Ohio, and I witnessed raccoons break into coolers, unzip tents, and do many more tricks, but I had never seen one drink from a can.

Within minutes of the incident, we heard feet scurrying as more raccoons came down from the trees. A few brave creatures wandered near us like the Pepsi drinker. I took it as a sign to clean up for the night and move closer to the fire. Talks of raccoons and demons had brought us closer together that night, and I thanked God for bringing her back to me. We continued our conversation for a few hours before turning in for the night. The next stop was Ohio, where I planned to visit a few friends. The journey neared the end, but I trusted God to put more people in my life for His glory. I praised and prayed before falling asleep.

Chapter

29

A cool brisk morning greeted us as we stepped out of the tent. Dewdrops fell from the tent onto my head and made me shudder. Charlotte poked at the fire, attempting to extinguish it further, and I checked for signs of break-ins. The raccoons must have moved onto a new campsite when they did not find anything valuable with us.

After Charlotte had gone back to Denver, I formed a habit of praising God each morning for the blessings in my life. With her back in my care, the temptation to cease this practice arose in my spirit, but I quickly extinguished the idea and went back to the tent to pray. I did so aloud so Charlotte could hear.

When I finished, she stepped in and asked if I did that every day. I told her I did, and it was a good practice that she should consider. "It starts my day off on the right foot."

As human beings, so much in this life can distract us, but if we focus on God in the mornings, He will direct our days. She said she wanted to know God better, and she would try it. She stepped away but returned with a question.

"Do you think," she said, as she searched for the right words,

"That we could maybe visit a hospital? But not any hospital. Can we go to a children's hospital?"

"Sure, are you okay?"

"Yes, I am fine. But I have this. I don't know what you call it. A nudging? I keep thinking in my mind I would like to visit sick children. Is that from God?

"That is 100% from God."

"But, how do you know? I mean, I didn't hear a voice."

"Okay, let me ask you this way. Would you have ever considered visiting a child in a hospital before you started getting closer to God?"

She raised the left side of her lower lip and turned her eyebrows in like she always did when she was deep in thought. "Hmm, I don't think it is something I would have done. I mean, I am not an uncaring person, but I would never have thought of it."

"No, it's not about being caring or uncaring, but the fact you are now thinking of it is because you are open to the Holy Spirit to come and work His work in your life."

"Hmm, well, that's cool because I feel good. Know what I mean?"

"I know exactly what you mean. That's the Spirit of God changing you. You are renewing your mind. So, have you considered what age or what do you want to do?"

"What do you mean?"

"When we get to the hospital. What age group? Do you want to read a book, do you want to pray with them, do you want to hear their stories?"

"Oh, I can't pray with them. I am not a pastor. That's your job." She turned and walked out of the tent. I followed her. She quickly moved away from me, and I could tell I had made her a little nervous. I didn't say she had to pray. I wondered if she had considered praying.

"You don't have to pray. You can visit or read a book or whatever God wants."

217

"What does He want?"

"Why don't you ask Him?"

She walked over to the tall tree from where many raccoons had descended upon us last evening. She stood at the base, looked up, and said, "God? What do you want me to do?"

Inside, I laughed at the somewhat unorthodox approach, but I also prayed God would speak to her. I waited for her reply.

"Well, I didn't hear anything."

"You will. Trust me. You will."

We cleaned up our campsite. When the sun dried the evening dew, we broke down the tent and packed it up. We didn't talk much while we drove toward the interstate. God spoke and informed me I should be ready for her questions.

As we crossed into Ohio, I said, "Welcome to the heart of it all."

"State bird is the cardinal. Columbus is the capital, but it used to be Coshocton. Chartered in 1803, the three major cities start with C, and the Broncos beat the Browns twice in the AFC championship game in the eighties and again in 1990."

"Impressive. It seems your knowledge goes beyond the states bordering your home."

"Not really. I looked it all up. I have Maryland, too. I knew you were born here and lived in Maryland, and I wanted to know all about where you were from and where you live now. I want to know all I can about the dad I never knew. Oh, and yes, I love that the Broncos owned the Browns."

I wasn't sure whether to be excited or sad. I was both at the same time. Sorry that she never knew her real dad, but excited that she called me dad more often now. I was thankful to God for the beautiful blessing to be for her what she had missed. However, I felt a fleeting moment of anxiety at the thought of her living in Maryland with me. It would be a significant change for both of us.

I ignored her Broncos owning the Browns comment.

I planned to spend a week in Ohio, spread between Columbus,

Zanesville, and Bellaire. A day visiting Wheeling, West Virginia, followed by one or two days in Pennsylvania and driving to Baltimore for the remaining one or two days. Formulating the plans in my mind caused me to face a unique realization. I would have to drive by the crash site. I didn't feel ready for it. Not even close. I let it go. I knew in my heart that God had brought me that far. He would get me through the rest.

Charlotte added another post to Facebook. I assumed she told people we were in Ohio.

"So, about that Broncos thing," I mentioned.

"Oh, you liked my comment?"

"No, I hated it. That's something we never discuss after today. We never talk about 'The Drive.'" I started laughing.

"Well, Dad, you have been on a long drive here lately." We laughed together.

The drive I was referring to was the name of the famous five minute and two second offensive football drive that John Elway orchestrated in the 1986 AFC Championship game against the Cleveland Browns. The Denver Broncos tied the game with seconds left and eventually won in overtime and claimed their spot in the Super Bowl that year. I was young, but old enough to be completely heart-broken when the Browns missed their best opportunity to go to the NFL championship game.

I looked at her, and for the first time since I first met her in the church several weeks earlier, I saw her as more than a broken little girl. I saw her as my daughter. The feeling was incredible. *Thank you, God.* I waited and heard in reply: *You both need me.* That hit me hard, but I recognized the truth. I needed God and always would. I knew Charlotte needed Him now, and she found Him. He said though, "You both need me."

We both need you? Am I missing your point? I didn't get an answer. That always told me I would have to pray about it more. I made a mental note.

A storm developed, and raindrops hit the windshield.

Together, we heard a loud screech, and we looked at one another. She grabbed her phone and reported what the noise was "Tornado Warning: A tornado has been spotted within a four-mile radius of your location. Please seek shelter immediately."

Her eyes gave her away, and her blushing cheeks followed. She was nervous. It was a perfect time to let her know I would protect her.

We approached a rest area and I pulled in. When I put the car in park, the rain poured out like someone had opened the Hoover Dam.

We ran for the building as the rain pelted against us with a mighty force. When we reached the building, a small crowd had already assembled inside while waiting for the storm to let up. Another man and his young daughter stood near the opposite entrance. They both experienced the punishing rain as well.

"I guess God wanted us to stop here," Charlotte said.

"It's a storm, a naturally occurring event."

The voice came from a middle-aged man standing near the entrance. Miffed not by what the stranger had said but by how he said it, I gave him a dirty look to let him know my displeasure.

"What? You believe your sky daddy made you stop?"

"Sir, I have no beef with you. I am sorry you are having a bad day."

"Bad day? I am having a great day. It's you Christians who make it bad."

The look on Charlotte's face indicated she wanted to dispense with his. I knew she would have had some choice words for the man, so I gradually stepped between her and the anti-Christian man. I gathered my thoughts and remained calm.

"That's rather offensive, my friend. But it's okay" My love waned. Bitterness settled in, and I caught myself before I spoke my mind. "Sir, I am going to go over here," I pointed to a corner as far from him as possible, "And wait out the storm. I pray your day gets better for you."

"Pray all you want. No one is listening."

I turned back. I took a deep breath. "Okay I can see you don't believe in God. But, can we agree to disagree? You came at my daughter the moment she walked in. We would never have talked at all had you not spoken to us first. I will pray you someday come to know God."

"God doesn't exist." He started shaking side to side and snidely spoke, "Mr. Pop-up Pastor." He must have read my facial expression. "Yeah, I saw you pull in with your fancy red car. You think you are a celebrity because your mystical fairy-tale being in heaven is guiding..." He didn't finish his sentence because of the flash and eardrum-breaking sound that came with it.

"Oh God!" he yelled.

I didn't say a word. I smiled, put my arm around Charlotte, and guided her to the corner of the rest area. Someone clapped, but the second crash of thunder deafened their attempt to cheer me on.

"I would have given him a piece of my mind."

"I thought so. That's why I stepped in. Jesus told us to love our enemies."

"But he is worse than an enemy. He doesn't even believe in God."

"Oh, but he sure called on him when the thunder clapped, didn't he?"

"So, that was why you smiled. Nice!"

"I don't believe in atheism, and I don't believe anyone truly is an atheist. I don't believe God created us with the ability to not believe in Him. If you think about it, the concept of gods has been around for all time. Long before, people thought critically like we do today. God let us know He is the one true God. We were created to believe in a creator. It's our choice if we believe that The LORD is God or not. But all of us believe in a creator. To say you are an atheist is a fancy way of saying, I choose to deny what I know is true. When the time comes, we all call on God."

"Wow that was profound."

"Thanks." It was another one of those thoughts that came from God. I wondered how I could have been a pastor for twelve years and not have had this kind of wisdom. God provided.

"Pretty cool that he knew you from Facebook, though. Recognized the car."

"Yeah, pretty cool." When an atheist calls you out because he recognizes you from social media, it's not because he likes what you are doing. He saw me as a celebrity, which I never desired, but it did show his jealousy. I didn't know, but I would have guessed he tried to have a Facebook following but failed. That or he led a miserable life. Either way, he was jealous.

The storm started letting up. The atheist looked back at me. I smiled, and he departed. I said a prayer for him, asking he would be safe on the road. Charlotte looked at the map of Ohio on the wall and moved her finger along Interstate 70.

"That's a long way."

"Colorado is longer."

"Yeah, I know, but I am eager to get to Maryland."

I was, too.

Ohio's state flower, the red carnation, was designated in 1904 to honor the memory of William McKinley. Assassinated in Buffalo, New York, in 1901, he was the twenty-fifth president of the United States and a native of Niles, Ohio, on the state's east side. However, many natives of Ohio would argue and do annually agree the orange barrel should be the state flower. These pliant polymer objects seemingly grow from the roads every spring and last until late autumn.

The construction in Columbus caused us substantial delays. I had promised Charlotte we would stop at Nationwide Children's hospital to visit with a child. She had decided she wanted to read a children's book to a group of "ten or under" as she referred to them. From Rome-Hilliard Road, outside of Interstate 270, until we neared our exit of Main Street in Bexley, we paced at an average of ten miles per hour. I feared we might run out of gas before we exited.

When I grew up in Whitehall, Interstate 70 and Interstate 71, which connects Cleveland and Cincinnati to Columbus, had been two-lane highways with simple ramps. Interstate 70 lanes were on the right, and Interstate 71 routes were on the left. I believed some engineers thought it wise to make the interchange much more complicated while taking in the scenery during our snailish tour through downtown. I-70 now went in two directions, and I-71 was going above I-70, and an enormous pile of dirt lay in between them. I shook my head as we passed it. I tried to imagine the headache commuters faced each day. It boggled my mind.

Free from the numbing pain of slow traffic, we arrived at the hospital. A nurse escorted us to a solarium, where we saw three young children. One used a wheelchair, her left leg raised and an IV connected to her right arm. Another had a feeding tube in his nose but sat on a sofa. The third sat on the floor pushing a firetruck along the flat blue carpet. Seeing no hair, I could not determine the patient's gender. Charlotte engaged this child first.

"What's your name?"

"Megan," the shy girl replied. "I have leukemia. What's wrong with you?"

"I am here to read you a book. Would you like that?" Megan nodded with a smile.

"How about you? What's your name?"

In a nasal voice, the young boy on the sofa answered her, "I am David. My stomach doesn't work right, but my mom says they are going to fix me, and I can go home soon."

"Ohhhhh, I pray you get to go home soon, David. Poor thing."

"And how about you?" She walked over and knelt beside the girl's wheelchair. "What's your name?"

The girl turned her head. Charlotte glanced at me, then at Megan, who ignored her as she continued to push the truck along the floor.

"She's Wendy. But she can't talk."

"She can talk, David. She chooses not to." The voice came from behind us. I turned to see who had spoken.

"I am Dr. Rogers. I am a pediatric oncologist here at the hospital. Thank you so much for coming in. The children love when people come to share stories. Are you from a local church?"

Charlotte sat on the couch next to David and opened the book. I shook the doctor's hand. "I am Jake Anderson, and this is Charlotte. We are not from a local church. We are from..." I paused and looked at Charlotte. I was not sure how I should say it. She interpreted my dilemma well.

"We are from Baltimore. But we are here visiting friends."

It was not a lie. After the hospital visit, the plan was to visit a friend of mine.

"Well, I am glad you came to call on us. I hope you enjoy your stay, and I apologize for the traffic. I hope it didn't cause too much of a delay."

"It was challenging, but we forgot all about it when we got here. Right, Dad?"

"Oh, this is your daughter. I am sorry, I missed that."

"My fault I should have introduced her. Yes, this is my daughter."

I was ashamed of my lack of formality.

I saw an empty recliner across the room, and I knew it called me. It also had a television in front of it as a bonus. I wanted to give Charlotte her space, but I was also interested in hearing how she handled the children, so I left the television off.

Wholly natural and nurturing, she grabbed their attention without fail. Even Wendy was captivated by the story. Charlotte had chosen a book that subtly told the story of Jesus without ever mentioning his name. She would occasionally ask the children if they understood, and they nodded. Her engaging demeanor reminded me of Jane reading to Timmy. When she finished the story, she explained to them what she had read. She asked if they knew who Jesus was.

"I do," said Wendy. It was the first time she spoke.

"Good. So, you know you will go to heaven then?"

"Yes, he died for me. If I don't survive, I will see him soon. But I am a fighter, and Mommy and Daddy pray for me every day.

They said Jesus loves me, and that's all that matters right now."

"Awe. You sweet thing, let's pray together. Can we?"

They all nodded. As I closed my eyes, I could hear Charlotte praying. "God, please heal these children. Please make them strong and protect them. Send Jesus to tell them about him and help them know it's him. God, if you would send them an angel, too, I would be thrilled. Also please help the man from the rest area. In Jesus' name, Amen."

She spoke a beautiful prayer, but I did notice she did not refer to God as Father. I didn't think much of it because not everyone prays the same way, but being someone who starts his prayers with "Heavenly Father," it caught my attention.

As she said goodbye to the children and returned to where I sat, I stood up and told her how proud I was of her. "You've come a long way, kid."

"Thanks, Dad. I owe it all to you and God. You both have had a tremendous impact on my life."

"And you have on mine, too. More than you know."

We left the hospital, and after stopping for food and gas, we were on our way to my friend's house. We stayed with him two days, talking about the old days and catching up on our lives to that point. He had a seventeen-year-old daughter who hit it off well with Charlotte.

Before leaving, I showed Charlotte where I grew up and took her to my favorite ice cream store. We visited many shops at the various locations outside of Columbus, and she talked me into a new dress I purchased. She said she wanted to wear it on day forty when we arrived at the Park and Ride. After updating her now 350 thousand-follower Facebook page, we headed east. The large number blew my mind.

Chapter

31

Being the state I grew up in, I am fond of Ohio. Even more, I am fond of the friendships I made during my childhood through my college years. But John Thornhill was a man I met many years ago at his soup kitchen in North Carolina. Sean and I donated to his endeavor, and he and I hit it off well. We have remained in close contact since. I recently heard he became a pastor in the Methodist Church after he moved to Ohio, and I was intrigued to find out the backstory. He asked me to come by for a visit sometime, but I never had the opportunity. Having called him before leaving Zanesville, we made arrangements to meet at the church he served...the First United Methodist Church of Bellaire.

Bellaire, I could tell right away, was a town that had seen better days. Many streets had poles where street signs had once directed visitors, but the horizontal plates were missing. Businesses had abandoned the city, and the roads remained in disrepair. Ironic as it may seem, as I moved closer to the church, the atmosphere changed. I sensed greater joy, and I knew God's Spirit had fallen on this part of town. Not that God was not interested in the rest of Bellaire, as I knew He was. Something about the work God performed from this church impacted the spiritual well-being of all who came near. I heard the word *epicenter* as I approached.

The large orange brick building built in the late 1800s was a beautiful sight to behold as we pulled into the south parking lot. Above the door, a maroon awning with "United Methodist Church" printed on it indicated we had arrived in the correct place. An unlocked door showed it was permissible to enter, so we did. After traversing the few steps, I proceeded through the double doors and turned to the left. A gorgeous seating area welcomed visitors and members alike. The captivating view as I turned to the right took my breath away. The beautiful architecture in the auditorium-style sanctuary caught my attention immediately. The pews and style of the windows indicated the building's age, but it was clear much time and effort had gone into keeping it maintained. The ceiling seemed to go on forever. Poles held up arches that were like the catacombs of the United States capitol building. A wonderful smell of fresh air from the janitor's hard work was also apparent. Sitting in the front pew was my friend John. Charlotte took a seat on one couch in the seating area, and I walked down the center aisle toward the altar area. John stood and hugged me.

"So, you are the pop-up pastor everyone is talking about?"

I laughed and looked back at Charlotte. She heard the comment, stood up, and took a bow before sitting down.

"That is Charlotte and the brainchild of the Facebook group. I will catch you up on her story, too, but first, let's talk about you. How did you become a pastor here?"

"Great! But I have to tell you the concept of 'pop-up pastor,' came from a parishioner here."

"Are you kidding me?"

"No, seriously. He has been keeping me posted on you and your journey. He is the one who commented early on and referred to you as the pop-up pastor."

"Wow, is there any way I can meet him?

"Well, actually, I was going to ask you if you can join us this evening. He is part of a community men's group that meets at the gazebo across the street. We'll meet at seven o'clock. Can you join us?"

I paused while I thought about our schedule. "I think we probably can."

"Great! I hope you can. He would love to meet you. Want to sit here or go to my office?

I sat down on the front pew. "Let's talk."

"Sure thing." He sat down. "Where do I begin? Well, as you know, I moved here about four years ago. I walked around town praying, and God directed me to this church. They had a meal giveaway to the public, and I was interested in helping because of my time with the soup kitchen my wife and I created. So, I visited the church, and it was the start of a big change."

"I am sure you didn't become pastor that night, though, correct? I mean, I know how the UMC works. In fact, I am shocked you are even here with your Baptist background. This is going to be a great story."

"Yeah, sure. The UMC has its standards, and props to them for how they work. But a need existed here, and God made it happen. So basically, I got to be close with the pastor who served here. He felt a calling to do more in the community, and I kept hearing God say pastor for me. One night, we sat in the gazebo and realized we both thought I should see about being the pastor here."

"Well, God sure had to be involved."

"Oh yes, there is no way this would have happened without him. All the pieces fell into place, and I went through interviews and shared my credentials. Having an M.Div. helped a lot, too. But in the end, I was installed as pastor, and he was released to do more work in the community."

"That's fantastic. So, are you licensed or ordained?"

"No, I am licensed. I don't have any desire to be ordained. I want part-time and want to have freedom over where I serve."

Being from the United Methodist Church, I understood what he meant. As a Methodist ordained pastor, you may be asked to go anywhere within your conference. Conferences are geographical regions, so had I been ordained in Maryland, I could have been in Deep Creek or Bethesda and wouldn't have a great deal of say in it. That was also the reason I stayed part-time. Sean and I had talked about having remote offices, but in the end, we always decided our Baltimore headquarters was the best for the business, so I could not allow the church to have the decision if I moved or stayed.

"There is a need for part-time pastors in all denominations these days, so I am sure they appreciated you taking this position."

"Yes, it was a win-win situation. God continued to move in this church, too, and He is building many people up to do and be what He intended them to be and do. This brings me to the next topic."

"Okay, I am listening."

"Well, the pastor who stepped down came back here as a member."

"Shut up!"

"No, I am not joking. He's our tech guy here."

For a pastor to leave a church and become a church member at the church he once served was unheard of in the United Methodist Church. But if he had been a part-time pastor as well and licensed, it would be possible. I had never heard of this happening.

"That's definitely God."

"Yes, it is. Well, there is more. He and I started a radio station."

"Wait, a radio station? Like with the tower and all? Where did you get the money?"

"No, an Internet radio station. But now that you mention it, every Monday at the radio station up on the hill above Bellaire, a secular station, country, pop, has a segment I call "The 60-Second Uplift." I am on the radio around 7:30 a.m. each Monday, talking about God and offering encouragement."

"Wow, over the air? That's awesome. I am shocked they let you."

"Yeah, I was pleased. Again, glory to God for making it happen."

"Okay, you said Internet radio. What is that?"

"Yes, Uplifting and Empowering Fulcrum Radio. It's on the Live365 app. You can search for Fulcrum Radio and hear uplifting Christian music and empowering Christian talk. It's 24/7, too."

"Man, John, that is fantastic. It sounds like you have been busy."

Before either of us could speak again, we heard a door open in the back. A young man walked in and up to Charlotte. I could not distinguish what he said to her, but her expression told me it was good.

"Really? That's awesome." She jumped up and walked to the edge of the pews. "Dad, this is Brad McLellan. Brad is the guy that labeled you the pop-up pastor. Can you believe this? He is the one that came up with the idea, and here he is. Did you know he was coming?"

"Dad?" John looked me at with shock.

"Yeah, I can explain. Long story." I stood up and went to meet the man who helped turn me into a celebrity.

"So, you are Jake Anderson?"

"Yes, sir. It's nice to meet you, Brad."

"Likewise. I have been following you since I caught a glimpse of you. I had no idea the term pop-up pastor would go viral."

"Or the page Charlotte created. I am amazed, but in it all, I see how God has worked it out for me to meet new people."

"Amen. God is good for sure. I have been praying Psalm 91 over you both since I saw the page."

"Oh man, thank you. I have sure felt His protection on this journey. I appreciate your prayers."

"Sure. I just met Charlotte. She is prettier than I anticipated."

Charlotte blushed. "Well, thank you, sir." She turned and walked back to the seating area.

I whispered so she couldn't hear us, "You should have seen her with purple hair."

We all laughed. The conversation continued for approximately thirty minutes. My stomach screamed, and my brain interpreted it as hunger, so I thanked both John and Brad for allowing us to visit. Day forty quickly approached, and I wanted to see a few more cities before driving into the Park and Ride at Security Boulevard, so we excused ourselves. After eating "Gullah Dogs" at a local restaurant on Belmont, we traveled north on Route 7. Since I had met Brad, I excused us from their men's group meeting.

We crossed the Ohio River and made our way to Wheeling, West Virginia. We spent the night in the famous McClure House Hotel. Presidents and actors alike have stayed in this renowned hotel. The lobby is home to a fantastic spiral staircase leading to the rooms. They have an elevator, but most guests take the stairs for the experience.

In the evening, we sat along the Ohio River and caught a glimpse of the famous Suspension Bridge that allowed traffic from Wheeling Island to travel to Wheeling City. The bridge resembles the Brooklyn Bridge but is much smaller.

"Did you know this was the first major bridge to span the Ohio River, and it tied national road on the east to the west? It was the longest suspension bridge of its kind for a while, and it was a huge deal for the Civil War."

"I did not know. That's awesome. So, it is quite historic."

"Yes, it is. If you search Wikipedia, you will find a lot about it. It's fascinating."

Like Bellaire, Wheeling had once been a significant city,

complete with streetcars. Over time, people gravitated to larger cities like Pittsburgh or Columbus, and industry and population declined considerably in the Ohio Valley area. I was glad to take a break and enjoy the warm July evening along the river. The Colorado, Missouri, and Mississippi Rivers were all impressive to see, but mighty Ohio was always my favorite. I never brought Timmy to see it. We were going to stop in Wheeling on our way to Yellowstone. He so desperately wanted to see a barge so he could entice them to honk their air horn.

Reliving the thought of the moment did not bring the sadness it had early in my journey. I realized healing was happening for me, and I had God to thank for it. I didn't want to make this journey and wanted to return home twice. But now, over 1,800 miles from where I began, I was sensing not only accomplishment but incredible healing. My faith took me to Utah, and God brought me where I sat that evening, watching the water flow. My mind wandered to the verse where God says, "Blessed is the one who puts his trust in The LORD. He is like a tree planted by the water, Jeremiah 17:4. I felt like a tree planted by the water.

A local business sponsored the community investment program to build the quaint brown wooden chairs along the riverbank where we sat. I don't know whether they intended the chairs to be as relaxing as we found them, but they sure were comfortable. My eyes closed, and my mind slipped into a state of unconsciousness. I would have been asleep within minutes had I not felt a vibration in my pocket. Typically, I would ignore text messages, but The LORD spoke to my spirit, and I awoke. I unlocked my phone and read my message. Sadness covered me as I read the text.

"Devon has gone home to be with God. Diane and I thank you for visiting us. I realize we don't know each other than our brief conversation, but I connected with you, and so did Diane. She is going to let God help her heal from this ordeal. You will forever be a part of the cherished memories of Devon's life. I only wish we could have met under better circumstances. Your time and your prayers meant so much to both of us. Devon would have liked you. I am happy he is not suffering any longer, but my heart aches terribly."

If I wasn't near my goal and so close to day forty, I would have returned to St. Louis to be with Devon's family. I remembered the words God spoke to me that night. *My grace is sufficient for you and will be for them as well.* I prayed God would indeed shed His grace on them because He had upon me. I knew too well what it was like to lose an eight-year-old son, and now they did, too. God brought me through over a year later, and I knew He would be with them.

I shed a couple of tears. Life is precious, but it is also tricky. In many ways, Devon missed out, but in many more ways, he was further ahead. When a child is lost, the parents often have agonizing questions and pain. Ralph once said acetaminophen could not take away. It's a pain unlike any other, but I am witness to the fact it is a pain that is mendable. I will always cherish my eight years with Timmy, as I know Diane and

Dominic will treasure their time with Devon. But the more excellent knowledge of eternal life without pain and tears will keep them going until that day comes for them.

Chapter

32

When I was younger, my parents took me to Ocean City, Maryland, and we traveled on Interstate 68 in West Virginia and into Maryland, where we once again picked up Interstate 70. Interstate 70 and Interstate 76 become one in Western Pennsylvania until Interstate 70 breaks south to Maryland and travels along the border of West Virginia. Many consider Interstate 70 does this to be the "long way" to get to Maryland. The truth is, I believe it took us an additional fifteen minutes.

Before reaching Maryland, however, we took a slight detour in Sommerset, Pennsylvania, and visited the site of the crash of United 93. Charlotte was a toddler on September 11, 2001, but I remember the day quite well. I had always wanted to visit New York and see the freedom tower, and someday I will. I had been to the Pentagon, and that day I was able to visit Shanksville and pay my respects.

Charlotte asked about the historic day as we walked along the white wall memorial in the field where United 93 crashed.

"I was twenty at the time. I was getting ready for my ten o'clock class. On Tuesdays and Thursdays, I had class at ten and one, and the rest of the day off. I turned on the television as I woke up and saw the world trade center on fire."

"Were you scared?"

"Well, yeah, a little. I wondered if Columbus would be attacked."

"Did you go to class?"

"Oh no. I skipped. I was shocked like everyone else, but something unique happened to me the night before. Something I didn't know how to explain. Well, not until recently, I guess."

"What was it?"

"Well, I had a thought come to mind. I walked up a flight of stairs, and as clear as I heard your voice, I heard a voice in my head say, 'Things are going to explode soon.' I remember specifically stopping in the middle of the steps and looking around, thinking the dorm I was in would explode. I stood there for five minutes until nothing happened. The next day I saw two planes hit the World Trade Center, and one flew into the Pentagon."

"And the one that crashed here. The people who fought back crashed here, right?"

"Yes. They fought back. It was a tragic day. But you know what? The next day, there were churches filled across the United States. America's Congress gathered on the steps of the Capitol and prayed. People came together united as I have never seen in my life."

"Really? What happened after that?"

"Well, I don't know how long it took. But we are humans, and we went back to our old ways. Our world changed that day, and not for good. Many people changed that day and for good, but unless we put our complete trust in God, we will never be like we all were."

"So, it's not likely to happen?"

"I don't give up that easily. I still pray for a 9/12 revival. I still believe revival will come to this nation. God is not done with us yet."

We spent forty-five minutes at the site reading the names on the wall before getting back on the road.

Arriving in Maryland, we stopped in Frederick to fill up the car and to eat. As Charlotte and I sat at an outside picnic table at Scheetz, eating our cheese curds and chicken sandwiches, nervousness rose in me, and adrenaline coursed through my veins. I prayed, this time not asking for courage but thanking God for His healing. The worry, I knew, came from the enemy. My worshipful prayers for healing and thanking God for the journey turned my anxiety into joy.

"You may want to put your dress on now."

"What? Why?"

"I figured you didn't realize it, but we will pass the site of the crash in a little less than an hour, and about ten minutes later, we will reach the eastern end of Interstate 70."

"Really? Are we that close? Okay then, I will do it." She walked out to the car, retrieved her dress. Before stepping inside, she stopped at the table. "Are you ready for this?"

I smiled with as large a smile as I could muster. "Darling, I am more than ready for this. Go change, and we will head out."

"Ok, Dad. If you say so."

I was ready. I could not have been more prepared. Forty days earlier, I drove onto Interstate 70 as a scared, broken man. Today, I would exit Interstate 70 healed, restored, feeling closer to God than I ever had in my life. As I waited for Charlotte to return, I thought about relationships I had established and how God strengthened my relationship with Him.

The sun beat down on my arm, and I felt its heat. I pulled it back into the shade, and the heat subsided. I moved it back once again, and the temperature change was noticeable.

The LORD spoke. *When you spend time in the sun, you risk*

burning—your body changes. When you spend time working on a relationship with Me, you change.

It made perfect sense to me. It was what I had been trying to tell people, without even realizing what I told them. Speaking of how a relationship with God is essential was one thing but did they understand? *Thank you, Lord. I love the analogy.*

When we dedicate our lives to anything, we will improve. If we work hard at our jobs, we will become masters at what we do. If we spend time in the sun, we will see physical changes in our bodies. If we dedicate ourselves to driving across the country, we will see new places and experience new people. Whatever we put our energy and devotion to, there we will grow.

When we pray and read the Bible, God will change us. I put the pieces together. Ralph's prejudice will fall away as he draws near to God. Sheila, if she presses into God, may come out of her lifestyle. Diane, when seeking God in prayer, will find healing for losing her son. Though her husband is not of the right mind, Martha can be comforted by pushing in on God, for He is the great healer.

If a force as powerful as the sun can change our bodies by spending time in it, imagine how much more God can change us if we spend time with Him. He created the sun, after all. I clapped my hands together with a loud snap as it all dawned on me. "Yes!" I finally shouted. Time didn't heal me; God healed me. The journey did not ease my mind; obedience to God did.

As Charlotte returned, wearing her stunning blue dress with white vertical stripes, she twirled around for me to see.

"Beautiful, darling."

"Thank you, sir."

"I had a wonderful moment while you were gone. I finally know why God asked me to come on this journey."

"Great! Are you going to share or keep it to yourself?"

"Let's get going, and I will explain it all on the way."

I walked about six inches off the ground as I approached the car. Our amazing God had helped me realize a little more about what life means in the past forty days. He created us with His love, and He restored us with that same love. Now, when we spend time with Him in prayer, we grow, heal, and love Him even more. It had been a fantastic journey with amazing people. I was sad the end was so near, but I was also eager to begin this new life closer to God and strengthen my relationship with Him daily.

Chapter
33

We pulled off the side of the road where a dedicated spot waited for us, and a Maryland State Trooper directed me into it. My adrenal glands pumped hormones as fast as they could. Tears formed in my eyes, but I pushed them back. It was the site where Jane and Timmy had crashed. I looked to the East and could see the exit where the young man had driven the wrong way was closed off. The highway had been taken down to one lane with construction barrels for two miles, but when we had seen them, I didn't know it was for us.

Charlotte's pop-up pastor Facebook page had over one million likes, and it showed. We found out later only residents and my coworkers could attend the media driven celebration that had been planned. If someone could not prove employment with Morris and Anderson or that they were a resident of Albeth Heights, admission was not allowed and asked to continue down the road.

Someone or some group had put together a fantastic event. I didn't want the spotlight and never was a fan of the fame. I wanted everyone to know Jesus, not Jake. Jesus died on a cross, not Jake.

I didn't rise from the grave. God is my Father, but not my biological father.

Escorted by the state trooper, he informed us the media wanted to interview both of us.

God, I don't want this. I prayed as I walked.

Give me the glory. I am with you.

Every time He spoke to me, I felt comforted. Every negative feeling in me melted away, and now pure joy filled my blood vessels. Courage and strength renewed in my heart, and I walked up to the reporter.

"Mr. Anderson, day forty is here. How do you feel?"

"Restored, renewed, rejuvenated. I feel touched by the hand of God."

"That's great. Will you adopt Charlotte as your daughter?"

"As God has adopted us into His family, I do the same with Charlotte. Adoption is a binding agreement and a permanent one. Charlotte is as much my child as we are all children of God."

"That sounds like a yes. Do you miss your family? Do you wish Timmy and Jane were still here?"

I was angry. Why would she ask such a question? But I remembered, "I am with you." I raised a warm smile. "Praise the King of Glory. He has redeemed me from my sins. He has restored my fortune with His shed blood. The name of Jesus is above all names."

Charlotte stomped her foot and clapped her hands. I reached my hand out to grab hers, and we walked hand in hand back to the car with the state trooper following closely behind. I walked Charlotte to the passenger side, opened the door, and walked around the back of the car because I saw the reporter running toward me.

"You better stop her, officer." I pointed to the reporter and the camera operator trying to keep up, pulling cords behind him. "We are leaving."

I sat down and pulled out into traffic. The trooper turned and placed his hand up, motioning for the reporter to stop.

"If they are at the Park and Ride, I am going to go around the loop and keep going. Be ready because I don't want to deal with them right now."

"I don't blame you. It was a bit much."

"It was unnecessary. Let's see how much of my last statement makes the news tonight."

We laughed as another state trooper stopped traffic behind me and waved me on. Eight minutes later, we arrived at the Park and Ride. A forty-day journey of faith and healing had ended. Thankfully there were several parked cars but no sizeable crowds. No police and no cameras. I pulled up to the spot nearest the Gwynns Falls Trail entrance and stopped. I glanced at my odometer reading. 2,742 miles.

Significant accomplishments like getting married, having a child, and starting your own business can fill our lives. But driving from one end of the United States to the other, that's quite an accomplishment. Others have completed this task, and professional drivers may do it several times a year, but the journey was never about the miles. I believe nothing is more significant than obeying the voice of God no matter what He asks of us in our lives.

Charlotte and I exited the car. I stretched and pointed to the trail. "So, what do you think? Up for an eighteen-mile hike?"

She glanced at the trailhead and back at me. "Tell me you are joking."

I intended it to be a joke, but I didn't tell her. I started walking toward the path, and she stayed behind to see how far I would take the trick. Before entering, I stopped and turned back to see her. My heart started racing as exhaustive memories returned to me. Almost whiplashing my neck, I turned to see a beagle howling at me as it walked toward me. This time, instead of running, I bent down and welcomed my friend.

"Hello, Zion. How on Earth did you get here?" There could

be no mistake about it. It was the dog that had chased me to my car at Cove Fort, Utah. I had come a long way, and I did not run from him this time. I embraced him. How he stood before me and not in Denver did not remain a mystery for long. His new owner came through the clearing looking for him.

"There you are."

"I am sorry. I didn't know he would chase anyone. I have only had him for two and a half weeks."

"Let me guess. You got him from an older gentleman in Denver. Chances are he wore blue jeans, a white T-Shirt, Angel's cap, and something orange. Am I right?"

"Umm…"

"Sorry, I didn't mean to startle you."

"Are you Jake Anderson?"

I smirked and raised to my feet. I didn't want to deal with this. "Let me guess, you saw me on Facebook?"

"Facebook? No! I am Steve, Randall's son. He told me about you."

I didn't know that Randall had a son. I didn't even know, until that moment, if Randall was even human. I thought for sure he was an angel. Now, I felt better, but it didn't explain how Zion had arrived from Denver. "What are you doing in Baltimore?"

"I just moved here. I guess Sean didn't tell you that I took a position with Morris and Anderson and started two weeks ago."

Would it have been cliché to say it's a small world? Joe Smith didn't think so. I didn't use those words as I know now when God involves Himself, everything is significantly small. It's His world, and we live in it. He is our creator and our giver of life.

Everything He created belongs to Him. Whether it be:

    a Mormon wife,

    a kidnapped child,

    a stranger with a dog,

    a self-centered pastor,

a child that sees into the spirit world,
a lady whose husband has dementia,
a lesbian struggling with her lifestyle,
a child that died from an injury,
a man selling tires,
or an atheist at a roadside rest stop.

We are all God's children, and He cares so deeply for us that He works daily in our lives to bring us closer to people who will encourage, strengthen, and empower us to know Him better.

It's all about relationships. Our relationships with one another build and strengthen us. God said to love our neighbors, but He also said to love Him, too. That is of utmost importance—not only loving Him but having a daily, intimate, strong relationship with Him through prayer. When we work on our relationship with Him, we change. We heal, and we find the freedom readily available in The LORD, Jesus Christ.

Epilogue

It's been five and a half months since I returned home. I returned to work. Charlotte is settling in, and life is returning to normal. She still has a long way to go in establishing a solid relationship with our Father in heaven, but as she sees me more like a father, she will see God as such in time.

I left my apartment and purchased a house in Albeth Heights—a lovely two-bedroom, two-story home in the country. Charlotte is excited to have a bedroom she says is larger than the living room at her mom's house. She was also excited to see the subscription channels I had on television so she could catch up on Marvel movies. She insists the pop-up pastor should be the next one added to the comic universe. I don't see it this way, though I have grown accustomed to the nickname.

I am no longer a pastor in the traditional sense, but I am still a pastor. My forty-day journey helped me rediscover when God calls you to be a pastor, you don't have to serve a church to be one, still. I visit various churches to speak, and I travel to people's homes to answer questions or be in their presence so we can talk.

I never was able to reach Joe Smith. Ralph and Marian tell me

Sara is in counseling and is doing well. I occasionally chat with Dominic and encourage him in his recovery and healing. Randall's son never showed up for work the day I returned. We had to let him go. I told Sean I did not find it surprising that he "suddenly disappeared." Unfortunately, I think Zion disappeared with him.

Life is good. I miss Jane and Timmy every day, and I have their pictures and the one picture of Patricia Taylor that Charlotte brought with her hanging on our living room wall. Charlotte had the four heart tattoos removed from her arm along with the squiggly lines. She opted to keep the heart in the middle. She has never considered purple hair again. Thankfully.

We had to fight off reporters for three weeks. Finally, I put a sign on the door and a message on my voice mail that said, "Praise the King of Glory. He has redeemed me from my sins. He has restored my fortune with His shed blood. The name of Jesus is above all names."

By the way, that part was not on the news story the night we returned. Go figure.

Acknowledgments

First, I want to thank Ian and Gracie for convincing me to take my idea and put it on paper. I needed your inspiration.

Thank you to Kande, Adam, Kathy, Terry, Ashley, and Randy for volunteering for my beta readers.

Thank you, Chad, for the idea of the pop-up pastor. I love the concept.

Thank you, Jerry for your friendship, prayers, and inspiration while writing this book.

Thank you to Fulcrum Publishing for allowing my book to be your first project. May you have many more that you can come alongside and help. Thank you, Ian and Frank, for your proofing skills. Very valuable.

And finally, for my wife, Tonya. Thank you for allowing me to take the time to write this book. I couldn't have done it without your loving support.

About the Author

Philip D Bliss served in the United Methodist Church as a part-time pastor for twenty years while he raised a family and worked on his career in Information Technology. He was inspired to write this book ten years ago when one night he wanted to see where Interstate 70 began, thinking it was in California. He received the idea to tell a story of a man traveling across the country after a tragedy. After years of jotting down ideas, he told the idea to a friend and his friend's daughter, who had just finished writing a book of her own. They both loved the idea so much and told him he should write the book. It took 3 more years, but *Forty On 70* became a reality.

He is actively involved in The Bellaire First United Methodist Church and an active participant in activities related to The Fulcrum Center. The Fulcrum Center is a non-profit organization that helps people be and do what God has designed them to be and do. They do this by coming along side people and assisting in various ways. He and his friend, Ian Thornton, started Fulcrum Radio in April 2021. He is the host of the podcast "Bible Time" and co-host of the podcast, "Uplift" on the Fulcrum Radio platform and the Fulcrum Radio YouTube channel. His lifelong desire has been to help people know The LORD and establish a deeper relationship with Him. He and his wife, Tonya, live in St. Clairsville, Ohio.

About The Publisher

Fulcrum Publishing is a division of The Fulcrum Center, a non-profit 501c(3) organization created to help people be and do what God designed them to be and do.

Fulcrum Publishing has the same heartbeat, to help others with their publishing needs so that the message God has given you can be launched into a waiting world and create an impact for the Kingdom of God. We are excited to walk alongside you on your journey and help you with your publishing needs.

The Fulcrum Center has many areas to help you. Whether it be determining your purpose or identity in Christ, life-coaching, strategic planning / assistance in the fulfillment of vision, personal growth or mentorship and even featuring you on our internet radio station – Fulcrum Radio on the Live365 platform.

For more information about The Fulcrum Center, please visit us at our website:

www.thefulcrumcenter.org.

May God bless you and keep you, and allow His face to shine upon you, giving you the peace you need as you journey with Him along the road He has for you.

Coming Soon From Philip D Bliss
Four Hearts
The backstory of Charlotte Taylor

He felt the darkness, as he always did when one of this kind came near. The presence of the beast did not inhibit his plans to watch the unfolding event before him. Matana had dealt with evil and had overcome it many times. Nothing new came before him, but oh how he desperately desired to be free of their presence in this hour.

The feeling of darkness grew as the demon drew nearer. Would the evil creature start a fight, would he observe, or would he try intervening? Matana knew all three were possible, and none would have a desirable outcome. Trying to ignore the beast, he remained focused on the birth. There would be time to prevent anything the dark spirit tried to accomplish.

Finally, with a scream and a push of all her might, the time had come. Patricia tried delivering the baby, and the doctor coached her to push while nurses held her hands. The dark beast moved closer, Matana observed his foe. He would take all necessary action if the spirit crossed the line. Patricia had not given her authority to stop the beast, but Matana was authorized to engage in battle if needed.

"One more push and that should do it. On three, Okay?" Patricia screamed in agony.

"Take a deep breath and push. You can do it," said the nurse on Patricia's right.

Patricia did as instructed. Matana watched the beast, as well as Patricia. Though he knew the child would be safe and protected, he still would be ready if needed. He could see hair as the baby crowned. His eyes shifted back to the room's darkness. It remained still, knowing Matana was watching. Matana had seen this tactic before.

They would remain still, pretending to observe. But in the moment of ultimate weakness, would whisper in the ear of a human to cause a mistake. Even worse, they may try to inhibit the baby at the moment of birth. Matana was ready for either, and he would not stand for it.

Patricia pushed as she screamed. The doctor secured the baby's neck and gradually applied pressure, pulling gently as the delivery came.

"It's a girl."

The spirit seized the opportunity, and with all his might, he pushed and whispered into the doctor's ear. Matana instantly swooped in and pushed against the doctor's right arm, holding him steady. The doctor's arm only slightly fell and was so subtle no one in the room even noticed. With a growl of disgust, the darkness snarled at Matana, and within seconds, left the room.

Matana observed as the baby was given to the nurses to hold. The doctor grabbed a nearby pair of surgical scissors and cut the umbilical cord of the newborn. Matana went on alert. The child separated from her mother, breathing on her own, and highly vulnerable to the enemy that would begin its relentless journey to sabotage the child's life. He saw no darkness, he did not feel its presence, but he remained on alert.

Patricia held her child for the first time as the first nurse announced the initial APGAR score, a five. With a smile and forgetting the pain of labor instantly, Patricia smiled and welcomed her child to the world.

"Hello, Charlotte. I am so glad to meet you finally."

"A beautiful name. What's her middle name?" asked the first nurse.

"Susan."

"Welcome to the world, Charlotte Susan Taylor," she said before jotting down the information.

"Welcome to the world, Charlotte," Matana spoke in angelic speak. None of the four remaining humans in the room could hear his voice. "I am glad to be your guardian angel. You will never know me, but I will always be ready to protect you when you need me."

Darkness returned—this time with two more entities. Two demons attempted to shake Patricia, and one tried to block Matana from retaliating. This tactic never worked against him, and moments before they returned, The Holy Spirit spoke to him, alerting him of their arrival. With a quick swipe of his sword, the lesser demon attacking him disappeared into spiritual darkness. Covering the new mother and her child with his body, his sword outstretched before him, Matana took his station, and in angel speak, he said, "The Lord rebuke you. Return to your source. The protection of God surrounds this family today with the authority of the Son of God."

The demons left quicker than they returned. Matana raised higher to gain a better view and observed once again. He knew this life would be a challenge. God had spoken that this young girl would belong to Him, and this angered the enemy. Matana reflected on his assignment. He had protected many lives during his eternal existence, and this one would not be different. He thought he was ready for the challenge.

Made in the USA
Coppell, TX
04 October 2022

84056691R00144